WHAT AN UNBRANDED COW HAS COST

From a sketch by Frederic Remington

The Writings of Owen Wister

of The American Academy of Arts and Letters

*Membre Correspondant de la Société
des Gens de Lettres*

Honorary Fellow of the Royal Society of Literature

—

Hank's Woman

PRINTED IN THE UNITED STATES OF AMERICA BY
R. R. DONNELLEY & SONS CO., AT THE LAKESIDE PRESS, CHICAGO

TO

MESSRS. HARPER & BROTHERS
AND
HENRY MILLS ALDEN

WHOSE FRIENDLINESS AND FAIR DEALING
I AM GLAD OF THIS CHANCE
TO RECORD

OWEN WISTER

> ... *mihi parva rura et*
> *Spiritum Graiae tenuem Camenae*
> *Parca non mendax dedit, et malignum*
> *Spernere vulgus.*

PREFACE—*Twenty-eight years after*

ON May 3rd, 1900, this collection was pub-lished. The eight sketches were written between September, 1891, and August, 1899, interspersed with others which belonged to *Lin McLean* or *The Virginian*. *Hank's Woman* was my first attempt at a Western sketch, and after its appearance in *Harper's Weekly*, I grew dissatisfied with it, and revised it.

The temptation to retouch early work in later years must often assail the writer. On the whole, he had better not yield to it. If it won the interest of his readers once, long ago, that is enough; it was then the best he knew how to do. The subsequent years, during which he may feel that he has learned more of his Art, have also made another person of *him*—old hands must keep off young work! No matter how clearly your spectacled eye may see imperfections which to your youthful eye were invisible, let them alone, you're different now, you can't go back, be thankful if you can still go forward, and put your matured experience and skill to new adventure!

Why do I say this here? Because in 1906, when I stood morning after morning in Lamb House at Rye, and saw Henry James bedevilling his beautiful earlier prose with patches and inversions and perversions, I didn't dare say it to him! I did dare to say a good deal, emboldened by our long associa-tion—I had begun to know him when I was twelve.

There in Lamb House with the old work pasted in strips on big sheets in front of him, and with pen in hand, he hovered over these defenseless creatures of his literary past, swooping down upon them from time to time and rending their original symmetry to new and disturbing shapes. Or, to take another simile, into the veins of such a work as *The Tragic Muse* he injected serum from *The Golden Bowl,* and the effect was disastrous. How could an artist and a critic so subtle and so con-summate ever perpetrate such an outrage on his own flesh and blood? Nobody knows that I have ever asked, and I have asked many.

Yes; it's a temptation to expand, to condense, to polish these old pages, as well as many others of *Lin McLean* and *The Virginian;* but they shall be left pretty much as they stood, even in spite of the mournful fate which befell them. As they appeared separately, they met with both private and public approval: this the scrap-book shows: together in the volume, about as many people seem to have bought the book as might comfortably enter a hotel eleva-tor. The disappointed author could only accept his fate and murmur like a great predecessor whose ambition was likewise to chronicle the life of his old border, "if it's no weel bobbit, we'll bob it again."

In these late years, consolation has come through *The Golden Book,* where, as in the case of *Red Men and White,* nearly all the sketches find themselves re-published in the best company.

As in that first group, so in this one, almost every tale might be called "a foot-note to history." I have taken hardly any liberties with the actual facts: the capture of Toussaint the "breed" was told me by one of the officers who caught him, and who also witnessed his interview with Red Cloud: it is chiefly with the characters that my imagination has busied itself; and their faithfulness to the life of our old frontier has been attested by those who were a part of that life themselves; the scrapbooks leave small doubt as to that.

One more instance, and the patience of the reader (if patient readers are not extinct) shall not be tried any further.

The sketch entitled *The Promised Land* was published in *Harper's Magazine* for April, 1894. There were only about a couple of drops of invention in it; everything happened, as there described; happened to intimate friends, who told it all to me; the last hours of Wild Goose Jake were invented—for the original character was still in good health when the tale was written; and Leander the feeble-minded boy was also invented.

"P. O. Marcus Wash., Feb. 6, '95.
"Midway, B. C.

"Mr. Wister:

"The enclosed clipping is from the Spokane *Review*.

"We read your story last year of 'Wild Goose Jake,' and recognised the characters, and surroundings as we have lived in this vicinity for a long time. I was much interested in the story, and I think you will see a startling similarity to this, the real end of a locally famous character. . . .

"I think you, yourself must certainly have visited the locality to have drawn the surroundings and characters so vividly.

"I have enjoyed very much those of your writings that have come my way, and hope you may live long to write much more of the same.

"Respectfully. . . ."

"WILD GOOSE BILL

"Details of the deadly duel that snuffed out two Lives.
"Bill's Mistress Had Left him and he was crazed with jealousy and drink.

"The tragedy that ended in the death of 'Wild Goose Bill,' whose true name was S. W. Condon and another man, and the serious wounding of the former's mistress, was the result of jealousy according to particulars that have come to light recently. It happened Monday noon at the King ranch, in the camp of Bill's enemies, and there were but four witnesses to the fray, the woman, Millie Dunn; the other participant in the duel, Barton Parks, a former stage-driver on the Conconully line; and Jack Bratton, who took to his heels when the shooting began. Mrs. Dunn had been Condon's mistress until, according to the rumor in that neighborhood, she deserted him for Bratton. Parks was a suitor for her favors, too, and so was drawn into the duel of death.

"Condon was a squaw man until some time in the summer of 1893, when he met Mrs. Dunn and took her to his ferry on the Columbia, where he was then living with his second dusky mate, to nurse an invalid child. It was but a short time until she had alienated his affections from his Indian wife, whom he persuaded, by a liberal alimony of ponies, to return to her people on the reservation. Condon loved his white mistress with a new-born passion that had slumbered during 40 years of conjugal companionship with the feminine aborigines. Mrs. Dunn secured a final decree of divorce last September, and Condon frequently declared that he would marry her as soon as the statutory prohibition of

six months had expired. When she deserted him
he sought solace in the bowl, as many a man has
done and oft, before. Crazed by liquor and love and
jealousy, three things that do not quite harmonize,
he returned from Wilbur, where he had been on a
spree, and went directly to the Hollis King Ranch,
where the tragedy occurred.

"Parks' presence in the house is not satisfacto-
rily accounted for. It is said by some that he was
employed by the woman to break a team of horses,
and that he had attached himself to her retinue.
He was reclining on a bunk at one side of the room.
Mrs. Dunn was seated opposite. Bratton was in the
rear doorway. Condon entered with a cordial greet-
ing, shook hands all around and stopped, as if de-
bating what he had better do. Drawing his six-
shooter with a quickness born of long practice, he
fired at his mistress first, it is said. Bratton felt that
his time would come next, and, remembering the
injunction about dead heroes, quietly fell back and
sought refuge in a safe place. Condon fired again
at the woman, the shot shattering her left arm.

"Parks took a hand then, emptying six chambers
of his revolver at Bill, who retreated when he had
exhausted his ammunition. Wounded as he was,
Parks ran for a Henry rifle, with which he fired
twice at the retreating figure. Both men died almost instantly.

"A messenger was dispatched to the Nes Pelum agency for a doctor but none was there, and he went on to Wilbur. Dr. Yount responded. Mrs. Belle Woodin, sister of Mrs. Dunn, was among those who accompanied the party that went out to care for the wounded and bring in the dead.

"Wild Goose Bill's name was Samuel Wilbur Condon. The town of Wilbur took its name from him. He was a native of Orange, N. J., and joined the rush of the Argonauts to the West in '49. After varied fortunes in California he came north, and engaged in freighting from Walla Walla to the placers of the Columbia. After establishing his ranch he furnished supplies to the placer miners for many miles both ways."

Why is it that coincidences, so constantly to be met with in the experience of us all, so invariably surprise us? But it's small surprise to be reminded by the scrap-book, that genteel critics in the East found these sketches "melodramatic." Poor sketches, how could they help it and remain truthful?

OWEN WISTER.

Long House, Bryn Mawr, 1928.

PREFACE

It's very plain that if a thing's the fashion—
    Too much the fashion—if the people leap
To do it, or to be it, in a passion
    Of haste and crowding, like a herd of sheep,
Why then that thing becomes through imitation
    Vulgar, excessive, obvious, and cheap.
No gentleman desires to be pursuing
What every Tom and Dick and Harry's doing.

Stranger, do you write books? I ask the question,
    Because I'm told that everybody writes;
That what with scribbling, eating, and digestion,
    And proper slumber, all our days and nights
Are wholly fulled. It seems an odd suggestion—
    But if you do write, stop it, leave the masses,
    Read me, and join the small selected classes.
  1900

TABLE OF CONTENTS

HANK'S WOMAN

I

MANY fish were still in the pool; and though luck seemed to have left me, still I stood at the end of the point, casting and casting my vain line, while the Virginian lay and watched. Noonday's extreme brightness had left the river and the plain in cooling shadow, but spread and glowed over the yet undimmed mountains. Westward, the Tetons lifted their peaks pale and keen as steel through the high, radiant air. Deep down between the blue gashes of their cañons the sun sank long shafts of light, and the glazed laps of their snow-fields shone separate and white upon their lofty vastness, like handkerchiefs laid out to dry. Opposite, above the valley, rose that other range, the Continental Divide, not sharp, but long and ample. It was bare in some high places, and below these it stretched everywhere, high and low, in brown and yellow parks, or in purple

1

miles of pine, a world of serene undulations, a great sweet country of silence.

A passing band of antelope stood herded suddenly together at sight of us; then a little breeze blew for a moment from us to them, and they drifted like phantoms away, and were lost in the levels of the sage-brush.

"If humans could do like that," said the Virginian, watching them go.

"Run, you mean?" said I.

"Tell a foe by the smell of him," explained the cow-puncher; "at fifty yards—or a mile."

"Yes," I said; "men would be hard to catch."

"A woman needs it most," he murmured. He lay down again in his lounging sprawl, with his grave eyes intently fixed upon my fly-casting.

The gradual day mounted up the hills farther from the floor of earth. Warm airs eddied in its wake slowly, stirring the scents of the plain together. I looked at the Southerner; and there was no guessing what his thoughts might be at work upon behind that drowsy glance. Then for a moment a trout rose, but only to look and whip down again into the pool that wedged its calm into the riffle from below.

"Second thoughts," mused the Virginian; and as the trout came no more, "Second thoughts," he repeated; "and even a fish will have them sooner than folks has them in this mighty hasty country." And he rolled over into a new position of ease.

At whom or what was he aiming these shafts of truth? Or did he moralize merely because health and the weather had steeped him in that serenity which lifts us among the spheres? Well, sometimes he went on from these beginnings and told me wonderful things.

"I reckon," said he, presently, "that knowing when to change your mind would be pretty near knowledge enough for plain people."

Since my acquaintance with him—this was the second summer of it—I had come to understand him enough to know that he was unfathomable. Still, for a moment it crossed my thoughts that perhaps now he was discoursing about himself. He had allowed a jealous foreman to fall out with him at Sunk Creek ranch in the spring, during Judge Henry's absence. The man, having a brief authority, parted with him. The Southerner had chosen that this should be the means of ultimately getting the foreman dismissed and

himself recalled. It was strategic. As he put
it to me: "When I am gone, it will be right
easy for the Judge to see which of us two he
wants. And I'll not have done any talking."
All of which duly befell in the autumn as he
had planned: the foreman was sent off, his
assistant promoted, and the Virginian again
hired. But this was meanwhile. He was in-
dulging himself in a several months' drifting,
and while thus drifting he had written to me.
That is how we two came to be on our way
from the railroad to hunt the elk and the
mountain-sheep, and were pausing to fish
where Buffalo Fork joins its waters with
Snake River. In those days the antelope still
ran there in hundreds, the Yellowstone Park
was a new thing, and mankind lived very far
away. Since meeting me with the horses in
Idaho the Virginian had been silent, even for
him. So now I stood casting my fly, and trust-
ing that he was not troubled with second
thoughts over his strategy.

"Have yu' studied much about marriage?"
he now inquired. His serious eyes met mine as
he lay stretched along the ground.

"Not much," I said; "not very much."

"Let's swim," he said. "They have changed
their minds."

Forthwith we shook off our boots and dropped our few clothes, and heedless of what fish we might now drive away, we went into the cool, slow, deep breadth of backwater which the bend makes just there. As he came up near me, shaking his head of black hair, the cow-puncher was smiling a little.

"Not that any number of baths," he remarked, "would conceal a man's objectionableness from an antelope—not even a she-one."

Then he went under water, and came up again a long way off.

We dried before the fire, without haste. To need no clothes is better than purple and fine linen. Then he tossed the flap-jacks, and I served the trout, and after this we lay on our backs upon a buffalo-hide to smoke and watch the Tetons grow more solemn, as the large stars opened out over the sky.

"I don't care if I never go home," said I.

The Virginian nodded. "It gives all the peace o' being asleep with all the pleasure o' feeling the widest kind of awake," said he. "Yu' might say the whole year's strength flows hearty in every waggle of your thumb." We lay still for a while. "How many things surprise yu' any more?" he next asked.

I began considering; but his silence had at length worked round to speech.

"Inventions, of course," said he, "these hyeh telephones an' truck yu' see so much about in the papers—but I ain't speaking o' such things of the brain. It is just the common things I mean. The things that a livin', noticin' man is liable to see and maybe sample for himself. How many o' them kind can surprise yu' still?"

I still considered.

"Most everything surprised me wunst," the cow-puncher continued, in his gentle Southern voice. "I must have been a mighty green boy. Till I was fourteen or fifteen I expect I was astonished by ten o'clock every morning. But a man begins to ketch on to folks and things afteh a while. I don't consideh that when—that afteh a man is, say twenty-five, it is creditable he should get astonished too easy. And so yu've not examined yourself that-a-way?"

I had not.

"Well, there's two things anyway—I know them for sure—that I expect will always get me—don't care if I live to thirty-five, or forty-five, or eighty. And one's the ways lightning can strike." He paused. Then he got up and kicked the fire, and stood by it, staring at me. "And the other is the people that other people will marry."

He stopped again; and I said nothing.

"The people that other people will marry," he repeated. "That will surprise me till I die."

"If my sympathy—" I began.

But the brief sound that he gave was answer enough, and more than enough cure for my levity.

"No," said he, reflectively; "not any such thing as a fam'ly for me, yet. Never, it may be. Not till I can't help it. And *that* woman has not come along so far. But I have been sorry for a woman lately. I keep thinking what she will do. For she will have to do something. Do yu' know Austrians? Are they quick in their feelings, like I-talians? Or are they apt to be sluggish, same as Norwegians and them other Dutch-speakin' races?"

I told him what little I knew about Austrians.

"This woman is the first I have ever saw of 'em," he continued. "Of course men will stampede into marriage in this hyeh Western country, where a woman is a scanty thing. It ain't what Hank has done that surprises me. And it is not on him that the sorrow will fall.

For she is good. She is very good. Do yu'
remember little black Hank? From Texas he
claims he is. He was working on the main
ditch over at Sunk Creek last summer when
that Em'ly hen was around. Well, seh, yu'
would not have pleasured in his company.
And this year Hank is placer-mining on Galena Creek, where we'll likely go for sheep.
There's Honey Wiggin and a young fello'
named Lin McLean, and some others along
with the outfit. But Hank's woman will not
look at any of them, though the McLean boy
is a likely hand. I have seen that; for I have
done a right smart o' business that-a-way
myself, here and there. She will mend their
clothes for them, and she will cook lunches for
them any time o' day, and her conduct gave
them hopes at the start. But I reckon Austrians have good religion.''

''No better than Americans,'' said I.

But the Virginian shook his head. ''Better'n what I've saw any Americans have. Of
course I am not judging a whole nation by one
citizen, and especially her a woman. And of
course in them big Austrian towns the folks
has shook their virtuous sayin's loose from
their daily doin's, same as we have. I expect
selling yourself brings the quickest returns to

man or woman all the world over. But I am speakin' not of towns, but of the back country, where folks don't just merely arrive on the cyars, but come into the world the natural way, and grow up slow. Wunst a week anyway they see the bunch of old grave-stones that marks their fam'ly. Their blood and name are knowed about in the neighborhood, and it's not often one of such will sell themselves. But their religion ain't to them like this woman's. They can be rip-snortin' or'n'ary in ways. Now she is getting naught but hindrance and temptation and meanness· from her husband and every livin' thing around her—yet she keeps right along, nor does she mostly bear any signs in her face. She has cert'nly come from where they are used to believing in God and a hereafter mighty hard, and all day long. She has got one o' them crucifixes, and Hank can't make her quit prayin' to it. But what is she going to do?"

"He will probably leave her," I said.

"Yes," said the Virginian—"leave her. Alone; her money all spent; knowin' maybe twenty words of English; and thousands of miles away from everything she can understand. For our words and ways is all alike strange to her."

"Then why did he want such a person?" I exclaimed.

There was surprise in the grave glance which the cow-puncher gave me. "Why, any man would," he answered. "I wanted her myself, till I found she was good."

I looked at this son of the wilderness, standing thoughtful and splendid by the fire, and unconscious of his own religion that had unexpectedly shone forth in these last words. But I said nothing; for words too intimate, especially words of esteem, put him invariably to silence.

"I had forgot to mention her looks to yu'," he pursued, simply. "She is fit for a man." He stopped again.

"Then there was her wages that Hank saw paid to her," he resumed. "And so marriage was but a little thing to Hank—agaynst such a heap of advantages. As for her idea in takin' such as him—maybe it was that he was small and she was big; tall and big. Or maybe it was just his white teeth. Them ridiculous reasons will bring a woman to a man, haven't yu' noticed? But maybe it was just her sorrowful, helpless state, left stranded as she was, and him keeping himself near her and sober for a week.

"I had been seein' this hyeh Yellowstone Park, takin' in its geysers, and this and that, for my enjoyment; and when I found what they claimed about its strange sights to be pretty near so, I landed up at Galena Creek to watch the boys prospectin'. Honey Wiggin, yu' know, and McLean, and the rest. And so they got me to go down with Hank to Gardner for flour and sugar and truck, which we had to wait for. We lay around the Mammoth Springs and Gardner for three days, playin' cyards with friends. And I got plumb interested in them tourists. For I had partly forgot about Eastern people. And hyeh they came fresh every day to remind a man of the great size of his country. Most always they would talk to yu' if yu' gave 'em the chance; and I did. I have come mighty nigh regrettin' that I did not keep a tally of the questions them folks asked me. And as they seemed genu-winely anxious to believe anything at all, and the worser the thing the believinger they'd grow, why I—well, there's times when I have got to lie to keep in good health.

"So I fooled and I fooled. And one noon I was on the front poach of the big hotel they have opened at the Mammoth Springs for tourists, and the hotel kid, bein' on the watch-out, he sees the dust comin' up the hill, and he yells out, 'Stage!'

"Yu've not saw that hotel yet, seh? Well, when the kid says, 'Stage,' the consequences is most sudden. About as con-spicuous, yu' may say, as when Old Faithful Geyser lets loose. Yu' see, one batch o' tourists pulls out right after breakfast for Norris Basin, leavin' things empty and yawnin'. By noon the whole hotel outfit has been slumberin' in its chairs steady for three hours. Maybe yu' might hear a fly buzz, but maybe not. Everything's liable to be restin', barrin' the kid. He's a-watchin' out. Then he sees the dust, and he says, 'Stage!' and it touches the folks off like a hot pokeh. The Syndicate manager he lopes to a lookin'-glass, and then organizes himself behind the book; and the young photograph chap bounces out o' his private door like one o' them cuckoo-clocks; and the fossil man claws his specimens and curiosities into shape, and the porters line up same as parade, and away goes the piano and fiddles up-stairs. It is mighty con-spicuous. So Hank he come runnin' out from somewheres, too, and the stage drives up.

"Then out gets a tall woman, and I noticed her yello' hair. She was kind o' dumb-eyed,

yet fine to see. I reckon Hank noticed her, too,
right away. And right away her trouble begins. For she was a lady's maid, and her lady
was out of the stage and roundin' her up
quick. And it's 'Where have you put the keys,
Willomene?' The lady was rich and stinkin'
lookin', and had come from New Yawk in her
husband's private cyar.

"Well, Willomene fussed around in her
pockets, and them keys was not there. So she
started explaining in tanglefoot English to
her lady how her lady must have took them
from her before leavin' the cyar. But the lady
seemed to relish hustlin' herself into a rage.
She got tolerable con-spicuous, too. And after
a heap o' words, 'You are discharged,' she
says; and off she struts. Soon her husband
came out to Willomene, still standin' like stat-
uary, and he pays her a good sum of cash, and
he goes away, and she keeps a-standing yet
for a spell. Then all of a sudden she says
something I reckon was 'O, Jesus,' and sits
down and starts a cryin'.

"I would like to have given her comfort.
But we all stood around on the hotel poach,
and the right thing would not come into my
haid. Then the baggage-wagon came in from
Cinnabar, and they had picked the keys up on

the road between Cinnabar and Gardner. So
the lady and her toilet was rescued, but that
did no good to Willomene. They stood her
trunk down along with the rest—a brass-
nailed little old concern—and there was Willomene out of a job and afoot a long, long
ways from her own range; and so she kept
sitting, and wunst in a while she'd cry some
more. We got her a room in the cheap hotel
where the Park drivers sleeps when they're in
at the Springs, and she acted grateful like,
thanking the boys in her tanglefoot English.
Next mawnin' her folks druv off in a private
team to Norris Basin, and she seemed dazed.
For I talked with her then, and questioned her
as to her wishes, but she could not say what
she wished, nor if it was east or west she
would go; and I reckon she was too stricken
to have wishes.

"Our stuff for Galena Creek delayed on the
railroad, and I got to know her, and then I
quit givin' Hank cause for jealousy. I kept
myself with the boys, and I played more
cyards, while Hank he sca'cely played at all.
One night I came on them—Hank and Willomene—walkin' among the pines where the
road goes down the hill. Yu' should have saw
that pair o' lovers. Her big shape was plain

and kind o' steadfast in the moon, and alongside of her little black Hank! And there it
was. Of course it ain't nothing to be surprised
at that a mean and triflin' man tries to seem
what he is not when he wants to please a good
woman. But why does she get fooled, when
it's so plain to other folks that are not givin'
it any special thought? All the rest of the
men and women at the Mammoth understood
Hank. They knowed he was a worthless proposition. And I cert'nly relied on his gettin'
back to his whisky and openin' her eyes that
way. But he did not. I met them next evening
again by the Liberty Cap. Supposin' I'd been
her brother or her mother, what use was it
me warning her? Brothers and mothers don't
get believed.

"The railroad brought the stuff for Galena
Creek, and Hank would not look at it on account of his courtin'. I took it alone myself
by Yancey's and the second bridge and Miller
Creek to the camp, nor I didn't tell Willomene
good-bye, for I had got disgusted at her blind-
ness."

The Virginian shifted his position, and
jerked his overalls to a more comfortable fit.
Then he continued:

"They was married the Tuesday after at

Livingston, and Hank must have been pow'ful
pleased at himself. For he gave Willomene a
wedding present, with the balance of his cash,
spending his last nickel on buying her a red-
tailed parrot they had for sale at the First
National Bank. The son-of-a-gun hollad so
freely at the bank, the president awde'd the
cashier to get shed of the out-ragious bird, or
he would wring its neck.

"So Hank and Willomene stayed a week up
in Livingston on her money, and then he
fetched her back to Gardner, and bought their
grub, and bride and groom came up to the
camp we had on Galena Creek.

"She had never slep' out before. She had
never been on a hawss, neither. And she
mighty near rolled off down into Pitchstone
Cañon, comin' up by the cut-off trail. Why,
seh, I would not willingly take you through
that place, except yu' promised me yu' would
lead your hawss when I said to. But Hank
takes the woman he had married, and he takes
heavy-loaded pack-hawsses. 'Tis the first time
such a thing has been known of in the country.
Yu' remember them big tall grass-topped
mountains over in the Hoodoo country, and
how they descends slam down through the
cross-timber that yu' can't sca'cely work

through afoot, till they pitches over into lots an' lots o' little cañons, with maybe two inches of water runnin' in the bottom? All that is East Fork water, and over the divide is Clark's Fork, or Stinkin' Water, if yu' take the country yondeh tŏ the southeast. But any place yu' go is them undesirable steep slopes, and the cut-off trail takes along about the worst in the business.

"Well, Hank he got his outfit over it somehow, and, gentlemen, hush! but yu'd ought t've seen him and that poor girl pull into our camp. Yu'd cert'nly never have conjectured them two was on a weddin' journey. He was leadin', but skewed around in his saddle to jaw back at Willomene for riding so ignorant. Suppose it was a thing she was responsible for, yu'd not have talked to her that-a-way even in private; and hyeh was the camp a-lookin', and a-listenin', and some of us ashamed. She was setting straddleways like a mountain, and between him and her went the three pack-animals, plumb shiverin' played out, and the flour—they had two hundred pounds—tilted over hellwards, with the red-tailed parrot shoutin' landslides in his cage tied on top o' the leanin' sacks.

"It was that mean to see, that shameless

and unkind, that even a thoughtless kid like
the McLean boy felt offended, and favorable
to some sort of remonstrance. 'The son-of-
a-bitch!' he said to me. 'The son-of-a-bitch!
If he don't stop, let's stop him.' And I reckon
we might have.

"But Hank he quit. 'Twas plain to see he'd
got a genu-wine scare comin' through Pitchstone Cañon, and it turned him sour, so he'd
hardly talk to us, but just mumbled 'How!'
kind o' gruff, when the boys come up to con-
gratulate him as to his marriage.

"But Willomene, she says when she saw me,
'Oh, I am so glad!' and we shook hands right
friendly. And I wished I'd told her good-bye
that day at the Mammoth. For she bore no
spite, and maybe I had forgot her feelings in
thinkin' of my own. I had talked to her down
at the Mammoth at first, yu' know, and she
said a word about old friends. Our friendship
was three weeks old that day, but I expect
her new experiences looked like years to her.
And she told me how near she come to gettin'
killed.

"'Yu' ain't ever been over that trail, seh?
Yu' cert'nly must see Pitchstone Cañon. But
we'll not go there with packs. And we will
get off our hawsses a good ways back. For

many animals feels that there's something the matter with that place, and they act very strange about it.

"The Grand Cañon is grand, and makes yu' feel good to look at it, and a geyser is grand and all right, too. But this hyeh Pitchstone hole, if Willomene had went down into that— well, I'll tell yu', that you may judge.

"She seen the trail a-drawin' nearer and nearer the aidge, between the timber and the jumpin'-off place, and she seen how them little loose stones and the crumble stuff would slide and slide away under the hawss's feet. She could hear the stuff rattlin' continually from his steps, and when she turned her haid to look, she seen it goin' down close beside her, but into what it went she could not see. Only, there was a queer steam would come up now and agayn, and her hawss trembled. So she tried to get off and walk without sayin' nothin' to Hank. He kep' on ahaid, and her hawss she had pulled up started to follo' as she was half off him, and that gave her a tumble, but there was an old crooked dead tree. It growed right out o' the aidge. There she hung.

"Down below is a little green water tricklin', green as the stuff that gets on brass, and tricklin' along over soft cream-colored forma-

tion, like pie. And it ain't so far to fall but
what a man might not be too much hurt for
crawlin' out. But there ain't no crawlin' out
o' Pitchstone Cañon, they say. Down in there
is caves that yu' cannot see. 'Tis them that
coughs up the steam now and agayn. With
the wind yu' can smell 'em a mile away, and
in the night I have been layin' quiet and heard
'em. Not that it's a big noise, even when a
man is close up. It's a fluffy kind of a sigh.
But it sounds as if some awful thing was
a-makin' it deep down in the guts of the world.
They claim there's poison air comes out o'
the caves and lays low along the water. They
claim if a bear or an elk strays in from below,
and the caves sets up their coughin', which
they don't regular every day, the animals die.
I have seen it come in two seconds. And when
it comes that-a-way risin' upon yu' with that
fluffy kind of a sigh, yu' feel mighty lonesome,
seh.

"So Hank he happened to look back and see
Willomene hangin' at the aidge o' them black
rocks. And his scare made him mad. And his
mad stayed with him till they come into camp.
She looked around, and when she seen Hank's
tent that him and her was to sleep in she
showed surprise. And he showed surprise
when he see the bread she cooked.

" 'What kind of a Dutch woman are yu',' says he, strainin' for a joke, 'if yu' can't use a Dutch-oven?'

" 'You say to me you have a house to live in,' says Willomene. 'Where is that house?'

" 'I did not figure on gettin' a woman when I left camp,' says Hank, grinnin', but not pleasant, 'or I'd have hurried up with the shack I'm a-buildin'.'

"He was buildin' one. When I left Galena Creek and come away from that country to meet you, the house was finished enough for the couple to move in. I hefted her brass-nailed trunk up the hill from their tent myself, and I watched her take out her crucifix. But she would not let me help her with that. She'd not let me touch it. She'd fixed it up agaynst the wall her own self her own way. But she accepted some flowers I picked, and set them in a can front of the crucifix. Then Hank he come in, and seein', says to me, 'Are you one of the kind that squats before them silly dolls?' 'I would tell yu',' I answered him; 'but it would not inter-est yu'.' And I cleared out, and left him and Willomene to begin their housekeepin'.

"Already they had quit havin' much to say to each other down in their tent. The only

steady talkin' done in that house was done by
the parrot. I've never saw any go ahaid of
that bird. I have told yu' about Hank, and
how when he'd come home and see her prayin'
to that crucifix he'd always get riled up. He
would mention it freely to the boys. Not that
she neglected him, yu' know. She done her
part, workin' mighty hard, for she was a willin' woman. But he could not make her quit
her religion; and Willomene she had got to
bein' very silent before I come away. She used
to talk to me some at first, but she dropped it.
I don't know why. I expect maybe it was hard
for her to have us that close in camp, witness-
in' her troubles every day, and she a for-
eigner. I reckon if she got any comfort, it
would be when we was off prospectin' or
huntin', and she could shut the cabin door and
be alone.''

The Virginian stopped for a moment.

''It will soon be a month since I left Galena
Creek,'' he resumed. ''But I cannot get the
business out o' my haid. I keep a-studyin'
over it.''

His talk was done. He had unburdened his
mind. Night lay deep and quiet around us,
with no sound far or near, save Buffalo Fork
plashing over its riffle.

II

We left Snake River. We went up Pacific
Creek, and through Two Ocean Pass, and
down among the watery willow-bottoms and
beaver-dams of the Upper Yellowstone. We
fished; we enjoyed existence along the lake.
Then we went over Pelican Creek trail and
came steeply down into the giant country of
grass-topped mountains. At dawn and dusk
the elk had begun to call across the stillness.
And one morning in the Hoodoo country,
where we were looking for sheep, we came
round a jut of the strange, organ-pipe forma-
tion upon a long-legged boy of about nineteen,
also hunting.

"Still hyeh?" said the Virginian, without
emotion.

"I guess so," returned the boy, equally
matter-of-fact. "Yu' seem to be around yourself," he added.

They might have been next-door neighbors,
meeting in a town street for the second time
in the same day.

The Virginian made me known to Mr. Lin
McLean, who gave me a brief nod.

"Any luck?" he inquired, but not of me.

"Oh," drawled the Virginian, "luck
enough."

Knowing the ways of the country, I said no word. It was bootless to interrupt their own methods of getting at what was really in both their minds.

The boy fixed his wide-open hazel eyes upon me. "Fine weather," he mentioned.

"Very fine," said I.

"I seen your horses a while ago," he said. "Camp far from here?" he asked the Virginian.

"Not specially. Stay and eat with us. We've got elk meat."

"That's what I'm after for camp," said McLean. "All of us is out on a hunt to-day—except him."

"How many are yu' now?"

"The whole six."

"Makin' money?"

"Oh, some days the gold washes out good in the pan, and others it's that fine it'll float off without settlin'."

"So Hank ain't huntin' to-day?"

"Huntin'! We left him layin' out in that clump o' brush below their cabin. Been drinkin' all night."

The Virginian broke off a piece of the Hoodoo mud-rock from the weird eroded pillar that we stood beside. He threw it into a bank of last year's snow. We all watched it as if it were important. Up through the mountain silence pierced the long quivering whistle of a bull-elk. It was like an unearthly singer practising an unearthly scale.

"First time she heard that," said McLean, "she was scared."

"Nothin' maybe to resemble it in Austria," said the Virginian.

"That's so," said McLean. "That's so, you bet! Nothin' just like Hank over there, neither."

"Well, flesh is mostly flesh in all lands, I reckon," said the Virginian. "I expect yu' can be drunk and disorderly in every language. But an Austrian Hank would be liable to respect her crucifix."

"That's so!"

"He ain't made her quit it yet?"

"Not him. But he's got meaner."

"Drunk this mawnin', yu' say?"

"That's his most harmless condition now."

"Nobody's in camp but them two? Her and him alone?"

"Oh, he dassent touch her."

"Who did he tell that to?"

"Oh, the camp is backin' her. The camp

has explained that to him several times, you
bet! And what's more, she has got the upper
hand of him herself. She has him beat."

"How beat?"

"She has downed him with her eye. Just
by endurin' him peacefully; and with her eye.
I've saw it. Things changed some after yu'
pulled out. We had a good crowd still, and it
was pleasant, and not too lively nor yet too
slow. And Willomene, she come more among
us. She'd not stay shut in-doors, like she done
at first. I'd have like to've showed her how to
punish Hank."

"Afteh she had downed yu' with her eye?"
inquired the Virginian.

Young McLean reddened, and threw a furtive look upon me, the stranger, the outsider.
"Oh, well," he said, "I done nothing onusual.
But that's all different now. All of us likes
her and respects her, and makes allowances
for her bein' Dutch. Yu' can't help but respect her. And she shows she knows."

"I reckon maybe she knows how to deal
with Hank," said the Virginian.

"Shucks!" said McLean, scornfully. "And
her so big and him so puny! She'd ought to
lift him off the earth with one arm and lam
him with a baste or two with the other, and
he'd improve."

"Maybe that's why she don't," mused the Virginian, slowly; "because she is so big. Big in the spirit, I mean. She'd not stoop to his level. Don't yu' see she is kind o' way up above him and camp and everything—just her and her crucifix?"

"Her and her crucifix!" repeated young Lin McLean, staring at this interpretation, which was beyond his lively understanding. "Her and her crucifix. Turruble lonesome company! Well, them are things yu' don't know about. I kind o' laughed myself the first time I seen her at it. Hank, he says to me soft, 'Come here, Lin,' and I peeped in where she was a-prayin'. She seen us two, but she didn't quit. So I quit, and Hank came with me, sayin' tough words about it. Yes, them are things yu' sure don't know about. What's the matter with you camping with us boys to-night?"

We had been going to visit them the next day. We made it to-day, instead. And Mr. McLean helped us with our packs, and we carried our welcome in the shape of elk meat. So we turned our faces down the grass-topped mountains towards Galena Creek. Once, far through an open gap away below us, we sighted the cabin with the help of our field-glasses.

"Pity we can't make out Hank sleepin' in
that brush," said McLean.

"He has probably gone into the cabin by
now," said I.

"Not him! He prefers the brush all day
when he's that drunk, you bet!"

"Afraid of her?"

"Well—oneasy in her presence. Not that
she's liable to be in there now. She don't stay
inside nowadays so much. She's been comin'
round the ditch, silent-like but friendly. And
she'll watch us workin' for a spell, and then
she's apt to move off alone into the woods,
singin' them Dutch songs of hern that ain't
got no toon. I've met her walkin' that way,
tall and earnest, lots of times. But she don't
want your company, though she'll patch your
overalls and give yu' lunch always. Nor she
won't take pay."

Thus we proceeded down from the open
summits into the close pines; and while we
made our way among the cross-timber and
over the little streams, McLean told us of
various days and nights at the camp, and how
Hank had come to venting his cowardice upon
his wife's faith.

"Why, he informed her one day when he
was goin' to take his dust to town, that if he

come back and found that thing in the house, he'd do it up for her. 'So yu' better pack off your wooden dummy somewheres,' says he. And she just looked at him kind o' stone-like and solemn. For she don't care for his words no more.

"And while he was away she'd have us all in to supper up at the shack, and look at us eatin' while she'd walk around puttin' grub on your plate. Day time she'd come around the ditch, watchin' for a while, and move off slow, singin' her Dutch songs. And when Hank comes back from spendin' his dust, he sees the crucifix same as always, and he says, 'Didn't I tell yu' to take that down?' 'You did,' says Willomene, lookin' at him very quiet. And he quit.

"And Honey Wiggin says to him, 'Hank, leave her alone.' And Hank, bein' all trembly from spreein' in town, he says, 'You're all agin me!' like as if he were a baby."

"I should think you would run him out of camp," said I.

"Well, we've studied over that some," Mc-Lean answered. "But what's to be done with Willomene?"

I did not know. None of us seemed to know.

"The boys got together night before last,"

continued McLean, "and after holdin' a unanimous meetin', we visited her and spoke to her
about goin' back to her home. She was slow
in corrallin' our idea on account of her bein'
no English scholar. But when she did, after
three of us takin' their turn at puttin' the
proposition to her, she would not accept any
of our dust. And though she started to thank
us the handsomest she knowed how, it seemed
to grieve her, for she cried. So we thought
we'd better get out. She's tried to tell us the
name of her home, but yu' can't pronounce
such outlandishness.''

As we went down the mountains, we talked
of other things, but always came back to this;
and we were turning it over still when the sun
had departed from the narrow cleft that we
were following, and shone only on the distant
grassy tops which rose round us into an upper
world of light.

"We'll all soon have to move out of this
camp, anyway," said McLean, unstrapping
his coat from his saddle and drawing it on.
"It gets chill now in the afternoons. D'yu'
see the quakin'-asps all turned yello', and the
leaves keeps fallin' without no wind to blow
'em down? We're liable to get snowed in on
short notice in this mountain country. If the

water goes to freeze on us we'll have to quit
workin'. There's camp.''

We had rounded a corner, and once more
sighted the cabin. I suppose it may have been
still half a mile away, upon the further side of
a ravine into which our little valley opened.
But field-glasses were not needed now to make
out the cabin clearly, windows and door.
Smoke rose from it; for supper-time was nearing and we stopped to survey the scene. As we
were looking, another hunter joined us, coming from the deep woods to the edge of the
pines where we were standing. This was
Honey Wiggin. He had killed a deer, and he
surmised that all the boys would be back
soon. Others had met luck besides himself; he
had left one dressing an elk over the next
ridge. Nobody seemed to have got in yet, from
appearances. Didn't the camp look lonesome?

''There's somebody, though,'' said McLean.

The Virginian took the glasses. ''I reckon
—yes, that's Hank. The cold has woke him
up, and he's comin' in out o' the brush.''

Each of us took the glasses in turn; and I
watched the figure go up the hill to the door
of the cabin. It seemed to pause and diverge
to the window. At the window it stood still,
head bent, looking in. Then it returned quickly

to the door. It was too far to discern, even
through the glasses, what the figure was
doing. Whether the door was locked, whether
he was knocking or fumbling with a key, or
whether he spoke through the door to the person within—I cannot tell what it was that
came through the glasses straight to my
nerves, so that I jumped at a sudden sound;
and it was only the distant shrill call of an
elk. I was handing the glasses to the Virginian
for him to see when the figure opened the door
and disappeared in the dark interior. As I
watched the square of darkness which the
door's opening made, something seemed to
happen there—or else it was a spark, a flash,
in my own straining eyes.

But at that same instant the Virginian
dashed forward upon his horse, leaving the
glasses in my hand. And with the contagion
of his act the rest of us followed him, leaving
the pack animals to follow us as they should
choose.

"Look!" cried McLean. "He's not shot
her."

I saw the tall figure of a woman rush out of
the door and pass quickly round the house.

"He's missed her!" cried McLean, again.
"She's savin' herself."

But the man's figure did not appear in pursuit. Instead of this, the woman returned as quickly as she had gone, and entered the dark interior.

"She had something," said Wiggin. "What would that be?"

"Maybe it's all right, after all," said McLean. "She went out to get wood."

The rough steepness of our trail had brought us down to a walk, and as we continued to press forward at this pace as fast as we could, we compared a few notes. McLean did not think he saw any flash. Wiggin thought that he had heard a sound, but it was at the moment when the Virginian's horse had noisily started away.

Our trail had now taken us down where we could no longer look across and see the cabin. And the half-mile proved a long one over this ground. At length we reached and crossed the rocky ford, overtaking the Virginian there.

"These hawsses," said he, "are played out. We'll climb up to camp afoot. And just keep behind me for the present."

We obeyed our natural leader, and made ready for whatever we might be going into. We passed up the steep bank and came again

in sight of the door. It was still wide open.
We stood, and felt a sort of silence which the
approach of two new-comers could not break.
They joined us. They had been coming home
from hunting, and had plainly heard a shot
here. We stood for a moment more after
learning this, and then one of the men called
out the names of Hank and Willomene. Again
we—or I at least—felt that same silence,
which to my disturbed imagination seemed to
be rising round us as mists rise from water.

"There's nobody in there," stated the Virginian. "Nobody that's alive," he added. And
he crossed to the cabin and walked into the
door.

Though he made no gesture, I saw astonish-
ment pass through his body, as he stopped
still; and all of us came after him. There
hung the crucifix, with a round hole through
the middle of it. One of the men went to it
and took it down; and behind it, sunk in the
log, was the bullet. The cabin was but a single
room, and every object that it contained could
be seen at a glance; nor was there hiding-
room for anything. On the floor lay the axe
from the wood-pile; but I will not tell of its
appearance. So he had shot her crucifix, her
Rock of Ages, the thing which enabled her to

bear her life, and that lifted her above life; and she—but there was the axe to show what she had done then. Was this cabin really empty? I looked more slowly about, half dreading to find that I had overlooked something. But it was as the Virginian had said; nobody was there.

As we were wondering, there was a noise above our heads, and I was not the only one who started and stared. It was the parrot; and we stood away in a circle, looking up at his cage. Crouching flat on the floor of the cage, his wings huddled tight to his body, he was swinging his head from side to side; and when he saw that we watched him, he began a low croaking and monotonous utterance, which never changed, but remained rapid and continuous. I heard McLean whisper to the Virginian, "You bet he knows."

The Virginian stepped to the door, and then he bent to the gravel and beckoned us to come and see. Among the recent footprints at the threshold the man's boot-heel was plain, as well as the woman's broad tread. But while the man's steps led into the cabin, they did not lead away from it. We tracked his course just as we had seen it through the glasses: up the hill from the brush to the window, and then

to the door. But he had never walked out
again. Yet in the cabin he was not; we tore
up the half-floor that it had. There was no use
to dig in the earth. And all the while that we
were at this search the parrot remained
crouched in the bottom of his cage, his black
eye fixed upon our movements.

"She has carried him," said the Virginian.
"We must follow up Willomene."

The latest heavy set of footprints led us
from the door along the ditch, where they
sank deep in the softer soil; then they turned
off sharply into the mountains.

"This is the cut-off trail," said McLean to
me. "The same he brought her in by."

The tracks were very clear, and evidently
had been made by a person moving slowly.
Whatever theories our various minds were
now shaping, no one spoke a word to his
neighbor, but we went along with a hush over
us.

After some walking, Wiggin suddenly
stopped and pointed.

We had come to the edge of the timber,
where a narrow black cañon began, and ahead
of us the trail drew near a slanting ledge,
where the footing was of small loose stones

I recognized the odor, the volcanic whiff, that so often prowls and meets one in the lonely woods of that region, but at first I failed to make out what had set us all running.

"Is he looking down into the hole himself?" some one asked; and then I did see a figure, the figure I had looked at through the glasses, leaning strangely over the edge of Pitchstone Cañon, as if indeed he was peering to watch what might be in the bottom.

We came near. But those eyes were sightless, and in the skull the story of the axe was carved. By a piece of his clothing he was hooked in the twisted roots of a dead tree, and hung there at the extreme verge. I went to look over, and Lin McLean caught me as I staggered at the sight I saw. He would have lost his own foothold in saving me had not one of the others held him from above.

She was there below; Hank's woman, brought from Austria to the New World. The vision of that brown bundle lying in the water will never leave me, I think. She had carried the body to this point; but had she intended this end? Or was some part of it an accident? Had she meant to take him with her? Had she meant to stay behind herself? No word

came from these dead to answer us. But as
we stood speaking there, a giant puff of breath
rose up to us between the black walls.

"There's that fluffy sigh I told yu' about,"
said the Virginian.

"He's talkin' to her! I tell yu' he's talkin'
to her!" burst out McLean, suddenly, in such
a voice that we stared as he pointed at the man
in the tree. "See him lean over! He's sayin',
'I have yu' beat after all.' " And McLean fell
to whimpering.

Wiggin took the boy's arm kindly and
walked him along the trail. He did not seem
twenty yet. Life had not shown this side of
itself to him so plainly before.

"Let's get out of here," said the Virginian.

It seemed one more pitiful straw that the
lonely bundle should be left in such a vault of
doom, with no last touches of care from its
fellow-beings, and no heap of kind earth to
hide it. But whether the place is deadly or
not, man dares not venture into it. So they
took Hank from the tree that night, and early
next morning they buried him near camp on
the top of a little mound.

But the thought of Willomene lying in
Pitchstone Cañon had kept sleep from me
through that whole night, nor did I wish to

attend Hank's burial. I rose very early, while the sunshine had still a long way to come down to us from the mountain-tops, and I walked back along the cut-off trail. I was moved to look once more upon that frightful place. And as I came to the edge of the timber, there was the Virginian. He did not expect any one. He had set up the crucifix as near the dead tree as it could be firmly planted.

"It belongs to her, anyway," he explained.

Some lines of verse came into my memory, and with a change or two I wrote them as deep as I could with my pencil upon a small board that he smoothed for me.

> "Call for the robin redbreast and the wren,
>   Since o'er shady groves they hover,
>   And with flowers and leaves do cover
> The friendless bodies of unburied men.
>   Call to this funeral dole
>   The ant, the field-mouse, and the mole,
> To rear her hillocks that shall keep her warm."

"That kind o' quaint language reminds me of a play I seen wunst in Saynt Paul," said the Virginian. "About young Prince Henry."

I told him that another poet was the author.

"They are both good writers," said the Virginian. And as he was finishing the monument that we had made, young Lin McLean joined us. He was a little ashamed of the feelings that he had shown yesterday, a little anxious to cover those feelings with brass.

"Well," he said, taking an offish, man-of-the-world tone, "all this fuss just because a woman believed in God."

"You have put it down wrong," said the Virginian; "it's just because a man didn't."

The Boy and the Buccaroos

I

ONE day at Nampa, which is in Idaho, a ruddy massive jovial old man stood by the Silver City stage, patting his beard with his left hand, and with his right the shoulder of a boy who stood beside him. He had come with the boy on the branch train from Boise, because he was a careful German and liked to say everything twice—twice at least when it was a matter of business. This was a matter of very particular business, and the German had repeated himself for nineteen miles. Presently the east-bound on the main line would arrive from Portland; then the Silver City stage would take the boy south on his new mission, and the man would journey by the branch train back to Boise. From Boise no one could say where he might not go, west or east. He was a great and pervasive cattle man in Oregon, California, and other places. Vogel and Lex—even to-day you may hear the two ranch partners spoken of. So the veteran Vogel was now once more going over his

41

notions and commands to his youthful deputy during the last precious minutes until the east-bound should arrive.

"Und if only you haf someding like dis," said the old man, as he tapped his beard and patted the boy, "it would be five hoondert more dollars salary in your liddle pants."

The boy winked up at his employer. He had a gray, humorous eye; he was slim and alert, like a sparrow-hawk—the sort of boy his father openly rejoices in and his mother is secretly in prayer over. Only, this boy had neither father nor mother. Since the age of twelve he had looked out for himself, never quite without bread, sometimes attaining champagne, getting along in his American way variously, on horse or afoot, across regions of wide plains and mountains, through towns where not a soul knew his name. He closed one of his gray eyes at his employer, and beyond this made no remark.

"Vat you mean by dat vink, anyhow?" demanded the elder.

"Say," said the boy, confidentially—"honest now. How about you and me? Five hundred dollars if I had your beard. You've got a record and I've got a future. And my bloom's on me rich, without a scratch. How

many dollars you gif me for dat bloom?'' The
sparrow-hawk sailed into a freakish imitation
of his master.

''You are a liddle rascal!'' cried the master,
shaking with entertainment. ''Und if der peoples vas to hear you sass old Max Vogel in dis
style they would say, 'Poor old Max, he lose
his gr-rip.' But I don't lose it.'' His great
hand closed suddenly on the boy's shoulder,
his voice cut clean and heavy as an axe, and
then no more joking about him. ''Haf you
understand that?'' he said.

''Yes, sir.''

''How old are you, son?''

''Nineteen, sir.''

''Oh my, that is offle young for the job I
gif you. Some of dose man you go to boss
might be your father. Und how much do you
weigh?''

''About a hundred and thirty.''

''Too light, too light. Und I haf keep my
eye on you in Boise. You are not so goot a
boy as you might be.''

''Well, sir, I guess not.''

''But you was not so bad a boy as you might
be, neider. You don't lie about it. Now it
must be farewell to all that foolishness. Haf
you understand? You go to set an example

where one is needed very bad. If those men see you drink a liddle, they drink a big lot. You forbid them, they laugh at you. You must not allow one drop of whisky at the whole place. Haf you well understand?"

"Yes, sir. Me and whisky are not necessary to each other's happiness."

"It is not you, it is them. How are you mit your gun?"

Vogel took the boy's pistol from its holster and aimed at an empty bottle which was sticking in the thin December snow. "Can you do this?" he said, carelessly, and fired. The snow struck the bottle, but the unharming bullet was buried half an inch to the left.

The boy took his pistol with solemnity. "No," he said. "Guess I can't do that." He fired, and the glass splintered into shapelessness. "Told you I couldn't miss as close as you did," said he.

"You are a darling," said Mr. Vogel. "Gif me dat lofely weapon."

A fortunate store of bottles lay, leaned, or stood about in the white snow of Nampa, and Mr. Vogel began at them.

"May I ask if anything is the matter?" inquired a mild voice from the stage.

"Stick that lily head in-doors," shouted

Vogel; and the face and eye-glasses withdrew
again into the stage. "The school-teacher he
will be beautifool virtuous company for you at
Malheur Agency," continued Vogel, shooting
again; and presently the large old German
destroyed a bottle with a crashing smack.
"Ah!" said he, in unison with the smack.
"Ah-ha! No von shall say der old Max lose
his gr-rip. I shoot it efry time now, but the
train she whistle. I hear her."

The boy affected to listen earnestly.

"Bah! I tell you I hear de whistle coming."

"Did you say there was a whistle?" ventured the occupant of the stage. The snow
shone white on his glasses as he peered out.

"Nobody whistle for you," returned the
robust Vogel. "You listen to me," he continued to the boy. "You are offle yoong. But
I watch you plenty this long time. I see you
work mit my stock on the Owyhee and the
Malheur; I see you mit my oder men. My
men they say always more and more, 'Yoong
Drake he is a goot one,' und I think you are a
goot one mine own self. I am the biggest cattle man on the Pacific slope, und I am also an
old devil. I have think a lot, und I like you."

"I'm obliged to you, sir."

"Shut oop. I like you, und therefore I make

you my new sooperintendent at my Malheur Agency r-ranch, mit a bigger salary as you don't get before. If you are a sookcess, I r-raise you some more.''

''I am satisfied now, sir.''

''Bah! Never do you tell any goot business man you are satisfied mit vat he gif you, for eider he don't believe you or else he think you are a fool. Und eider ways you go down in his estimation. You make those men at Malheur Agency behave themselves und I r-raise you. Only I do vish, I certainly vish you had some beard on that yoong chin.''

The boy glanced at his pistol.

''No, no, no, my son,'' said the sharp old German. ''I don't want gunpowder in this affair. You must act kviet und decisif und keep your liddle shirt on. What you accomplish shootin'? You kill somebody, und then, pop! somebody kills you. What goot is all that nonsense to me?''

''It would annoy me some, too,'' retorted the boy, eying the capitalist. ''Don't leave me out of the proposition.''

''Broposition! Broposition! Now you get hot mit old Max for nothing.''

''If you didn't contemplate trouble,'' pursued the boy, ''what was your point just now

in sampling my marksmanship?'' He kicked
some snow in the direction of the shattered
bottle. ''It's understood no whisky comes on
that ranch. But if no gunpowder goes along
with me, either, let's call the deal off. Buy
some other fool.''

''You haf not understand, my boy. Und
you get very hot because I happen to make
that liddle joke about somebody killing you.
Was you thinking maybe old Max not care
what happen to you?''

A moment of silence passed before the answer came: ''Suppose we talk business?''

''Very well, very well. Only notice this
thing. When oder peoples talk oop to me like
you haf done many times, it is not they who
does the getting hot. It is me—old Max. Und
when old Max gets hot he slings them out of
his road anywheres. Some haf been very
sorry they get so slung. You invite me to buy
some oder fool? Oh, my boy, I will buy no
oder fool except you, for that was just like me
when I was yoong Max!'' Again the ruddy
and grizzled magnate put his hand on the
shoulder of the boy, who stood looking away
at the bottles, at the railroad track, at anything save his employer.

The employer proceeded: ''I was afraid of

nobody und noding in those days. You are afraid of nobody and noding. But those days was different. No Pullman sleepers, no railroad at all. We come oop the Columbia in the steamboat, we travel hoonderts of miles by team, we sleep, we eat nowheres in particular mit many unexpected interrooptions. There was Indians, there was offle bad white men, und if you was not offle yourself you vanished quickly. Therefore in those days was Max Vogel hell und repeat.''

The magnate smiled a broad fond smile over the past which he had kicked, driven, shot, bled, and battled through to present power; and the boy winked up at him again now.

''I don't propose to vanish, myself,'' said he.

''Ah-ha! you was no longer mad mit der old Max! Of coorse I care what happens to you. I was alone in the world myself in those lofely wicked days.''

Reserve again made flinty the boy's face.

''Neider did I talk about my feelings,'' continued Max Vogel, ''but I nefer show them too quick. If I was injured I wait, and I strike to kill. We all paddles our own dug-out, eh? We ask no favors from nobody; we must win our spurs! Not so? Now I talk business with you

where you interroopt me. If cowboys was
not so offle scarce in the country, I would long
ago haf bounce the lot of those drunken fellows. But they cannot be spared; we must get
along so. I cannot send Brock, he is needed at
Harper's. The dumb fellow at Alvord Lake
is too dumb; he is not quickly coorageous.
They would play high jinks mit him. Therefore I send you. Brock he say to me you haf
joodgement. I watch, und I say to myself also,
this boy haf goot joodgement. Und when you
look at your pistol so quick, I tell you quick I
don't send you to kill men when they are so
scarce already! My boy, it is ever the moral,
the say-noding strength what gets there—mit
always the liddle pistol behind, in case—joost
in case. Haf you understand? I ask you to
shoot. I see you know how, as Brock told me.
I recommend you to let them see that aggom-
plishment in a friendly way. Maybe a shooting-match mit prizes—I pay for them—pretty
soon after you come. Und joodgement—und
joodgement. Here comes that train. Haf you
well understand?''

Upon this the two shook hands, looking
square friendship in each other's eyes. The
east-bound, long quiet and dark beneath its
flowing clots of smoke, slowed to a halt. A

few valises and legs descended, ascended, herding and hurrying; a few trunks were thrown resoundingly in and out of the train; a woolly, crooked old man came with a box and a bandanna bundle from the second-class car; the travellers of a thousand miles looked torpidly at him through the dim, dusty windows of their Pullman, and settled again for a thousand miles more. Then the east-bound, shooting heavier clots of smoke laboriously into the air, drew its slow length out of Nampa, and away.

"Where's that stage?" shrilled the woolly old man. "That's what I'm after."

"Why, hello!" shouted Vogel. "Hello, Uncle Pasco! I heard you was dead."

Uncle Pasco blinked his small eyes to see who hailed him. "Oh!" said he, in his light, crusty voice. "Dutchy Vogel. No, I ain't dead. You guessed wrong. Not dead. Help me up, Dutchy."

A tolerant smile broadened Vogel's face. "It was ten years since I see you," said he, carrying the old man's box.

"Shouldn't wonder. Maybe it'll be another ten till you see me next." He stopped by the stage step, and wheeling nimbly, surveyed his old-time acquaintance, noting the good hat, the prosperous watch-chain, the big, well-blacked boots. "Not seen me for ten years. Hee-hee! No. Usen't to have a cent more than me. Twins in poverty. That's how Dutchy and me started. If we was buried to-morrow they'd mark him 'Pecunious' and me 'Impecunious.' That's what. Twins in poverty."

"I stick to von business at a time, Uncle," said good-natured, successful Max.

A flicker of aberration lighted in the old man's eye. "H'm, yes," said he, pondering. "Stuck to one business. So you did. H'm." Then, suddenly sly, he chirped: "But I've struck it rich now." He tapped his box. "Jewelry," he half-whispered. "Miners and cowboys."

"Yes," said Vogel. "Those poor, deluded fellows, they buy such stuff." And he laughed at the seedy visionary who had begun frontier life with him on the bottom rung and would end it there. "Do you play that concertina yet, Uncle?" he inquired.

"Yes, yes. I always play. It's in here with my tooth-brush and socks." Uncle Pasco held up the bandanna. "Well, he's getting ready to start. I guess I'll be climbing inside. Holy Gertrude!"

This shrill comment was at sight of the

school-master, patient within the stage. "What business are you in?" demanded Uncle Pasco.

"I am in the spelling business," replied the teacher, and smiled, faintly.

"Hell!" piped Uncle Pasco. "Take this."

He handed in his bandanna to the traveller, who received it politely. Max Vogel lifted the box of cheap jewelry; and both he and the boy came behind to boost the old man up on the stage step. But with a nettled look he leaped up to evade them, tottered half-way, and then, light as a husk of grain, got himself to his seat and scowled at the school-master.

After a brief inspection of that pale, spectacled face, "Dutchy," he called out of the door, "this country is not what it was."

But old Max Vogel was inattentive. He was speaking to the boy, Dean Drake, and held a flask in his hand. He reached the flask to his new superintendent. "Drink hearty," said he. "There, son! Don't be shy. Haf you forgot it is forbidden fruit after now?"

"Kid sworn off?" inquired Uncle Pasco of the school-master.

"I understand," replied this person, "that Mr. Vogel will not allow his cowboys at the

Malheur Agency to have any whisky brought
there. Personally, I feel gratified." And Mr.
Bolles, the new school-master, gave his faint
smile.

"Oh," muttered Uncle Pasco. "Forbidden
to bring whisky on the ranch? H'm." His
eyes wandered to the jewelry-box. "H'm,"
said he again; and becoming thoughtful, he
laid back his moth-eaten sly head, and spoke
no further with Mr. Bolles.

Dean Drake climbed into the stage and the
vehicle started.

"Goot luck, goot luck, my son!" shouted
the hearty Max, and opened and waved both
his big arms at the departing boy. He stood
looking after the stage. "I hope he come
back," said he. "I think he come back. If he
come I r-raise him fifty dollars without any
beard."

II

The stage had not trundled so far on its
Silver City road but that a whistle from
Nampa station reached its three occupants.
This was the branch train starting back to
Boise with Max Vogel aboard; and the boy
looked out at the locomotive with a sigh.

"Only five days of town," he murmured.
"Six months more wilderness now."

"My life has been too much town," said the new school-master. "I am looking forward to a little wilderness for a change."

Old Uncle Pasco, leaning back, said nothing; he kept his eyes shut and his ears open.

"Change is what I don't get," sighed Dean Drake. In a few miles, however, before they had come to the ferry over Snake River, the recent leave-taking and his employer's kind but dominating repression lifted from the boy's spirit. His gray eye wakened keen again, and he began to whistle light opera tunes, looking about him alertly, like the sparrow-hawk that he was. "Ever see Jeannie Winston in 'Fatinitza'?" he inquired of Mr. Bolles.

The school-master, with a startled, thankful countenance, stated that he had never.

"Ought to," said Drake.

> " 'You a man? that can't be true!
> Men have never eyes like you.'

That's what the girls in the harem sing in the second act. Golly whiz!" The boy gleamed over the memory of that evening.

"You have a hard job before you," said the school-master, changing the subject.

"Yep. Hard." The wary Drake shook his head warningly at Mr. Bolles to keep off that subject, and he glanced in the direction of slumbering Uncle Pasco. Uncle Pasco was quite aware of all this. "I wouldn't take another lonesome job so soon," pursued Drake, "but I want the money. I've been working eleven months along the Owyhee as a sort of junior boss, and I'd earned my vacation. Just got it started hot in Portland, when biff! old Vogel telegraphs me. Well, I'll be saving instead of squandering. But it feels so good to squander!"

"I have never had anything to squander," said Bolles, rather sadly.

"You don't say! Well, old man, I hope you will. It gives a man a lot he'll never get out of spelling-books. Are you cold? Here." And despite the school-master's protest, Dean Drake tucked his buffalo coat round and over him. "Some day, when I'm old," he went on, "I mean to live respectable under my own cabin and vine. Wife and everything. But not, anyway, till I'm thirty-five."

He dropped into his opera tunes for awhile; but evidently it was not "Fatinitza" and his vanished holiday over which he was chiefly

meditating, for presently he exclaimed: "I'll
give them a shooting-match in the morning.
You shoot?"

Bolles hoped he was going to learn in this
country, and exhibited a .22 Smith & Wesson
revolver.

Drake grieved over it. "Wrap it up warm,"
said he. "Don't let it get a chill. I'll lend you
a grown up one when we get to the Malheur
Agency. But you can eat, anyhow. Christmas
being next week, you see, my programme is,
shoot all A.M. and eat all P.M. I wish you could
light on a notion what prizes to give my buccaroos."

"Buccaroos?" said Bolles.

"Yep. Cow-punchers. Vaqueros. Buccaroos in Oregon. Bastard Spanish word, you
see, drifted up from Mexico. Vogel would not
care to have me give 'em money as prizes."

At this Uncle Pasco opened an eye.

"How many buccaroos will there be?"
Bolles inquired.

"At the Malheur Agency? It's the headquarters of five of our ranches. There ought
to be quite a crowd. A dozen, probably, at
this time of year."

Uncle Pasco opened his other eye. "Here,
you!" he said, dragging at his box under the

seat. "Pull it, can't you? There. Just what
you're after. There's your prizes." Querulous
and watchful, like some aged, rickety ape,
the old man drew out his trinkets in shallow
shelves.

"Sooner give 'em nothing," said Dean
Drake.

"What's that? What's the matter with
them?"

"Guess the boys have had all the brass
rings and glass diamonds they want."

"That's all you know, then. I sold that
box clean empty through the Palouse country
last week, 'cept the bottom drawer, and an
outfit on Meacham's hill took that. Shows all
you know. I'm going clean through your
country after I've quit Silver City. I'll start
in by Baker City again, and I'll strike Harney,
and maybe I'll go to Linkville. I know what
buccaroos want. I'll go to Fort Rinehart, and
I'll go to the Island ranch, and first thing
you'll be seeing your boys wearing my stuff
all over their fingers and Sunday shirts, and
giving their girls my stuff right in Harney
City. That's what."

"All right, Uncle. It's a free country."

"Pshaw! Guess it is. I was in it before
you was, too. You were wet behind the ears

when I was jammin' all around here. How many are they up at your place, did you say?''

"I said about twelve. If you're coming our way, stop and eat with us.''

"Maybe I will and maybe I won't.'' Uncle Pasco crossly shoved his box back.

"All right, Uncle. It's a free country,'' repeated Drake.

Not much was said after this. Uncle Pasco unwrapped his concertina from the red handkerchief and played nimbly for his own benefit. At Silver City he disappeared, and, finding he had stolen nothing from them, they did not regret him. Dean Drake had some affairs to see to here before starting for Harper's ranch, and it was pleasant to Bolles to find how Drake was esteemed through this country. The school-master was to board at the Malheur Agency, and had come this way round because the new superintendent must so travel. They were scarcely birds of a feather, Drake and Bolles, yet since one remote roof was to cover them, the in-door man was glad this boy-host had won so much goodwill from high and low. That the shrewd old Vogel should trust so much in a nineteen-year-old was proof enough at least of his character; but when Brock, the foreman from Harper's,

came for them at Silver City, Bolles witnessed
the affection that the rougher man held for
Drake. Brock shook the boy's hand with that
serious quietness and absence of words which
shows the Western heart is speaking. After a
look at Bolles and a silent bestowing of the
baggage aboard the team, he cracked his long
whip and the three rattled happily away
through the dips of an open country where
clear streams ran blue beneath the winter
air. They followed the Jordan (that Idaho
Jordan) west towards Oregon and the Owyhee, Brock often turning in his driver's seat
so as to speak with Drake. He had a long,
gradual chapter of confidences and events;
through miles he unburdened these to his
favorite:

The California mare was doing well in har-
ness. The eagle over at Whitehorse ranch had
fought the cat most terrible. Gilbert had got
a mule-kick in the stomach, but was eating his
three meals. They had a new boy who played
the guitar. He used maple-syrup on his meat,
and claimed he was from Alabama. Brock
guessed things were about as usual in most
ways. The new well had caved in again.
Then, in the midst of his gossip, the thing he
had wanted to say all along came out: "We're

pleased about your promotion," said he; and, blushing, shook Drake's hand again.

Warmth kindled the boy's face, and next, with a sudden severity, he said: "You're keeping back something."

The honest Brock looked blank, then labored in his memory.

"Has the sorrel girl in Harney married you yet?" said Drake.

Brock slapped his leg, and the horses jumped at his mirth. He was mostly grave-mannered, but when his boy superintendent joked, he rejoiced with the same pride that he took in all of Drake's excellences.

"The boys in this country will back you up," said he, next day; and Drake inquired: "What news from the Malheur Agency?"

"Since the new Chinaman has been cooking for them," said Brock, "they have been peaceful as a man could wish."

"They'll approve of me, then," Drake answered. "I'm feeding 'em hyas Christmas muck-a-muck."

"And what may that be?" asked the schoolmaster.

"You no kumtux Chinook?" inquired Drake. "Travel with me and you'll learn all sorts of languages. It means just a big feed. All whisky is barred," he added to Brock.

"It's the only way," said the foreman. "They've got those Pennsylvania men up there."

Drake had not encountered these.

"The three brothers Potts," said Brock. "Full, Half-past Full, and Drunk are what they call them. Them's the names; they've brought them from Klamath and Rogue River."

"I should not think a Chinaman would enjoy such comrades," ventured Mr. Bolles.

"Chinamen don't have comrades in this country," said Brock, briefly. "They like his cooking. It's a lonesome section up there, and a Chinaman could hardly quit it, not if he was expected to stay. Suppose they kick about the whisky rule?" he suggested to Drake.

"Can't help what they do. Oh, I'll give each boy his turn in Harney City when he gets anxious. It's the whole united lot I don't propose to have cut up on me."

A look of concern for the boy came over the face of foreman Brock. Several times again before their parting did he thus look at his favorite. They paused at Harper's for a day to attend to some matters, and when Drake was leaving this place one of the men said to him: "We'll stand by you." But from his blithe appearance and talk as the slim boy journeyed to the Malheur River and Head-quárter ranch, nothing seemed to be on his mind. Oregon twinkled with sun and fine white snow. They crossed through a world of pines and creviced streams and exhilarating silence. The little waters fell tinkling through icicles in the loneliness of the woods, and snow-shoe rabbits dived into the brush. East Oregon, the Owyhee and the Malheur country, the old trails of General Crook, the willows by the streams, the open swales, the high woods where once Buffalo Horn and Chief E-egante and O-its the medicine-man prospered, through this domain of war and memories went Bolles the school-master with Dean Drake and Brock. The third noon from Harper's they came leisurely down to the old Malheur Agency, where once the hostile Indians had drawn pictures on the door, and where Castle Rock frowned down unchanged.

"I wish I was going to stay here with you," said Brock to Drake. "By Indian Creek you can send word to me quicker than we've come."

"Why, you're an old bat!" said the boy to

his foreman, and clapped him farewell on the
shoulder.

Brock drove away, thoughtful. He was not
a large man. His face was clean-cut, almost
delicate. He had a well-trimmed, yellow mustache, and it was chiefly in his blue eye and
lean cheek-bone that the frontiersman showed.
He loved Dean Drake more than he would ever
tell, even to himself.

The young superintendent set about his
ranch-work this afternoon of Brock's leaving,
and the buccaroos made his acquaintance one
by one and stared at him. Villainy did not sit
outwardly upon their faces; they were not vil-
lains; but they stared at the boy sent to control them, and they spoke together, laughing.
Drake took the head of the table at supper,
with Bolles on his right. Down the table some
silence, some staring, much laughing went on
—the rich brute laugh of the belly untroubled
by the brain. Sam, the Chinaman, rapid and
noiseless, served the dishes.

"What is it?" said a buccaroo.

"Can it bite?" said another.

"If you guess what it is, you can have it,"
said a third.

"It's meat," remarked Drake, incisively,
helping himself; "and tougher than it looks."

The brute laugh rose from the crowd and fell into surprised silence; but no rejoinder came, and they ate their supper somewhat thoughtfully. The Chinaman's quick, soft eye had glanced at Dean Drake when they laughed. He served his dinner solicitously. In his kitchen that evening he and Bolles unpacked the good things—the olives, the dried fruits, the cigars—brought by the new superintendent for Christmas; and finding Bolles harmless, like his gentle Asiatic self, Sam looked cautiously about and spoke:

"You not know why they laugh," said he. "They not talk about my meat then. They mean new boss, Misser Dlake. He velly young boss."

"I think," said Bolles, "Mr. Drake understood their meaning, Sam. I have noticed that at times he expresses himself peculiarly. I also think they understood his meaning."

The Oriental pondered. "Me like Misser Dlake," said he. And drawing quite close, he observed, "They not nice man velly much."

Next day and every day "Misser Dlake" went gayly about his business, at his desk or on his horse, vigilant, near and far, with no sign save a steadier keenness in his eye. For the Christmas dinner he provided still further, sending to the Grande Ronde country for turkeys and other things. He won the heart of Bolles by lending him a good horse; but the buccaroos, though they were boisterous over the coming Christmas joy, did not seem especially grateful. Drake, however, kept his worries to himself.

"This thing happens anywhere," he said one night in the office to Bolles, puffing a cigar. "I've seen a troop of cavalry demoralize itself by a sort of contagion from two or three men."

"I think it was wicked to send you here by yourself," blurted Bolles.

"Poppycock! It's the chance of my life, and I'll jam her through or bust."

"I think they have decided you are getting turkeys because you are afraid of them," said Bolles.

"Why, of course! But d' you figure I'm the man to abandon my Christmas turkey because my motives for eating it are misconstrued?"

Dean Drake smoked for a while; then a knock came at the door. Five buccaroos entered and stood close, as is the way with the guilty who feel uncertain.

"We were thinking as maybe you'd let us go over to town," said Half-past Full, the spokesman.

"When?"

"Oh, any day along this week."

"Can't spare you till after Christmas."

"Maybe you'll not object to one of us goin'?"

"You'll each have your turn after this week."

A slight pause followed. Then Half-past Full said: "What would you do if I went, anyway?"

"Can't imagine," Drake answered, easily. "Go, and I'll be in a position to inform you."

The buccaroo dropped his stolid bull eyes, but raised them again and grinned. "Well, I'm not particular about goin' this week, boss."

"That's not my name," said Drake, "but it's what I am."

They stood a moment. Then they shuffled out. It was an orderly retreat—almost.

Drake winked over to Bolles. "That was a graze," said he, and smoked for a while. "They'll not go this time. Question is, will they go next?"

III

Drake took a fresh cigar, and threw his legs over the chair arm.

"I think you smoke too much," said Bolles, whom three days had made familiar and friendly.

"Yep. Have to just now. That's what! as Uncle Pasco would say. They are a half-breed lot, though," the boy continued, returning to the buccaroos and their recent visit. "Weaken in the face of a straight bluff, you see, unless they get whisky-courageous. And I've called 'em down on that."

"Oh!" said Bolles, comprehending.

"Didn't you see that was their game? But he will not go after it."

"The flesh is all they seem to understand," murmured Bolles.

Half-past Full did not go to Harney City for the tabooed whisky, nor did any one. Drake read his buccaroos like the children that they were. After the late encounter of grit, the atmosphere was relieved of storm. The children, the primitive, pagan, dangerous children, forgot all about whisky, and lusted joyously for Christmas. Christmas was coming! No work! A shooting-match! A big feed!

Cheerfulness bubbled at the Malheur Agency. The weather itself was in tune. Castle Rock seemed no longer to frown, but rose into the shining air, a mass of friendly strength. Except when a rare sledge or horseman passed, Mr. Bolles's journeys to the school were all to show it was not some pioneer colony in a new, white, silent world that heard only the playful shouts and songs of the buccaroos. The sun overhead and the hard-crushing snow underfoot filled every one with a crisp, tingling hilarity.

Before the sun first touched Castle Rock on the morning of the feast they were up and in high feather over at the bunk-house. They raced across to see what Sam was cooking; they begged and joyfully swallowed lumps of his raw plum-pudding. "Merry Christmas!" they wished him, and "Melly Clismas!" said he to them. They played leap-frog over by the stable, they put snow down each other's backs. Their shouts rang round corners; it was like boys let out of school. When Drake gathered them for the shooting-match, they cheered him; when he told them there were no prizes, what did they care for prizes? When he beat them all the first round, they cheered

him again. Pity he hadn't offered prizes! He
wasn't a good business man, after all!

The rounds at the target proceeded through
the forenoon, Drake the acclaimed leader; and
the Christmas sun drew to mid-sky. But as
its splendor in the heavens increased, the
happy shoutings on earth began to wane. The
body was all that the buccaroos knew; well,
the flesh comes pretty natural to all of us—and
who had ever taught these men about the
spirit? The further they were from breakfast
the nearer they were to dinner; yet the happy
shoutings waned! The spirit is a strange
thing. Often it dwells dumb in human clay,
then unexpectedly speaks out of the clay's
darkness.

It was no longer a crowd Drake had at the
target. He became aware that quietness had
been gradually coming over the buccaroos.
He looked, and saw a man wandering by himself in the lane. Another leaned by the stable
corner, with a vacant face. Through the windows of the bunk-house he could see two or
three on their beds. The children were tired
of shouting. Drake went in-doors and threw
a great log on the fire. It blazed up high with
sparks, and he watched it, although the sun

shown bright on the window-sill. Presently he noticed that a man had come in and taken a chair. It was Half-past Full, and with his boots stretched to the warmth, he sat gazing into the fire. The door opened and another buccaroo entered and sat off in a corner. He had a bundle of old letters, smeared sheets tied with a twisted old ribbon. While his large, rope-toughened fingers softly loosened the ribbon, he sat with his back to the room and presently began to read the letters over, one by one. Most of the men came in before long, and silently joined the watchers round the great fireplace. Drake threw another log on, and in a short time this, too, broke into ample flame. The silence was long; a slice of shadow had fallen across the window-sill, when a young man spoke, addressing the logs:

"I skinned a coon in San Saba, Texas, this day a year."

At the sound of a voice, some of their eyes turned on the speaker, but turned back to the fire again. The spirit had spoken from the clay, aloud; and the clay was uncomfortable at hearing it.

After some more minutes a neighbor whispered to a neighbor, "Play you a game of crib."

The man nodded, stole over to where the board was, and brought it across the floor on creaking tip-toe. They set it between them, and now and then the cards made a light sound in the room.

"I treed that coon on Honey," said the young man, after a while—"Honey Creek, San Saba. Kind o' dry creek. Used to flow into Big Brady when it rained."

The flames crackled on, the neighbors still played their cribbage. Still was the day bright, but the shrinking wedge of sun had gone entirely from the window-sill. Half-past Full had drawn from his pocket a mouth-organ, breathing half-tunes upon it; in the middle of "Suwannee River" the man who sat in the corner laid the letter he was beginning upon the heap on his knees and read no more. The great genial logs lay glowing, burning; from the fresher one the flames flowed and forked; along the embered surface of the others ran red and blue shivers of iridescence. With legs and arms crooked and sprawled, the buccaroos brooded, staring into the glow with seldom-winking eyes, while deep inside the clay the spirit spoke quietly. Christmas Day was passing, but the sun shone still two good hours high. Outside, over the snow and pines, it was only in the deeper folds of the hills that the blue shadows had come; the rest of the world was gold and silver; and from far across that silence into this silence by the fire came a tinkling stir of sound. Sleigh-bells it was, steadily coming, too early for Bolles to be back from his school festival.

The toy-thrill of the jingling grew clear and sweet, a spirit of enchantment that did not wake the stillness, but cast it into a deeper dream. The bells came near the door and stopped, and then Drake opened it.

"Hello, Uncle Pasco!" said he. "Thought you were Santa Claus."

"Santa Claus! H'm. Yes. That's what. Told you maybe I'd come."

"So you did. Turkey is due in—let's see— ninety minutes. Here, boys! some of you take Uncle Pasco's horse."

"No, no, I won't. You leave me alone. I ain't stoppin' here. I ain't hungry. I just grubbed at the school. Sleepin' at Missouri Pete's to-night. Got to make the railroad to-morrow." The old man stopped his precip-itate statements. He sat in his sledge deeply muffled, blinking at Drake and the buccaroos, who had strolled out to look at him. "Done a big business this trip," said he. "Told

THE BOY AND THE BUCCAROOS 73

you I would. Now if you was only givin'
your children a Christmas-tree like that I
seen that feller yer school-marm doin' just
now—hee-hee!'' From his blankets he revealed the well-known case. ''Them things
would shine on a tree,'' concluded Uncle
Pasco.

''Hang 'em in the woods, then,'' said Drake.

''Jewelry, is it?'' inquired the young Texas
man.

Uncle Pasco whipped open his case. ''There
you are,'' said he. ''All what's left. That ring
'll cost you a dollar.''

''I've a dollar somewheres,'' said the young
man, fumbling.

Half-past Full, on the other side of the
sleigh, stood visibly fascinated by the wares
he was given a skilful glimpse of down among
the blankets. He peered and he pondered
while Uncle Pasco glibly spoke to him.

''Scatter your truck out plain!'' the buccaroo exclaimed, suddenly. ''I'm not buying in
the dark. Come over to the bunk-house and
scatter.''

''Brass will look just the same anywhere,''
said Drake.

''Brass!'' screamed Uncle. ''Brass your
eye!''

But the buccaroos, plainly glad for distraction, took the woolly scolding old man with them. Drake shouted that if getting cheated cheered them, by all means to invest heavily, and he returned alone to his fire, where Bolles soon joined him. They waited, accordingly, and by-and-by the sleigh-bells jingled again. As they had come out of the silence, so did they go into it, their little silvery tinkle dancing away in the distance, faint and fainter, then, like a breath, gone.

Uncle Pasco's trinkets had audibly raised the men's spirits. They remained in the bunkhouse, their laughter reaching Drake and Bolles more and more. Sometimes they would scuffle and laugh loudly.

"Do you imagine it's more leap-frog?" inquired the school-master.

"Gambling," said Drake. "They'll keep at it now till one of them wins everything the rest have bought."

"Have they been lively ever since morning?"

"Had a reaction about noon," said Drake. "Regular home-sick spell. I felt sorry for 'em."

"They seem full of reaction," said Bolles. "Listen to that!"

It was now near four o'clock, and Sam came in, announcing dinner.

"All leady," said the smiling Chinaman.

"Pass the good word to the bunk-house," said Drake, "if they can hear you."

Sam went across, and the shouting stopped. Then arose a thick volley of screams and cheers.

"That don't sound right," said Drake, leaping to his feet. In the next instant the Chinaman, terrified, returned through the open door. Behind him lurched Half-past Full, and stumbled into the room. His boot caught, and he pitched, but saved himself and stood swaying heavily, looking at Drake. The hair curled dense over his bull head, his mustache was spread with his grin, the light of cloddish humor and destruction burned in his big eye. The clay had buried the spirit like a caving pit.

" 'Twas false jewelry all right!" he roared, at the top of his voice. "A good old jimmy-john full, boss. Say, boss, goin' to run our jimmyjohn off the ranch? Try it on, kid. Come over and try it on!" The bull beat on the table.

Dean Drake had sat quickly down in his chair, his gray eye upon the hulking buccaroo.

Small and dauntless he sat, a sparrow-hawk
caught in a trap, and game to the end—whatever end.

"It's a trifle tardy to outline any policy
about your demijohn," said he, seriously.
"You folks had better come in and eat before
you're beyond appreciating."

"Ho, we'll eat your grub, boss. Sam's
cooking goes." The buccaroo lurched out and
away to the bunk-house, where new bellowing
was set up.

"I've got to carve this turkey, friend," said
the boy to Bolles.

"I'll do my best to help eat it," returned
the school-master, smiling.

"Misser Dlake," said poor Sam, "I solly
you. I velly solly you."

IV

"Reserve your sorrow, Sam," said Dean
Drake. "Give us your soup for a starter.
Come," he said to Bolles. "Quick."

He went into the dining-room, prompt in
his seat at the head of the table, with the
school-master next to him.

"Nice man, Uncle Pasco," he continued.
"But his time is not now. We have nothing
to do for the present but sit like every day
and act perfectly natural."

"I have known simpler tasks," said Mr. Bolles, "but I'll begin by spreading this excellently clean napkin."

"You're no school-marm!" exclaimed Drake; "you please me."

"The worst of a bad thing," said the mild Bolles, "is having time to think about it, and we have been spared that."

"Here they come," said Drake.

They did come. But Drake's alert strategy served the end he had tried for. The drunken buccaroos swarmed disorderly to the door and halted. Once more the new superintendent's ways took them aback. Here was the decent table with lights serenely burning, with unwonted good things arranged upon it—the olives, the oranges, the preserves. Neat as parade drill were the men's places, all the cups and forks symmetrical along the white cloth. There, waiting his guests at the far end, sat the slim young boss talking with his boarder, Mr. Bolles, the parts in their smooth hair going with all the rest of this propriety. Even the daily tin dishes were banished in favor of crockery.

"Bashful of Sam's napkins, boys?" said the boss. "Or is it the bald-headed china?"

At this bidding they came in uncertainly. Their whisky was ashamed inside. They took their seats, glancing across at each other in a transient silence, drawing their chairs gingerly beneath them. Thus ceremony fell unexpected upon the gathering, and for a while they swallowed in awkwardness what the swift, noiseless Sam brought them. He in a long white apron passed and repassed with his things from his kitchen, doubly efficient and civil under stress of anxiety for his young master. In the pauses of his serving he watched from the background, with a face that presently caught the notice of one of them.

"Smile, you almond-eyed highbinder," said the buccaroo. And the Chinaman smiled his best.

"I've forgot something," said Half-past Full, rising. "Don't let 'em skip a course on me." Half-past left the room.

"That's what I have been hoping for," said Drake to Bolles.

Half-past returned presently and caught Drake's look of expectancy. "Oh, no, boss," said the buccaroo, instantly, from the door. "You're on to me, but I'm on to you." He slammed the door with ostentation and dropped with a loud laugh into his seat.

"First smart thing I've known him do," said Drake to Bolles. "I am disappointed."

Two buccaroos next left the room together.

"They may get lost in the snow," said the humorous Half-past. "I'll just show 'em the trail." Once more he rose from the dinner and went out.

"Yes, he knew too much to bring it in here," said Drake to Bolles. "He knew none but two or three would dare drink, with me looking on."

"Don't you think he is afraid to bring it in the same room with you at all?" Bolles suggested.

"And me temperance this season? Now, Bolles, that's unkind."

"Oh, dear, that is not at all what—"

"I know what you meant, Bolles. I was only just making a little merry over this casualty. No, he don't mind me to that extent, except when he's sober. Look at him!"

Half-past was returning with his friends. Quite evidently they had all found the trail.

"Uncle Pasco is a nice old man!" pursued Drake. "I haven't got my gun on. Have you?"

"Yes," said Bolles, but with a sheepish swerve of the eye.

Drake guessed at once. "Not Baby Bunting? Oh, Lord! and I promised to give you an adult weapon!—the kind they're wearing now by way of full-dress.''

"Talkin' secrets, boss?" said Half-past Full.

The well-meaning Sam filled his cup, and this proceeding shifted the buccaroo's truculent attention.

"What's that mud?" he demanded.

"Coffee," said Sam, politely.

The buccaroo swept his cup to the ground, and the next man howled dismay.

"Burn your poor legs?" said Half-past. He poured his glass over the victim. They wrestled, the company pounded the table, betting hoarsely, until Half-past went to the floor, and his plate with him.

"Go easy," said Drake. "You're smashing the company's property."

"Bald-headed china for sure, boss!" said a second of the brothers Potts, and dropped a dish.

"I'll merely tell you," said Drake, "that the company don't pay for this china twice."

"Not twice?" said Half-past Full, smashing some more. "How about thrice?"

"Want your money now?" another inquired.

A riot of banter seized upon all of them, and they began to laugh and destroy.

"How much did this cost?" said one, prying askew his three-tined fork.

"How much did you cost yourself?" said another to Drake.

"What, our kid boss? Two bits, I guess."

"Hyas markook. Too dear!"

They bawled at their own jokes, loud and ominous; threat sounded beneath their lightest word, the new crashes of china that they threw on the floor struck sharply through the foreboding din of their mirth. The spirit that Drake since his arrival had kept under in them day by day, but not quelled, rose visibly each few succeeding minutes, swelling upward as the tide does. Buoyed up on the whisky, it glittered in their eyes and yelled mutinously in their voices.

"I'm waiting all orders," said Bolles to Drake.

"I haven't any," said Drake. "New ones, that is. We've sat down to see this meal out. Got to keep sitting."

He leaned back, eating deliberately, saying no more to the buccaroos; they saw he would never leave the room till they did. As he had taken his chair the first, so was the boy bound to quit it the last. The game of prying fork-tines staled on them one by one, and they took to songs, mostly of love and parting. With the red whisky in their eyes they shouted plaintively of sweethearts, and vows, and lips, and meeting in the wildwood. From these they went to ballads of the cattle-trail and the Yuba River, and so inevitably worked to the old coast song, made of three languages, with its verses rhymed on each year since the first beginning. Tradition laid it heavy upon each singer in his turn to keep the pot a-boiling by memory or by new invention, and the chant went forward with hypnotic cadence to a tune of larkish, ripping gayety. He who had read over his old stained letters in the homesick afternoon had waked from such dreaming and now sang:

"Wunst, Oh wunst in the year o' '49,
    I did meet a fancy thing by the name o' Keroline;
    I prayed her on my knees for to go and leave me be;
    But she wouldn't, no she wouldn't, and she took and married me."

His neighbor was ready with an original contribution:

"Wunst, Oh wunst in the year o' '64,
    By the city of Whatcom down along the shore—
    I never could persuade 'em for to leave me be—
    A Siwash squaw she went and took and married me."

"What was you doin' between all them years?" called Half-past Full.

"Shut yer mouth," said the next singer:

"Wunst, Oh wunst in the year o' '71,
    ('Twas the suddenest deed that I ever done)—
I never could persuade 'em for to leave me be—
A rich banker's daughter she took and married me."

"This is looking better," said Bolles to Drake.

"Don't you believe it," said the boy.

Ten or a dozen years were thus sung.

"I never could persuade 'em for to leave me be," tempestuously brought down the chorus and the fists, until the drunkards could sit no more, but stood up to sing, tramping the tune heavily together. Then, just as the turn came round to Drake himself, they dashed their chairs down and herded out of the room behind Half-past Full, slamming the door.

Drake sat a moment at the head of his Christmas dinner, the fallen chairs, the lumpy wreck. Blood charged his face from his hair to his collar. "Let's smoke," said he. They went from the dinner through the room of the great fireplace to his office beyond.

"Have a mild one?" he said to the schoolmaster.

"No, a strong one to-night, if you please."
And Bolles gave his mild smile.

"You do me good now and then," said
Drake.

"Dear me," said the teacher, "I have found
it the other way."

All the rooms fronted on the road with
doors—the old-time agency doors, where the
hostiles had drawn their pictures in the days
before peace had come to reign over this country. Drake looked out, because the singing
had stopped and they were very quiet in the
bunk-house. He saw the Chinaman steal from
his kitchen.

"Sam is tired of us," he said to Bolles.

"Tired?"

"Running away, I guess. I'd prefer a new
situation myself. That's where you're defi-
cient, Bolles. Only got sense enough to stay
where you happen to be. Hello. What is he
up to?"

Sam had gone beside a window of the bunk-
house and was listening there, flat like a
shadow. Suddenly he crouched, and was gone
among the sheds. Out of the bunk-house immediately came a procession, the buccaroos
still quiet, a careful, gradual body.

Drake closed his door and sat in the chair

again. "They're escorting that jug over here," said he. "A new move, and a big one."

He and Bolles heard them enter the next room, always without much noise or talk—the loudest sound was the jug when they set it on the floor. Then they seemed to sit, talking little.

"Bolles," said Drake, "the sun has set. If you want to take after Sam—"

But the door of the sitting-room opened and the Chinaman himself came in. He left the door a-swing and spoke clearly. "Misser Dlake," said he, "slove bloke" (stove broke).

The superintendent came out of his office, following Sam to the kitchen. He gave no look or word to the buccaroos with their demi-john; he merely held his cigar sidewise in his teeth and walked with no hurry through the sitting-room. Sam took him through to the kitchen and round to a hind corner of the stove, pointing.

"Misser Dlake," said he, "slove no bloke. I hear them inside. They going kill you."

"That's about the way I was figuring it," mused Dean Drake.

"Misser Dlake," said the Chinaman, with appealing eyes, "I velly solly you. They no hurtee me. Me cook."

"Sam, there is much meat in your words. Condensed beef don't class with you. But reserve your sorrows yet a while. Now what's my policy?" he debated, tapping the stove here and there for appearances; somebody might look in. "Shall I go back to my office and get my guns?"

"You not goin' run now?" said the Chinaman, anxiously.

"Oh, yes, Sam. But I like my gun travelling. Keeps me kind of warm. Now if they should get a sight of me arming—no, she's got to stay here till I come back for her. So long, Sam! See you later. And I'll have time to thank you then."

Drake went to the corral in a strolling manner. There he roped the strongest of the horses, and also the school-master's. In the midst of his saddling, Bolles came down.

"Can I help you in any way?" said Bolles.

"You've done it. Saved me a bothering touch-and-go play to get you out here and seem innocent. I'm going to drift."

"Drift?"

"There are times to stay and times to leave, Bolles; and this is a case of the latter. Have you a real gun on now?"

Poor Bolles brought out guiltily his .22

Smith & Wesson. "I don't seem to think of things," said he.

"Cheer up," said Drake. "How could you thought-read me? Hide Baby Bunting, though. Now we're off. Quietly, at the start. As if we were merely jogging to pasture."

Sam stood at his kitchen door, mutely wishing them well. The horses were walking without noise, but Half-past Full looked out of the window.

"We're by, anyhow," said Drake. "Quick now. Burn the earth." The horse sprang at his spurs. "Dust, you son-of-a-gun! Rattle your hocks! Brindle! Vamoose!" Each shouted word was a lash with his quirt. "Duck!" he called to Bolles.

Bolles ducked, and bullets grooved the spraying snow. They rounded a corner and saw the crowd jumping into the corral, and Sam's door empty of that prudent Celestial.

"He's a very wise Chinaman!" shouted Drake, as they rushed.

"What?" screamed Bolles.

"Very wise Chinaman. He'll break that stove now to prove his innocence."

"Who did you say was innocent?" screamed Bolles.

"Oh, I said you were," yelled Drake,

disgusted; and he gave over this effort at conversation as their horses rushed along.

V

It was a dim, wide stretch of winter into which Drake and Bolles galloped from the howling pursuit. Twilight already veiled the base of Castle Rock, and as they forged heavily up a ridge through the caking snow, and the yells came after them, Bolles looked seriously at Dean Drake; but that youth wore an expression of rising merriment. Bolles looked back at the dusk from which the yells were sounding, then forward to the spreading skein of night where the trail was taking him and the boy, and in neither direction could he discern cause for gayety.

"May I ask where we are going?" said he.

"Away," Drake answered. "Just away, Bolles. It's a healthy resort."

Ten miles were travelled before either spoke again. The drunken buccaroos yelled hot on their heels at first, holding more obstinately to this chase than sober ruffians would have attempted. Ten cold, dark miles across the hills it took to cure them; but when their shoutings, that had followed over heights where the pines grew and down through the open swales between, dropped off, and died finally away among the willows along the south fork of the Malheur, Drake reined in his horse with a jerk.

"Now isn't that too bad!" he exclaimed.

"It is all very bad," said Bolles, sorry to hear the boy's tone of disappointment.

"I didn't think they'd fool me again," continued Drake, jumping down.

"Again?" inquired the interested Bolles.

"Why, they've gone home!" said the boy, in disgust.

"I was hoping so," said the school-master.

"Hoping? Why, it's sad, Bolles. Four miles farther and I'd have had them lost."

"Oh!" said Bolles.

"I wanted them to keep after us," complained Drake. "Soon as we had a good lead I coaxed them. Coaxed them along on purpose by a trail they knew, and four miles from here I'd have swung south into the mountains they don't know. There they'd have been good and far from home in the snow without supper, like you and me, Bolles. But after all my trouble they've gone back snug to that fireside. Well, let us be as cosey as we can."

He built a bright fire, and he whistled as he kicked the snow from his boots, busying over the horses and the blankets. "Take a rest," he said to Bolles. "One man's enough to do the work. Be with you soon to share our little cottage." Presently Bolles heard him reciting confidentially to his horse, "'Twas the night after Christmas, and all in the house—only we are not all in the house!" He slapped the belly of his horse Tyee, who gambolled away to the limit of his picket-rope.

"Appreciating the moon, Bolles?" said he, returning at length to the fire. "What are you so gazeful about, father?"

"This is all my own doing," lamented the school-master.

"What, the moon is?"

"It has just come over me," Bolles continued. "It was before you got in the stage at Nampa. I was talking. I told Uncle Pasco that I was glad no whisky was to be allowed on the ranch. It all comes from my folly!"

"Why, you hungry old New England conscience!" cried the boy, clapping him on the shoulder. "How in the world could you foresee the crookedness of that hoary Beelzebub?"

"That's all very well," said Bolles, miserably. "You would never have mentioned it yourself to him."

"You and I, Bolles, are different. I was raised on miscellaneous wickedness. A look at my insides would be liable to make you say your prayers."

The school-master smiled. "If I said any prayers," he replied, "you would be in them."

Drake looked moodily at the fire. "The Lord helps those who help themselves," said he. "I've prospered. For a nineteen-year-old I've hooked my claw fairly deep here and there. As for to-day—why, that's in the game, too. It was their deal. Could they have won it on their own play? A joker dropped into their hand. It's my deal now, and I have some jokers myself. Go to sleep, Bolles. We've a ride ahead of us."

The boy rolled himself in his blanket skilfully. Bolles heard him say once or twice in a sort of judicial conversation with the blanket —"and all in the house—but we were not all in the house. Not all. Not a full house—" His tones drowsed comfortably into murmur, and then to quiet breathing. Bolles fed the fire, thatched the unneeded wind-break (for the calm, dry night was breathless), and for a long while watched the moon and a tuft of the sleeping boy's hair.

"If he is blamed," said the school-master,

"I'll never forgive myself. I'll never forgive myself anyhow."

A paternal, or rather maternal, expression came over Bolles's face, and he removed his large, serious glasses. He did not sleep very well.

The boy did. "I'm feeling like a bird," said he, as they crossed through the mountains next morning on a short cut to the Owyhee. "Breakfast will brace you up, Bolles. There'll be a cabin pretty soon after we strike the other road. Keep thinking hard about coffee."

"I wish I could," said poor Bolles. He was forgiving himself less and less.

Their start had been very early; as Drake bid the school-master observe, to have nothing to detain you, nothing to eat and nothing to pack, is a great help in journeys of haste. The warming day, and Indian Creek well behind them, brought Drake to whistling again, but depression sat upon the self-accusing Bolles. Even when they sighted the Owyhee road below them, no cheerfulness waked in him; not at the nearing coffee, nor yet at the companionable tinkle of sleigh-bells dancing faintly upward through the bright, silent air.

"Why, if it ain't Uncle Pasco!" said Drake, peering down through a gap in the foot-hill.

"We'll get breakfast sooner than I expected. Quick! Give me Baby Bunting!"

"Are you going to kill him?" whispered the school-master, with a beaming countenance. And he scuffled with his pocket to hand over his hitherto belittled weapon.

Drake considered him. "Bolles, Bolles," said he, "you have got the New England conscience rank. Plymouth Rock is a pudding to your heart. Remind me to pray for you first spare minute I get. Now follow me close. He'll be much more useful to us alive."

They slipped from their horses, stole swiftly down a shoulder of the hill, and waited among some brush. The bells jingled unsuspectingly onward to this ambush.

"Only hear 'em!" said Drake. "All full of silver and Merry Christmas. Don't gaze at me like that, Bolles, or I'll laugh and give the whole snap away. See him come! The old man's breath streams out so calm. He's not worried with New England conscience. One, two, three—" Just before the sleigh came opposite, Dean Drake stepped out. "Morning, Uncle!" said he. "Throw up your hands!"

Uncle Pasco stopped dead, his eyes blinking. Then he stood up in the sleigh among his blankets. "H'm," said he. "The Kid."

"Throw up your hands! Quit fooling with that blanket!" Drake spoke dangerously now. "Bolles," he continued, "pitch everything out of the sleigh while I cover him. "He's got a shot-gun under that blanket. Sling it out."

It was slung. The wraps followed. Uncle Pasco stepped obediently down, and soon the chattels of the emptied sleigh littered the snow. The old gentleman was invited to undress until they reached the six-shooter that Drake suspected. Then they ate his lunch, drank some whisky that he had not sold to the buccaroos, told him to repack the sleigh, allowed him to wrap up again, bade him take the reins, and they would use his six-shooter and shot-gun to point out the road to him.

He had said very little, had Uncle Pasco, but stood blinking, obedient and malignant. "H'm" said he now, "goin' to ride with me, are you?"

He was told yes, that for the present he was their coachman. Their horses were tired and would follow, tied behind. "We're weary, too," said Drake, getting in. "Take your legs out of my way or I'll kick off your shins. Bolles, are you fixed warm and comfortable? Now start her up for Harper ranch, Uncle."

"What are you proposing to do with me?" inquired Uncle Pasco.

"Not going to wring your neck, and that's enough for the present. Faster, Uncle. Get a gait on. Bolles, here's Baby Bunting. Much obliged to you for the loan of it, old man."

Uncle Pasco's eye fell on the .22-caliber pistol. "Did you hold me up with that lemonade straw?" he asked, huskily.

"Yep," said Drake. "That's what."

"Oh, hell!" murmured Uncle Pasco. And for the first time he seemed dispirited.

"Uncle, you're not making time," said Drake after a few miles. "I'll thank you for the reins. Open your bandanna and get your concertina. Jerk the bellows for us."

"That I'll not!" screamed Uncle Pasco.

"It's music or walk home," said the boy. "Take your choice."

Uncle Pasco took his choice, opening with the melody of "The Last Rose of Summer." The sleigh whirled up the Owyhee by the winter willows, and the levels, and the meadow pools, bright frozen under the blue sky. Late in this day the amazed Brock by his corrals at Harper's beheld arrive his favorite, his boy superintendent, driving in with the schoolmaster staring through his glasses, and Uncle Pasco throwing out active strains upon his concertina. The old man had been bidden to bellows away for his neck.

Drake was not long in explaining his need to the men. "This thing must be worked quick," said he. "Who'll stand by me?"

All of them would, and he took ten, with the faithful Brock. Brock would not allow Gilbert to go, because he had received another mule-kick in the stomach. Nor was Bolles permitted to be of the expedition. To all his protests, Drake had but the single word: "This is not your fight, old man. You've done your share with Baby Bunting."

The school-master was in sorrow compelled to see them start back to Indian Creek and the Malheur without him. With him Uncle Pasco would have joyfully exchanged. He was taken along with the avengers. They would not wring his neck, but they would play cat and mouse with him and his concertina; and they did. But the conscience of Bolles still toiled. When Drake and the men were safe away, he got on the wagon going for the mail, thus making his way next morning to the railroad and Boise, where Max Vogel listened to him; and together this couple hastily took train and team for the Malheur Agency.

The avengers reached Indian Creek duly, and the fourth day after his Christmas din-

ner Drake came once more in sight of Castle
Rock.

"I am doing this thing myself, understand," he said to Brock. "I am responsible."

"We're here to take your orders," returned
the foreman. But as the agency buildings
grew plain and the time for action was coming, Brock's anxious heart spoke out of its ful-
ness. "If they start in to—to—they might—
I wish you'd let me get in front," he begged,
all at once.

"I thought you thought better of me," said
Drake.

"Excuse me," said the man. Then presently: "I don't see how anybody could 'a' told
he'd smuggle whisky that way. If the old man
[Brock meant Max Vogel] goes to blame you,
I'll give him my opinion straight."

"The old man's got no use for opinions,"
said Drake. "He goes on results. He trusted
me with this job, and we're going to have results now."

The drunkards were sitting round outside
the ranch house. It was evening. They cast
a sullen inspection on the new-comers, who returned them no inspection whatever. Drake
had his men together and took them to the
stable first, a shed with mangers. Here he

had them unsaddle. "Because," he mentioned to Brock, "in case of trouble we'll be sure of their all staying. I'm taking no chances now."

Soon the drunkards strolled over, saying good-day, hazarding a few comments on the weather and like topics, and meeting sufficient answers.

"Goin' to stay?"

"Don't know."

"That's a good horse you've got."

"Fair."

But Sam was the blithest spirit at the Malheur Agency. "Hiyah!" he exclaimed. "Misser Dlake! How fashion you come quick so?" And the excellent Chinaman took pride in the meal of welcome that he prepared.

"Supper's now," said Drake to his men. "Sit anywhere you feel like. Don't mind whose chair you're taking—and we'll keep our guns on."

Thus they followed him, and sat. The boy took his customary perch at the head of the table, with Brock at his right. "I miss old Bolles," he told his foreman. "You don't appreciate Bolles."

"From what you tell of him," said Brock, "I'll examine him more careful."

Seeing their boss, the sparrow-hawk, back

in his place, flanked with supporters, and his
gray eye indifferently upon them, the buccaroos grew polite to oppressiveness. While
Sam handed his dishes to Drake and the new-
comers, and the new-comers ate what was
good before the old inhabitants got a taste,
these latter grew more and more solicitous.
They offered sugar to the strangers, they offered their beds; Half-past Full urged them
to sit companionably in the room where the
fire was burning. But when the meal was over,
the visitors went to another room with their
arms, and lighted their own fire. They brought
blankets from their saddles, and after a little
concertina they permitted the nearly perished
Uncle Pasco to slumber. Soon they slumbered
themselves, with the door left open, and Drake
watching. He would not even share vigil with
Brock, and all night he heard the voices of the
buccaroos, holding grand, unending council.

When the relentless morning came, and
breakfast with the visitors again in their
seats, unapproachable, the drunkards felt the
crisis to be a strain upon their sobered nerves.
They glanced up from their plates, and down;
along to Dean Drake eating his hearty por-
ridge, and back at one another, and at the
hungry, well-occupied strangers.

"Say, we don't want trouble," they began to the strangers.

"Course you don't. Breakfast's what you're after."

"Oh, well, you'd have got gay. A man gets gay."

"Sure."

"Mr. Drake," said Half-past Full, sweating with his effort, "we were sorry while we was a-fogging you up."

"Yes," said Drake. "You must have been just overcome by contrition."

A large laugh went up from the visitors, and the meal was finished without further diplomacy.

"One matter, Mr. Drake," stammered Half-past Full, as the party rose. "Our jobs. We're glad to pay for any things what got sort of broke."

"Sort of broke," repeated the boy, eying him. "So you want to hold your jobs?"

"If—" began the buccaroo, and halted.

"Fact is, you're a set of cowards," said Drake, briefly. "I notice you've forgot to remove that whisky jug."

The demijohn still stood by the great fireplace. Drake entered and laid hold of it, the crowd standing back and watching. He took it out, with what remained in its capacious bottom, set it on a stump, stepped back, levelled his gun, and shattered the vessel to pieces. The whisky drained down, wetting the stump, creeping to the ground.

Much potency lies in the object-lesson, and a grin was on the faces of all present, save Uncle Pasco's. It had been his demijohn, and when the shot struck it he blinked nervously.

"You ornery old mink!" said Drake, looking at him. "You keep to the jewelry business hereafter."

The buccaroos grinned again. It was reassuring to witness wrath turn upon another.

"You want to hold your jobs?" Drake resumed to them. "You can trust yourselves?"

"Yes, sir," said Half-past Full.

"But I don't trust you," stated Drake, genially; and the buccaroos' hopeful eyes dropped. "I'm going to divide you," pursued the new superintendent. "Split you far and wide among the company's ranches. Stir you in with decenter blood. You'll go to Whitehorse ranch, just across the line of Nevada," he said to Half-past Full. "I'm tired of the brothers Potts. You'll go—let's see—"

Drake paused in his apportionment, and a sleigh came swiftly round the turn, the horse loping and lathery.

"What vas dat shooting I hear joost now?" shouted Max Vogel, before he could arrive. He did not wait for any answer. "Thank the good God!" he exclaimed, at seeing the boy Dean Drake unharmed, standing with a gun. And to their amazement he sped past them, never slacking his horse's lope until he reached the corral. There he tossed the reins to the placid Bolles, and springing out like a sure-footed elephant, counted his saddle-horses; for he was a general. Satisfied, he strode back to the crowd by the demijohn. "When dem men get restless," he explained to Drake at once, "always look out. Somebody might steal a horse."

The boy closed one gray, confidential eye at his employer. "Just my idea," said he, "when I counted 'em before breakfast."

"You liddle r-rascal," said Max, fondly. "What you shoot at?"

Drake pointed at the demijohn. "It was bigger than those bottles at Nampa," said he. "Guess you could have hit it yourself."

Max's great belly shook. He took in the

situation. It had a flavor that he liked. He paused to relish it a little more in silence.

"Und you have killed noding else?" said he, looking at Uncle Pasco, who blinked copiously. "Mine old friend, you never get rich if you change your business so frequent. I tell you that thirty years now." Max's hand found Drake's shoulder, but he addressed Brock. "He is all what you tell me," said he to the foreman. "He have joodgement."

Thus the huge, jovial Teuton took command, but found Drake had left little for him to do. The buccaroos were dispersed at Harper's, at Fort Rinehart, at Alvord Lake, towards Stein's peak, and at the Island ranch by Harney Lake. And if you know east Oregon, or the land where Chief E-egante helped out Specimen Jones, his white soldier friend, when the hostile Bannocks were planning his immediate death as a spy, you will know what wide regions separated the buccaroos. Bolles was taken into Max Vogel's esteem; also was Chinese Sam. But Max sat smoking in the office with his boy superintendent, in particular satisfaction.

"You are a liddle r-rascal," said he. "Und I r-raise you fifty dollars."

A Kinsman of Red Cloud

I

IT was thirty minutes before a June sundown at the post, and the first call had
sounded for parade. Over in the barracks
the two companies and the single troop
lounged a moment longer, then laid their
police literature down, and lifted their stocking feet from the beds to get ready. In the
officers' quarters the captain rose regretfully
from after-dinner digestion, and the three
lieutenants sought their helmets with a sigh.
Lieutenant Balwin had been dining an unconventional and impressive guest at the
mess, and he now interrupted the anecdote
which the guest was achieving with frontier
deliberation.

"Make yourself comfortable," he said.
"I'll have to hear the rest about the half-
breed when I get back."

"There ain't no more—yet. He got my cash
with his private poker deck that wunst, and
I'm fixing for to get his'n."

Second call sounded; the lines filed out and

formed, the sergeant of the guard and two privates took their station by the flag, and when battalion was formed the commanding officer, towering steeple-stiff beneath his plumes, received the adjutant's salute, ordered him to his post, and began drill. At all this the unconventional guest looked on comfortably from Lieutenant Balwin's porch.

"I doubt if I could put up with that there discipline all the week," he mused. "Carry—*arms!* Present—*arms!* I guess that's all I know of it." The winking white line of gloves stirred his approval. "Pretty good that. Gosh, see the sun on them bayonets!"

The last note of retreat merged in the sonorous gun, and the flag shining in the light of evening slid down and rested upon the earth. The blue ranks marched to a single bugle—the post was short of men and officers—and the captain, with the released lieutenants, again sought digestion and cigars. Balwin returned to his guest, and together they watched the day forsake the plain. Presently the guest rose to take his leave. He looked old enough to be the father of the young officer, but he was a civilian, and the military man proceeded to give him excellent advice.

"Now don't get into trouble, Cutler."

The slouch-shouldered scout rolled his quid gently, and smiled at his superior with indulgent regard.

"See here, Cutler, you have a highly unoccupied look about you this evening. I've been studying the customs of this population, and I've noted a fact or two."

"Let 'em loose on me, sir."

"Fact one: When any male inhabitant of Fort Laramie has a few spare moments, he hunts up a game of cards."

"Well, sir, you've called the turn on me."

"Fact two: At Fort Laramie a game of cards frequently ends in discussion."

"Fact three: Mr. Balwin, in them discussions Jarvis Cutler has the last word. You put that in your census report alongside the other two."

"Well, Cutler, if somebody's gun should happen to beat yours in an argument, I should have to hunt another wagon-master."

"I'll not forget that. When was you expecting to pull out north?"

"Whenever the other companies get here. May be three days—may be three weeks."

"Then I will have plenty time for a game to-night."

With this slight dig of his civilian independ-

ence into the lieutenant's military ribs, the
scout walked away, his long, lugubrious frock-
coat (worn in honor of the mess) occasionally
flapping open in the breeze, and giving a view
of a belt richly fluted with cartridges, and the
ivory handle of a pistol looking out of its holster. He got on his horse, crossed the flat, and
struck out for the cabin of his sociable friends,
Loomis and Kelley, on the hill. The open door
and a light inside showed the company, and
Cutler gave a grunt, for sitting on the table
was the half-breed, the winner of his un-
avenged dollars. He rode slower, in order to
think, and arriving at the corral below the
cabin, tied his horse to the stump of a cotton-
wood. A few steps towards the door, and he
wheeled on a sudden thought and under cover
of the night did a crafty something which to
the pony was altogether unaccountable. He
unloosed both front and rear cinch of his saddle, so they hung entirely free in wide bands
beneath the pony's belly. He tested their
slackness with his hand several times, stopping instantly when the more and more surprised pony turned his head to see what new
thing in his experience might be going on, and,
seeing, gave a delicate bounce with his hind-
quarters.

"Never you mind, Duster," muttered the scout. "Did you ever see a skunk-trap? Oughts is for mush-rats, and number ones is mostly used for 'coons and 'possums, and I guess they'd do for a skunk. But you and me'll call this here trap a number two, Duster, for the skunk I'm after is a big one. All you've to do is to act natural."

Cutler took the rope off the stump by which Duster had been tied securely, wound and strapped it to the tilted saddle, and instead of this former tether, made a weak knot in the reins, and tossed them over the stump. He entered the cabin with a countenance sweeter than honey.

"Good-evening, boys," he said. "Why, Toussaint, how do you do?"

The hand of Toussaint had made a slight, a very slight, movement towards his hip, but at sight of Cutler's mellow smile resumed its clasp upon his knee.

"Golly, but you're gay-like this evenin'!" said Kelley.

"Blamed if I knowed he could look so frisky," added Loomis.

"Sporting his onced-a-year coat," Kelley pursued. "That ain't for our benefit, Joole."

"No, we're not that high in society." Both

these cheerful waifs had drifted from the Atlantic coast westward.

Cutler looked from them to his costume, and then amiably surveyed the half-breed.

"Well, boys, I'm in big luck, I am. How's yourn nowadays, Toussaint?"

"Pretty good sometime. Sometime heap hell." The voice of the half-breed came as near heartiness as its singularly false quality would allow, and as he smiled he watched Cutler with the inside of his eyes.

The scout watched nobody and nothing with great care, looked about him pleasantly, inquired for the whisky, threw aside hat and gloves, sat down, leaning the chair back against the wall, and talked with artful candor. "Them sprigs of lieutenants down there," said he, "they're a surprising lot for learning virtue to a man. You take Balwin. Why, he ain't been out of the Academy only two years, and he's been telling me how card-playing ain't good for you. And what do you suppose he's been and offered Jarvis Cutler for a job? I'm to be wagon-master." He paused, and the half-breed's attention to his next words increased. "Wagon-master, and good pay, too. Clean up to the Black Hills; and the troops'll move soon as ever them

reinforcements come. Drinks on it, boys! Set
'em up, Joole Loomis. My contract's sealed
with some of Uncle Sam's cash, and I'm going
to play it right here. Hello! Somebody coming to join us? He's in a hurry.''

There was a sound of lashing straps and
hoofs beating the ground, and Cutler looked
out of the door. As he had calculated, the
saddle had gradually turned with Duster's
movements and set the pony bucking.

"Stampeded!" said the scout, and swore
the proper amount called for by such circumstances. "Some o' you boys help me stop the
durned fool.''

Loomis and Kelley ran. Duster had jerked
the prepared reins from the cotton-wood, and
was lurching down a small dry gulch, with
the saddle bouncing between his belly and the
stones.

Cutler cast a backward eye at the cabin
where Toussaint had stayed behind alone.
"Head him off below, boys, and I'll head him
off above,'' the scout sang out. He left his
companions, and quickly circled round behind
the cabin, stumbling once heavily, and hurrying on, anxious lest the noise had reached the
lurking half-breed. But the ivory-handled
pistol, jostled from its holster, lay unheeded

among the stones where he had stumbled. He
advanced over the rough ground, came close
to the logs, and craftily peered in at the small
window in the back of the cabin. It was evi-
dent that he had not been heard. The sinister
figure within still sat on the table, but was
crouched, listening like an animal to the
shouts that were coming from a safe distance
down in the gulch. Cutler, outside of the window, could not see the face of Toussaint, but
he saw one long brown hand sliding up and
down the man's leg, and its movement put him
in mind of the tail of a cat. The hand stopped
to pull out a pistol, into which fresh cartridges
were slipped. Cutler had already done this
same thing after dismounting, and he now
felt confident that his weapon needed no further examination. He did not put his hand
to his holster. The figure rose from the table,
and crossed the room to a set of shelves in
front of which hung a little yellow curtain.
Behind it were cups, cans, bottles, a pistol,
counters, red, white, and blue, and two fresh
packs of cards, blue and pink, side by side.
Seeing these, Toussaint drew a handkerchief
from his pocket, and unwrapped two further
packs, both blue; and at this Cutler's intent
face grew into plain shape close to the window,

but receded again into uncertain dimness.
From down in the gulch came shouts that
the runaway horse was captured. Toussaint
listened, ran to the door, and quickly returning, put the blue pack from the shelf into
his pocket, leaving in exchange one of his own.
He hesitated about altering the position of
the cards on the shelf, but Kelley and Loomis
were unobservant young men, and the half-
breed placed the pink cards on top of his blue
ones. The little yellow curtain again hung
innocently over the shelves, and Toussaint,
pouring himself a drink of whisky, faced
round, and for the first time saw the window
that had been behind his back. He was at it
in an instant, wrenching its rusty pin, that did
not give, but stuck motionless in the wood.
Cursing, he turned and hurried out of the door
and round the cabin. No one was there. Some
hundred yards away the noiseless Cutler
crawled farther among the thickets that filled
the head of the gulch. Toussaint whipped out
a match, and had it against his trousers to
strike and look if there were footprints, when
second thoughts warned him this might be
seen, and was not worth risking suspicion
over, since so many feet came and went by
this cabin. He told himself no one could have

been there to see him, and slowly returned inside, with a mind that fell a hair's-breadth short of conviction.

The boys, coming up with the horse, met Cutler, who listened to how Duster had stood still as soon as he had kicked free of his saddle, making no objection to being caught. They suggested that he would not have broken loose had he been tied with a rope; and hearing this, Cutler bit off a piece of tobacco, and told them they were quite right: a horse should never be tied by his bridle. For a savory moment the scout cuddled his secret, and turned it over like the tobacco lump under his tongue. Then he explained, and received serenely the amazement of Loomis and Kelley.

"When you kids have travelled this Western country awhile you'll keep your cards locked," said he. "He's going to let us win first. You'll see, he'll play a poor game with the pink deck. Then, if we don't call for fresh cards, why, he'll call for 'em himself. But, just for the fun of the thing, if any of us loses steady, why, we'll call. Then, when he gets hold of his strippers, watch out. When he makes his big play, and is stretchin' for to rake the counters in, you grab 'em, Joole; for by then I'll have my gun on him, and if he makes any trouble we'll feed him to the coyotes. I expect that must have been it, boys,'' he continued, in a new tone, as they came within possible ear-shot of the half-breed in the cabin. "A coyote come around him where he was tied. The fool horse has seen enough of 'em to git used to 'em, you'd think, but he don't. There; that'll hold him. I guess he'll have to pull the world along with him if he starts to run again.''

The lamp was placed on the window-shelf, and the four took seats, Cutler to the left of Toussaint, with Kelley opposite. The pink cards fell harmless, and for a while the game was a dull one to see. Holding a pair of kings, Cutler won a little from Toussaint, who remarked that luck must go with the money of Uncle Sam. After a few hands, the half-breed began to bet with ostentatious folly, and, losing to one man and another, was joked upon the falling off of his game. In an hour's time his blue chips had been twice reinforced, and twice melted from the neat often-counted pile in which he arranged them; moreover, he had lost a horse from his string down on Chug Water.

"Lend me ten dollar,'' he said to Cutler. "You rich man now.''

In the next few deals Kelley became poor. "I'm sick of this luck," said he.

"Then change it, why don't you? Let's have a new deck." And Loomis rose.

"Joole, you always are for something new," said Cutler. "Now I'm doing pretty well with these pink cards. But I'm no hog. Fetch on your fresh ones."

The eyes of the half-breed swerved to the yellow curtain. He was by a French trapper from Canada out of a Sioux squaw, one of Red Cloud's sisters, and his heart beat hot with the evil of two races, and none of their good. He was at this moment irrationally angry with the men who had won from him through his own devices, and malice undisguised shone in his lean flat face. At sight of the blue cards falling in the first deal, silence came over the company, and from the distant parade-ground the bugle sounded the melancholy strain of taps. Faint, far, solemn, melodious, the music travelled unhindered across the empty night.

"Them men are being checked off in their bunks now," said Cutler.

"What you bet this game?" demanded Toussaint.

"I've heard 'em play that same music over a soldier's grave," said Kelley.

"You goin' to bet?" Toussaint repeated.

Cutler pushed forward the two necessary white chips. No one's hand was high, and Loomis made a slight winning. The deal went its round several times, and once, when it was Toussaint's, Cutler suspected that special cards had been thrown to him by the half-breed as an experiment. He therefore played the gull to a nicety, betting gently upon his three kings; but when he stepped out boldly and bet the limit, it was not Toussaint but Kelley who held the higher hand, winning with three aces. Why the *coup* should be held off longer puzzled the scout, unless it was that Toussaint was carefully testing the edges of his marked cards to see if he controlled them to a certainty. So Cutler played on calmly. Presently two aces came to him in Toussaint's deal, and he wondered how many more would be in his three-card draw. Very pretty! One only, and he lost to Loomis, who had drawn three, and held four kings. The hands were getting higher, they said. The game had "something to it now." But Toussaint grumbled, for his luck was bad all this year, he said. Cutler had now made sure that the aces and kings went where the half-breed wished, and could be slid undetected from the top or the middle or the bottom of the pack; but he had no test yet how far down the scale the marking went. At Toussaint's next deal Cutler judged the time had come, and at the second round of betting he knew it. The three white men played their parts, raising each other without pause, and again there was total silence in the cabin. Every face bent to the table, watching the turn repeat its circle with obstinate increase, until new chips and more new chips had been brought to keep on with, and the heap in the middle had mounted high in the hundreds, while in front of Toussaint lay his knife and a match-box—pledges of two more horses which he had staked. He had drawn three cards, while the others took two, except Cutler, who had a pair of kings again, and drawing three, picked up two more. Kelley dropped out, remarking he had bet more than his hand was worth, which was true, and Loomis followed him. Their persistence had surprised Toussaint a little. He had not given every one suspicious hands: Cutler's four kings were enough. He bet once more, was raised by the scout, called, and threw down his four aces.

"That beats me," said Cutler, quietly, and his hand moved under his frock-coat, as the

half-breed, eying the central pile of counters
in triumph, closed his fingers over it. They
were dashed off by Kelley, who looked ex-
pectantly across at Cutler, and seeing the
scout's face wither into sudden old age, cried
out, "For God's sake, Jarvis, where's your
gun?"

Kelley sprang for the yellow curtain, and
reeled backward at the shot of Toussaint.
His arm thrashed along the window-sill as he
fell, sweeping over the lamp, and flaring chan-
nels of oil ran over his body and spread on the
ground. But these could no longer hurt him.
The half-breed had leaped outside the cabin,
enraged that Cutler should have got out during the moment he had been dealing with Kelley. The scout was groping for his ivory-
handled pistol off in the darkness. He found
it, and hurried to the little window at a second
shot he heard inside. Loomis, beating the rising flame away, had seized the pistol from the
shelf, and aimlessly fired into the night at
Toussaint. He fired again, running to the door
from the scorching heat. Cutler got round
the house to save him if he could, and saw
the half-breed's weapon flash, and the body
pitch out across the threshold. Toussaint,
gaining his horse, shot three times and missed

Cutler, whom he could not clearly see; and he heard the scout's bullets sing past him as his horse bore him rushing away.

II

Jarvis Cutler lifted the dead Loomis out of the cabin. He made a try for Kelley's body, but the room had become a cave of flame, and he was driven from the door. He wrung his hands, giving himself bitter blame aloud, as he covered Loomis with his saddle-blanket, and jumped bareback upon Duster to go to the post. He had not been riding a minute when several men met him. They had seen the fire from below, and on their way up the half-breed had passed them at a run.

"Here's our point," said Cutler. "Will he hide with the Sioux, or will he take to the railroad? Well, that's my business more than being wagon-master. I'll get a warrant. You tell Lieutenant Balwin—and somebody give me a fresh horse."

A short while later, as Cutler, with the warrant in his pocket, rode out of Fort Laramie, the call of the sentinels came across the night: "Number One. Twelve o'clock, and all's well." A moment, and the refrain sounded more distant, given by Number Two. When the fourth took it up, far away along the line, the words were lost, leaving something like the faint echo of a song. The half-breed had crossed the Platte, as if he were making for his kindred tribe, but the scout did not believe in this too plain trail.

"There's Chug Water lying right the other way from where he went, and I guess it's there Mr. Toussaint is aiming for." With this idea Cutler swung from north to southwest along the Laramie. He went slowly over his short-cut, not to leave the widely circling Toussaint too much in his rear. The fugitive would keep himself carefully far on the other side of the Laramie, and very likely not cross it until the forks of Chug Water. Dawn had ceased to be gray, and the doves were cooing incessantly among the river thickets, when Cutler, reaching the forks, found a bottom where the sage-brush grew seven and eight feet high, and buried himself and his horse in its cover. Here was comfort; here both rivers could be safely watched. It seemed a good leisure-time for a little fire and some breakfast. He eased his horse of the saddle, sliced some bacon, and put a match to his pile of small sticks. As the flame caught, he stood up to enjoy the cool of a breeze that was passing through the stillness, and he suddenly stamped his fire out. The smell of another fire had come across Chug Water on the wind. It was incredible that Toussaint should be there already. There was no seeing from this bottom, and if Cutler walked up out of it the other man would see, too. If it were Toussaint, he would not stay long in the vast exposed plain across Chug Water, but would go on after his meal. In twenty minutes it would be the thing to swim or wade the stream, and crawl up the mud bank to take a look. Meanwhile, Cutler dipped in water some old bread that he had and sucked it down, while the little breeze from opposite shook the cotton-wood leaves and brought over the smell of cooking meat. The sun grew warmer, and the doves ceased. Cutler opened his big watch, and clapped it shut as the sound of the mud heavily slopping into the other river reached him. He crawled to where he could look at the Laramie from among his sage-brush, and there was Toussaint leading his horse down to the water. The half-breed gave a shrill call, and waved his hat. His call was answered, and as he crossed the Laramie, three Sioux appeared, riding to the bank. They waited till he gained their level, when all four rode up the Chug Water, and went out of sight opposite the watching Cutler. The scout threw off some of his clothes, for the water was still high, and when he had crossed, and drawn himself to a level with the plain, there were the four squatted among the sage-brush beside a fire. They sat talking and eating for some time. One of them rose at last, pointed south, and mounting his horse, dwindled to a dot, blurred, and evaporated in the heated, trembling distance. Cutler at the edge of the bank still watched the other three, who sat on the ground. A faint shot came, and they rose at once, mounted, and vanished southward. There was no following them now in this exposed country, and Cutler, feeling sure that the signal had meant something about Toussaint's horses, made his fire, watered his own horse, and letting him drag a rope where the feed was green, ate his breakfast in ease. Toussaint would get a fresh mount, and proceed to the railroad. With the comfort of certainty and tobacco, the scout lolled by the river under the cotton-wood, and even slept. In the cool of the afternoon he reached the cabin of an acquaintance twenty miles south, and changed his horse. A man had passed by, he was told. Looked as if bound for Cheyenne.

"No," Cutler said, "he's known there"; and
he went on, watching Toussaint's tracks.
Within ten miles they veered away from
Cheyenne to the southeast, and Cutler struck
out on a trail of his own more freely. By midnight he was on Lodge-Pole Creek, sleeping
sound among the last trees that he would pass.
He slept twelve hours, having gone to bed
knowing he must not come into town by daylight. About nine o'clock he arrived, and went
to the railroad station; there the operator
knew him. The lowest haunt in the town was a
tent south of the Union Pacific tracks; and
Cutler, getting his irons, and a man from the
saloon, went there, and stepped in, covering
the room with his pistol. The fiddle stopped,
the shrieking women scattered, and Toussaint,
who had a glass in his hand, let it fly at Cutler's head, for he was drunk. There were two
customers besides himself.

"Nobody shall get hurt here," said Cutler,
above the bedlam that was now set up. "Only
that man's wanted. The quieter I get him,
the quieter it'll be for others."

Toussaint had dived for his pistol, but the
proprietor of the dance-hall, scenting law,
tapped the half-breed on the head with the
barrel of another, and he rolled over, and was

harmless for some minutes. Then he got on his legs, and was led out of the entertainment, which resumed more gayly than ever. Feet shuffled, the fiddle whined, and truculent treble laughter sounded through the canvas walls as Toussaint walked between Cutler and the saloon-man to jail. He was duly indicted, and upon the scout's deposition committed to trial for the murder of Loomis and Kelley. Cutler, hoping still to be wagon-master, wrote to Lieutenant Balwin, hearing in reply that the reinforcements would not arrive for two months. The session of the court came in one, and Cutler was the Territory's only witness. He gave his name and age, and hesitated over his occupation.

"Call it poker-dealer," sneered Toussaint's attorney.

"I would, but I'm such a fool one," observed the witness. "Put me down as wagon-master to the military outfit that's going to White River."

"What is your residence?"

"Well, I reside in the section that lies between the Missouri River and the Pacific Ocean."

"A pleasant neighborhood," said the judge, who knew Cutler perfectly, and precisely how well he could deal poker hands.

"It's not a pleasant neighborhood for some." And Cutler looked at Toussaint.

"You think you done with me?" Toussaint inquired, upon which silence was ordered in the court.

Upon Cutler's testimony the half-breed was found guilty, and sentenced to be hanged in six weeks from that day. Hearing this, he looked at the witness. "I see you one day agin," he said.

The scout returned to Fort Laramie, and soon the expected troops arrived, and the expedition started for White River to join Captain Brent. The captain was stationed there to impress Red Cloud, and had written to headquarters that this chief did not seem impressed very deeply, and that the lives of the settlers were insecure. Reinforcements were accordingly sent to him. On the evening before these soldiers left Laramie, news came from the south. Toussaint had escaped from jail. The country was full of roving, dubious Indians, and with the authentic news went a rumor that the jailer had received various messages. These were to the effect that the Sioux nation did not desire Toussaint to be killed by the white man, that Toussaint's mother was the sister of Red Cloud, and that many friends of Toussaint often passed the jailer's house. Perhaps he did get such messages. They are not a nice sort to receive. However all this may have been, the prisoner was gone.

III

Fort Robinson, on the White River, is backed by yellow bluffs that break out of the foot-hills in turret and toadstool shapes, with stunt pines starving between their torrid bastions. In front of the fort the land slants away into the flat unfeatured desert, and in summer the sky is a blue-steel cover that each day shuts the sun and the earth and mankind into one box together, while it lifts at night to let in the cool of the stars. The White River, which is not wide, runs in a curve, and around this curve below the fort some distance was the agency, and beyond it a stockade, inside which in those days dwelt the settlers. All this was strung out on one side of the White River, the outside of the curve; and at a point near the agency a foot-bridge of two cottonwood trunks crossed to the concave of the river's bend—a bottom of some extent, filled with growing cotton-woods, and the tepees of many Sioux families. Along the river and on the plain other tepees stood.

One morning, after Lieutenant Balwin had become established at Fort Robinson, he was talking with his friend Lieutenant Powell, when Cutler knocked at the wire door. The wagon-master was a privileged character, and he sat down and commented irrelevantly upon the lieutenant's pictures, Indian curiosities, and other well-meant attempts to conceal the walls.

"What's the trouble, Cutler?"

"Don't know as there's any trouble."

"Come to your point, man; you're not a scout now."

"Toussaint's here."

"What! in camp?"

"Hiding with the Sioux. Two Knives heard about it." (Two Knives was a friendly Indian.) "He's laying for me," Cutler added.

"You've seen him?"

"No. I want to quit my job and go after him."

"Nonsense!" said Powell.

"You can't, Cutler," said Balwin. "I can't spare you."

"You'll be having to fill my place, then, I guess."

"You mean to go without permission?" said Powell, sternly.

"Lord, no! He'll shoot me. That's all."

The two lieutenants pondered.

"And it's to-day," continued Cutler, plaintively, "that he should be gettin' decently hanged in Cheyenne."

Still the lieutenants pondered, while the wagon-master inspected a photograph of Marie Rose as Marguerite.

"I have it!" exclaimed Powell. "Let's kill him."

"How about the commanding officer?"

"He'd back us—but we'll tell him afterwards. Cutler, can you find Toussaint?"

"If I get the time."

"Very well, you're off duty till you do. Then report to me at once."

Just after guard-mounting two days later, Cutler came in without knocking. Toussaint was found. He was down on the river now, beyond the stockade. In ten minutes the wagon-master and the two lieutenants were rattling down to the agency in an ambulance, behind four tall blue government mules. These were handily driven by a seventeen-year-old boy whom Balwin had picked up, liking his sterling American ways. He had come West to be a cowboy, but a chance of helping to impress Red Cloud had seemed still dearer to his heart. They drew up at the agency store, and all went in, leaving the boy nearly out of his mind with curiosity, and pretending to be absorbed with the reins. Presently they came out, Balwin with field-glasses.

"Now," said he, "where?"

"You see the stockade, sir?"

"Well?" said Powell, sticking his chin on Cutler's shoulder to look along his arm as he pointed. But the scout proposed to be deliberate.

"Now the gate of the stockade is this way, ain't it?"

"Well, well?"

"You start there and follow the fence to the corner—the left corner, towards the river. Then you follow the side that's nearest the river down to the other corner. Now that corner is about a hundred yards from the bank. You take a bee-line to the bank and go down stream, maybe thirty yards. No; it'll be forty yards, I guess. There's a lone pine-tree right agin the edge." The wagon-master stopped.

"I see all that," said Lieutenant Balwin, screwing the field-glasses. "There's a buck and a squaw lying under the tree."

"Naw, sir," drawled Cutler, "that ain't no buck. That's him lying in his Injun blanket and chinnin' a squaw."

"Why, that man's an Indian, Cutler. I tell you I can see his braids."

"Oh, he's rigged up Injun fashion, fust rate, sir. But them braids of his ain't his'n. False hair."

The lieutenants passed each other the field-glasses three times, and glared at the lone pine and the two figures in blankets. The boy on the ambulance was unable to pretend any longer, and leaned off his seat till he nearly fell.

"Well," said Balwin, "I never saw anything look more like a buck Sioux. Look at his paint! Take the glasses yourself, Cutler."

But Cutler refused. "He's like an Injun," he said. "But that's just what he wants to be." The scout's conviction bore down their doubt.

They were persuaded. "You can't come with us, Cutler," said Powell. "You must wait for us here."

"I know, sir; he'd spot us, sure. But it ain't right. I started this whole business with my poker scheme at that cabin, and I ought to stay with it clear through."

The officers went into the agency store and took down two rifles hanging at the entrance, always ready for use. "We're going to kill a man," they explained, and the owner was entirely satisfied. They left the rueful Cutler inside, and proceeded to the gate of the stockade, turning there to the right, away from the river, and following the paling round the corner down to the farther right-hand corner. Looking from behind it, the lone pine-tree stood near, and plain against the sky. The striped figures lay still in their blankets, talking, with their faces to the river. Here and there across the stream the smoke-stained peak of a tepee showed among the green leaves.

"Did you ever see a more genuine Indian?" inquired Balwin.

"We must let her rip now, anyhow," said Powell, and they stepped out into the open. They walked towards the pine till it was a hundred yards from them, and the two beneath it lay talking all the while. Balwin covered the man with his rifle and called. The man turned his head, and seeing the rifle, sat up in his blanket. The squaw sat up also. Again the officer called, keeping his rifle steadily pointed, and the man dived like a frog

over the bank. Like magic his blanket had
left his limbs and painted body naked, except
for the breech-clout. Balwin's tardy bullet
threw earth over the squaw, who went flapping and screeching down the river. Balwin
and Powell ran to the edge, which dropped six
abrupt feet of clay to a trail, then shelved into
the swift little stream. The red figure was
making up the trail to the foot-bridge that led
to the Indian houses, and both officers fired.
The man continued his limber flight, and they
jumped down and followed, firing. They heard
a yell on the plain above, and an answer to it,
and then confused yells above and below,
gathering all the while. The figure ran on
above the river trail below the bank, and their
bullets whizzed after it.

"Indian!" asserted Balwin, panting.

"Ran away, though," said Powell.

"So'd you run. Think any Sioux'd stay
when army officer comes gunning for him?"

"Shoot!" said Powell. " 'S getting near
bridge," and they went on, running and firing.
The yells all over the plain were thickening.
The air seemed like a substance of solid flash-
ing sound. The naked runner came round the
river curve into view of the people at the
agency store.

"Where's a rifle?" said Cutler to the agent.

"Officers got 'em," the agent explained.

"Well, I can't stand this," said the scout, and away he went.

"That man's crazy," said the agent.

"You bet he ain't!" remarked the ambulance boy.

Cutler was much nearer to the bridge than was the man in the breech-clout, and reaching the bank, he took half a minute's keen pleasure in watching the race come up the trail. When the figure was within ten yards Cutler slowly drew an ivory-handled pistol. The lieutenants below saw the man leap to the middle of the bridge, sway suddenly with arms thrown up, and topple into White River. The current swept the body down, and as it came it alternately lifted and turned and sank as the stream played with it. Sometimes it struck submerged stumps or shallows, and bounded half out of water, then drew under with nothing but the back of the head in sight, turning round and round. The din of Indians increased, and from the tepees in the cottonwoods the red Sioux began to boil, swarming on the opposite bank, but uncertain what had happened. The man rolling in the water was close to the officers.

"It's not our man," said Balwin. "Did you or I hit him?"

"We're gone, anyhow," said Powell, quietly. "Look!"

A dozen rifles were pointing at their heads on the bank above. The Indians still hesitated, for there was Two Knives telling them these officers were not enemies, and had hurt no Sioux. Suddenly Cutler pushed among the rifles, dashing up the nearest two with his arm, and their explosion rang in the ears of the lieutenants. Powell stood grinning at the general complication of matters that had passed beyond his control, and Balwin made a grab as the head of the man in the river washed by. The false braid came off in his hand!

"Quick!" shouted Cutler from the bank. "Shove him up here!"

Two Knives redoubled his harangue, and the Indians stood puzzled, while the lieutenants pulled Toussaint out, not dead, but shot through the hip. They dragged him over the clay and hoisted him, till Cutler caught hold and jerked him to the level, as a new noise of rattling descended on the crowd, and the four blue mules wheeled up and halted. The boy had done it himself. Guessing the officers'

need, he had pelted down among the Sioux,
heedless of their yells, and keeping his gray
eyes on his team. In got the three, pushing
Toussaint in front, and scoured away for the
post as the squaw arrived to shriek the truth
to her tribe—that Red Cloud's relation had
been the victim.

Cutler sat smiling as the ambulance swung
along. "I told you I belonged in this here affair," he said. And when they reached the
fort he was saying it still, occasionally.

Captain Brent considered it neatly done.
"But that boy put the finishing touches," he
said. "Let's have him in."

The boy was had in, and ate a dinner with
the officers in glum embarrassment, smoking
a cigar after it without joy. Toussaint was
given into the doctor's hands, and his wounds
carefully dressed.

"This will probably cost an Indian out-
break," said Captain Brent, looking down at
the plain. Blanketed riders galloped over it,
and yelling filled the air. But Toussaint was
not destined to cause this further harm. An
unexpected influence intervened.

All afternoon the cries and galloping went
on, and next morning (worse sign) there
seemed to be no Indians in the world. The

, horizon was empty, the air was silent, the smoking tepees were vanished from the cotton-woods, and where those in the plain had been lay the lodge-poles, and the fires were circles of white, cold ashes. By noon an interpreter came from Red Cloud. Red Cloud would like to have Toussaint. If the white man was not willing, it should be war.

Captain Brent told the story of Loomis and Kelley. "Say to Red Cloud," he ended, "that when a white man does such things among us, he is killed. Ask Red Cloud if Toussaint should live. If he thinks yes, let him come and take Toussaint."

The next day, with ceremony and feathers of state, Red Cloud came, bringing his interpreter, and after listening until every word had been told him again, requested to see the half-breed. He was taken to the hospital. A sentry stood on post outside the tent, and inside lay Toussaint, with whom Cutler and the ambulance-boy were playing whisky-poker. While the patient was waiting to be hanged, he might as well enjoy himself within reason. Such was Cutler's frontier philosophy. We should always do what we can for the sick. At sight of Red Cloud looming in the doorway, gorgeous and grim as Fate, the game was suspended. The Indian took no notice

of the white men, and walked to the bed.
Toussaint clutched at his relation's fringe, but
Red Cloud looked at him. Then the mongrel
strain of blood told, and the half-breed poured
out a chattering appeal, while Red Cloud by
the bedside waited till it had spent itself. Then
he grunted, and left the room. He had not
spoken, and his crest of long feathers as it
turned the corner was the last vision of him
that the card-players had.

Red Cloud came back to the officers, and in
their presence formally spoke to his interpreter, who delivered the message: "Red
Cloud says Toussaint heap no good. No
Injun, anyhow. He not want him. White
man hunt pretty hard for him. Can keep
him."

Thus was Toussaint twice sentenced. He
improved under treatment, played many
games of whisky-poker, and was conveyed to
Cheyenne and hanged.

These things happened in the early seven-
ties; but there are Sioux still living who remember the two lieutenants, and how they
pulled the half-breed out of White River by
his false hair. It makes them laugh to this
day. Almost any Indian is full of talk when
he chooses, and when he gets hold of a joke
he never lets go.

Sharon's Choice

UNDER Providence, a man may achieve the making of many things—ships, books, fortunes, himself even, quite often enough to encourage others; but let him beware of creating a town. Towns mostly happen. No real-estate operator decided that Rome should be. Sharon was an intended town; a one man's piece of deliberate manufacture; his whim, his pet, his monument, his device for immortally continuing above ground. He planned its avenues, gave it his middle name, fed it with his railroad. But he had reckoned without the inhabitants (to say nothing of nature), and one day they displeased him. Whenever you wish, you can see Sharon and what it has come to, as I saw it when, as a visitor without local prejudices, they asked me to serve with the telegraph operator and the ticket-agent and the hotel-manager on the literary committee of judges at the school festival. There would be a stage, and flags, and elocution, and parents assembled, and afterwards ice-cream with strawberries from El Paso.

138

"Have you ever awarded prizes for school speaking?" inquired the telegraph-operator, Stuart.

"Yes," I told him. "At Concord in New Hampshire."

"Ever have a chat afterwards with a mother whose girl did not get the prize?"

"It was boys," I replied. "And parents had no say in it."

"It's boys and girls in Sharon," said he. "Parents have no say in it here, either. But that don't seem to occur to them at the moment. We'll all stick together, of course."

"I think I had best resign," said I. "You would find me no hand at pacifying a mother."

"There are fathers also," said Stuart. "But individual parents are small trouble compared with a big split in public opinion. We've missed that so far, though."

"Then why have judges? Why not a popular vote?" I inquired.

"Don't go back on us," said Stuart. "We are so few here. And you know education can't be democratic, or where will good taste find itself? Eastman knows that much, at least." And Stuart explained that Eastman was the head of the school and chairman of our committee. "He is from Massachusetts,

and his taste is good, but he is total absti-
nence. Won't allow any literature with the
least smell of a drink in it, not even in the
singing-class. Would not have 'Here's a
health to King Charles' inside the door. Nar-
rowing, that; as many of the finest classics
speak of wine freely. Eastman is useful, but a
crank. Now take 'Lochinvar.' We are to have
it on strawberry night; but say! Eastman
kicked about it. Told the kid to speak something else. Kid came to me, and I—''

A smile lurked for one instant in the corner
of Stuart's eye, and disappeared again. Then
he drew his arm through mine as we walked.

"You have never seen anything in your
days like Sharon," said he. "You could not sit
down by yourself and make such a thing up.
Shakespeare might have, but he would have
strained himself doing it. Well, Eastman says
'Lochinvar' will go in my expurgated version.
Too bad Sir Walter cannot know. Ever read
his *Familiar Letters?* Great grief! but he was
a good man. Eastman stuck about that mention of wine. Remember?

'So now am I come with this lost love of mine
To lead but one measure, drink one cup of wine.'

'Well,' thought I, 'Eastman would agree to
water. Water and daughter would go, but is

frequently used, and spoils the metre.' So I
fiddled with my pencil down in the telegraph-
office, and I fixed the thing up. How's this?

> 'So now am I come with this beautiful maid
> To lead but one measure, drink one lemonade.'

Eastman accepts that. Says it's purer. Oh,
it's not all sadness here!''

"How did you come to be in Sharon?" I
asked my exotic acquaintance.

"Ah, how did I? How did all our crowd at
the railroad? Somebody has got to sell tickets, somebody has got to run that hotel, and
telegraphs have got to exist here. That's how
we foreigners came. Many travellers change
cars here, and one train usually misses the
other, because the two companies do not love
each other. You hear lots of language,
especially in December. Eastern consump-
tives bound for southern California get left
here, and drummers are also thick. Remarks
range from 'How provoking!' to things I
would not even say myself. So that big hotel
and depot has to be kept running, and we
fellows get a laugh now and then. Our lot is
better than these people's.'' He made a general gesture at Sharon.

"I should have thought it was worse,''
said I.

"No, for we'll be transferred some day. These poor folks are shipwrecked. Though it is their own foolishness, all this."

Again my eye followed as he indicated the town with a sweep of his hand; and from the town I looked to the four quarters of heaven. I may have seen across into Old Mexico. No sign labels the boundary; the vacuum of continent goes on, you might think, to Patagonia. Symptoms of neighboring Mexico basked on the sand heaps along Sharon's spacious avenues—little torpid, indecent gnomes in sashes and open rags, with crowning-steeple straw hats, and murder dozing in their small black eyes. They might have crawled from holes in the sand, or hatched out of brown cracked pods on some weeds that trailed through the broken bottles, the old shoes, and the wire fences. Outside these ramparts began the vacuum, white, gray, indigo, florescent, where all the year the sun shines. Not the semblance of any tree dances in the heat; only rocks and lumps of higher sand waver and dissolve and reappear in the shaking crystal of mirage. Not the scar of any river-bed furrows the void. A river there is, flowing somewhere out of the shiny violet mountains to the North, but it dies subterraneously on its way to Sharon, misses the town, and emerges thirty miles south across the sunlight in a shallow, futile lake, a *cienega,* called Las Palomas. Then it evaporates into the ceaseless blue sky.

The water you get in Sharon is dragged by a herd of wind-wheels from the bowels of the sand. Over the town they turn and turn— Sharon's upper story—a filmy colony of slats. In some of the homes beneath them you may go up-stairs—in the American homes, not in the adobe Mexican caves of song, woman, and knives; and brick and stone edifices occur. Monuments of perished trade, these rise among their flatter neighbors cubical and stark; under-shirts, fire-arms, and groceries for sale in the ground-floor, blind dust-windows above. Most of the mansions, however, squat ephemerally upon the soil, no cellar to them, and no stair-case, the total fragile box ready to bounce and caracole should the wind drive hard enough. Inside them, eating, mending, the newspaper, and more babies, eke out the twelvemonth; outside, the citizens loiter to their errands along the brief wide avenues of Sharon that empty into space. Men, women, and children move about in the town, sparse and casual, and over their heads in a white tribe the wind-wheels on their rudders

veer to the breeze and indolently revolve
above the gaping obsoleteness. Through the
dumb town the locomotive bell tolls pervad-
ingly when a train of freight or passengers
trundles in from the horizon or out along the
dwindling fence of telegraph poles. No matter where you are, you can hear it come and
go, leaving Sharon behind, an airy carcass,
bleached and ventilated, setting on the sand,
with the sun and the hot wind pouring through
its bones.

This town was the magnate's child, the
thing that was to keep his memory green; and
as I took it in on that first walk of discovery,
Stuart told me its story: how the magnate
had decreed the railroad shops should be
here; how, at that, corner lots grew in a night;
how horsemen galloped the streets, shooting
for joy, and the hasty tents rose while the
houses were hammered together; how they
had song, dance, cards, whisky, license, murder, marriage, opera—the whole usual thing—
regular as the clock in our West, in Australia,
in Africa, in every virgin corner of the world
where the Anglo-Saxon rushes to spend his
animal spirits—regular as the clock, and in
Sharon's case about fifteen minutes long. For
they became greedy, the corner-lot people.

They ran up prices for land which the railroad, the breath of their nostrils, wanted. They grew ugly, forgetting they were dealing with a magnate, and that a railroad from ocean to ocean can take its shops somewhere else with appalling ease. Thus did the corner lots become sand again in a night. "And in the words of the poet," concluded Stuart, "Sharon has an immense future behind it."

Our talk was changed by the sight of a lady leaning and calling over a fence.

"Mrs. Jeffries," said she. "Oh, Mrs. Jeffries!"

"Well?" called a voice next door.

"I want to send Leola and Arvasita into your yard."

"Well?" the voice repeated.

"Our tool-house blew over into your yard last night. It's jammed behind your tank."

"Oh, indeed!"

A window in the next house was opened, a head put out, and this occasioned my presentation to both ladies. They were Mrs. Mattern and Mrs. Jeffries, and they fell instantly into a stiff caution of deportment; but they speedily found I was not worth being cautious over. Stuart whispered to me that they were widows of high standing, and mothers of

competing favorites for the elocution prize;
and I hastened to court their esteem. Mrs.
Mattern was in body more ample, standing
high and yellow and fluffy; but Mrs. Jeffries
was smooth and small, and behind her spec-
tacles she had an eye.

"You must not let us interrupt you, ladies,"
said I, after some civilities. "Did I understand that something was to be carried somewhere?"

"You did," said Mrs. Jeffries (she had
come out of her house); "and I am pleased to
notice no damage has been done to our fence
—this time."

"It would have been fixed right up at my
expense, as always, Mrs. Jeffries," retorted
her neighbor, and started to keep abreast of
Mrs. Jeffries as that lady walked and inspected the fence. Thus the two marched
parallel along the frontier to the rear of their
respective territories.

"You'll not resign?" said Stuart to me. "It
is 'yours till death,' ain't it?"

I told him that it was.

"About once a month I can expect this,"
said Mrs. Jeffries, returning along her frontier.

"Well, it's not the only case in Sharon,

Mrs. Jeffries," said Mrs. Mattern. "I'll remind you of them three coops when you kept
poultry, and they got away across the railroad, along with the barber's shop."

"But cannot we help you get it out?" said
I, with a zealous wish for peace.

"You are very accommodating, sir," said
Mrs. Mattern.

"One of the prize-awarding committee,"
said Stuart. "An elegant judge of oratory.
Has decided many contests at Concord, the
home of Emerson."

"Concord, New Hampshire," I corrected;
but neither lady heard me.

"How splendid for Leola!" cried Mrs. Mattern, instantly. "Leola! Oh, Leola! Come
right out here!"

Mrs. Jeffries had been more prompt. She
was already in her house, and now came
from it, bringing a pleasant-looking boy of
sixteen, it might be. The youth grinned at
me as he stood awkwardly, brought in shirt-
sleeves from the performance of some household work.

"This is Guy," said his mother. "Guy took
the prize last year. Guy hopes—"

"Shut up, mother," said Guy, with entire
sweetness. "I don't hope twice—"

"Twice or a dozen times should raise no hard feelings if my son is Sharon's best speaker," cried Mrs. Jeffries, and looked across the fence viciously.

"Shut up, mother; I ain't," said Guy.

"He is a master of humor recitations," his mother now said to me. "Perhaps you know, or perhaps you do not know, how high up that is reckoned."

"Why, mother, Leola can speak all around me. She can," Guy added to me, nodding his head confidentially.

I did not believe him, I think because I preferred his name to that of Leola.

"Leola will study in Paris, France," announced Mrs. Mattern, arriving with her child. "She has no advantages here. This is the gentleman, Leola."

But before I had more than noted a dark-eyed maiden who would not look at me, but stood in skirts too young for her figure, black stockings, and a dangle of hair that should have been up, her large parent had thrust into my hand a scrap-book.

"Here is what the Santa Fé *Observer* says"; and when I would have read, she read aloud for me. "The next is the Los Angeles *Christian Home*. And here's what they wrote about her in El Paso: 'Her histrionic genius for one so young'—it commences below that picture. That's Leola." I now recognized the black stockings and the hair. "Here's what a literary lady in Lordsburg thinks," pursued Mrs. Mattern.

"Never mind that," murmured Leola.

"I shall." And the mother read the letter to me. "Leola has spoke in five cultured cities," she went on. "Arvasita can depict how she was oncored at Albuquerque last Easter-Monday."

"Yes, sir, three recalls," said Arvasita, arriving at our group by the fence. An elder sister, she was, evidently. "Are you acquainted with 'Camill'?" she asked me, with a trifle of sternness; and upon my hesitating, "the celebrated French drayma of 'Camill,' " she repeated, with a trifle more of sternness. " 'Camill' is the lady in it who dies of consumption. Leola recites the letter-and-coughing scene, Act Third. Mr. Patterson of Coloraydo Springs pronounces it superior to Modjeska."

"That is Leola again," said Mrs. Mattern, showing me another newspaper cut—hair, stockings, and a candle this time.

"Sleep-walking scene, 'Macbeth,' " said

Arvasita. "Leola's great night at the church
fair and bazar, El Paso, in Shakespeare's acknowledged masterpiece. Leola's repetwar
likewise includes 'Catherine the Queen before
her Judges,' 'Quality of Mercy is not
Strained,' 'Death of Little Nell,' 'Death of
Paul Dombey,' 'Death of the Old Year,'
'Burial of Sir John Moore,' and other stand-
ard gems suitable for ladies.''

"Leola," said her mother, "recite 'When
the British Warrior Queen' to the gentleman.''

"No, momma, please not," said Leola, and
her voice made me look at her; something of
appeal sounded in it.

"Leola is that young you must excuse her,"
said her mother—and I thought the girl
winced.

"Come away, Guy," suddenly snapped little
Mrs. Jeffries. "We are wasting the gentleman's time. You are no infant prodigy, and
we have no pictures of your calves to show
him in the papers.''

"Why, mother!" cried the boy, and he gave
a brotherly look to Leola.

But the girl, scarlet and upset, now ran inside the house.

"As for wasting time, madam," said I, with

indignation, "you are wasting yours in attempting to prejudice the judges."

"There!" said Guy.

"And, Mrs. Mattern," I continued, "if I may say so without offence, the age (real or imaginary) of the speakers may make a difference in Albuquerque, but with our committee not the slightest."

"Thank you, I'm sure," said Mrs. Mattern, bridling.

"Eastern ideas are ever welcome in Sharon," said Mrs. Jeffries. "Good-morning." And she removed Guy and herself into her house, while Mrs. Mattern and Arvasita, stiffly ignoring me, passed into their own door.

"Come have a drink," said Stuart to me. "I am glad you said it. Old Mother Mattern will let down those prodigy skirts. The poor girl has been ashamed of them these two years, but momma has bulldozed her into staying young for stage effect. The girl's not conceited, for a wonder, and she speaks well. It is even betting which of the two widows you have made the maddest."

Close by the saloon we were impeded by a rush of small boys. They ran before and behind us suddenly from barrels and unforeseen places, and wedging and bumping between us, they shouted: "Chicken-legs! Ah, look at the chicken-legs!"

For a sensitive moment I feared they were speaking of me; but the folding slat-doors of the saloon burst open outward, and a giant barkeeper came among the boys and caught and shook them to silence.

"You want to behave," was his single remark; and they dispersed like spray from an atomizer.

I did not see why they should thus describe him. He stood and nodded to us, and jerked a big thumb towards the departing flock. "Funny how a boy will never think," said he, with amiability. "But they'll grow up to be about as good as the rest of us, I guess. Don't you let them monkey with you, Josey!" he called.

"Naw, I won't," said a voice. I turned and saw, by a barrel, a youth in knee-breeches glowering down the street at his routed enemies. He was possibly eight, and one hand was bound in a grimy rag. This was Chicken-legs.

"Did they harm you, Josey?" asked the giant.

"Naw, they didn't."

"Not troubled your hand any?"

"Naw, they didn't."

"Well, don't you let them touch you. We'll see you through." And as we followed him in towards our drink through his folding slat-doors he continued discoursing to me, the new-comer. "I am against interfering with kids. I like to leave 'em fight and fool just as much as they see fit. Now them boys ain't mali-cious, but they're young, you see, they're young, and misfortune don't appeal to them. Josey lost his father last spring, and his mother died last month. Last week he played with a freight-car and left two of his fingers with it. Now you might think that was enough hardship."

"Indeed yes," I answered.

"But the little stake he inherited was gam-bled away by his stinking old aunt."

"Well!" I cried.

"So we're seeing him through."

"You bet," said a citizen in boots and pistol, who was playing billiards.

"This town is not going to permit any man to fool with Josey," stated his opponent in the game.

"Or women either," added a lounger by the bar, shaggy-bearded and also with a pistol.

"Mr. Abe Hanson," said the barkeeper, presenting me to him. "Josey's father's partner. He's took the boy from the aunt and is going to see him through."

"How 'r' ye?" said Mr. Hanson, hoarsely, and without enthusiasm.

"A member of the prize-awarding committee," explained Stuart, and waved a hand at me.

They all brightened up and came round me.

"Heard my boy speak?" inquired one. "Reub Gadsden's his name."

I told him I had heard no speaker thus far; and I mentioned Leola and Guy.

"Hope the boy 'll give us 'The Jumping Frog' again," said one. "I near bust."

"What's the heifer speakin' this trip?" another inquired.

"Huh! Her!" said a third.

"You'll talk different, maybe, this time," retorted the other.

"Not agin 'The Jumping Frog,' he won't," the first insisted. "I near bust," he repeated.

"I'd like for you to know my boy Reub," said Mr. Gadsden to me, insinuatingly.

"Quit fixin' the judge, Al," said Leola's backer. "Reub forgets his words, an' says 'em over, an' balks, an' mires down, an' backs out, an' starts fresh, an' it's confusin' to foller him.''

"I'm glad to see you take so much interest, gentlemen," said I.

"Yes, we're apt to see it through," said the barkeeper. And Stuart and I bade them a good-morning.

As we neared the school-master's house, where Stuart was next taking me, we came again upon the boys with Josey, and no barkeeper at hand to "see him through." But Josey made it needless. At the word "Chicken-legs" he flew in a limber manner upon the nearest, and knocking him immediately flat, turned with spirit upon a second and kicked him. At this they set up a screeching and fell all together, and the school-master came out of his door.

"Boys, boys!" said he. "And the Sabbath, too!"

As this did not immediately affect them, Mr. Eastman made a charge, and they fled from him then. A long stocking of Josey's was torn, and hung in two streamers round his ankles; and his dangling shoe-laces were trodden to fringe.

"If you want your hand to get well for strawberry night—" began Mr. Eastman.

"Ah, bother strawberry night!" said Josey,

and hopped at one of his playmates. But Mr. Eastman caught him skilfully by the collar.

"I am glad his misfortunes have not crushed him altogether," said I.

"Josey Yeatts is an anxious case, sir," returned the teacher. "Several influences threaten his welfare. Yesterday I found tobacco on him. Chewing, sir."

"Just you hurt me," said Josey, "and I'll tell Abe."

"Abe!" exclaimed Mr. Eastman, lifting his brow. "He means a man old enough to be his father, sir. I endeavor to instill him with some few notions of respect, but the town spoils him. Indulges him completely, I may say. And when Sharon's sympathies are stirred, sir, it will espouse a cause very warmly— Give me that!" broke off the school-master, and there followed a brief wrestle. "Chewing again to-day, sir," he added to me.

"Abe lemme have it," shrieked Josey. "Lemme go, or he'll come over and fix you."

But the calm, chilly Eastman had ground the tobacco under his heel. "You can understand how my hands are tied," he said to me.

"Readily," I answered.

"The men give Josey his way in everything. He has a—I may say an unworthy aunt."

"Yes," said I. "So I have gathered."

At this point Josey ducked and slid free, and the united flock vanished with jeers at us. Josey forgot they had insulted him, they forgot he had beaten them; against a common enemy was their friendship cemented.

"You spoke of Sharon's warm way of espousing causes," said I to Eastman.

"I did, sir. No one could live here long without noticing it."

"Sharon is a quiet town, but sudden," remarked Stuart. "Apt to be sudden. They're beginning about strawberry night," he said to Eastman. "Wanted to know about things down in the saloon."

"How does their taste in elocution chiefly lie?" I inquired.

Eastman smiled. He was young, totally bald, the moral dome of his skull rising white above visionary eyes and a serious auburn beard. He was clothed in a bleak, smooth slate-gray suit, and at any climax of emphasis he lifted slightly upon his toes and relaxed again, shutting his lips tight on the finished sentence. "Your question," said he, "has often perplexed me. Sometimes they seem to prefer verse; sometimes prose stirs them greatly. We shall have a liberal crop of both

this year. I am proud to tell you I have aug-
mented our number of strawberry speakers
by nearly fifty per cent.''

''How many will there be?'' said I.

''Eleven. You might wish some could be
excused. But I let them speak to stimulate
their interest in culture. Will you not take
dinner with me, gentlemen? I was just sitting
down when little Josey Yeatts brought me
out.''

We were glad to do this, and he opened another can of corned beef for us. ''I cannot
offer you wine, sir,'' said he to me, ''though I
am aware it is a general habit in luxurious
homes.'' And he tightened his lips.

''General habit wherever they don't prefer
whisky,'' said Stuart.

''I fear so,'' the school-master replied, smiling. ''That poison shall never enter my house,
gentlemen, any more than tobacco. And as I
cannot reform the adults of Sharon, I am doing what I can for their children. Little Hugh
Straight is going to say his 'Lochinvar' very
pleasingly, Mr. Stuart. I went over it with
him last night. I like them to be word per-
fect,'' he continued to me, ''as failures on ex-
hibition night elicit unfavorable comment.''

"And are we to expect failures also?" I inquired.

"Reuben Gadsden is likely to mortify us. He is an earnest boy, but nervous; and one or two others. But I have limited their length. Reuben Gadsden's father declined to have his boy cut short, and he will give us a speech of Burke's; but I hope for the best. It narrows down, it narrows down. Guy Jeffries and Leola Mattern are the two."

"The parents seem to take keen interest," said I.

Mr. Eastman smiled at Stuart. "We have no reason to suppose they have changed since last year," said he. "Why, sir," he suddenly exclaimed, "if I did not feel I was doing something for the young generation here, I should leave Sharon to-morrow! One is not appreciated, not appreciated."

He spoke fervently of various local enterprises, his failures, his hopes, his achievements; and I left his house honoring him, but amazed—his heart was so wide and his head so narrow; a man who would purify with simultaneous austerity the morals of Lochinvar and of Sharon.

"About once a month," said Stuart, "I run

against a new side he is blind on. Take his puzzlement as to whether they prefer verse or prose. Queer and dumb of him that, you see. Sharon does not know the difference between verse and prose.''

''That's going too far,'' said I.

''They don't,'' he repeated, ''when it comes to strawberry night. If the piece is about something they understand, rhymes do not help or hinder. And of course sex is apt to settle the question.''

''Then I should have thought Leola—'' I began.

''Not the sex of the speaker. It's the listeners. Now you take women. Women generally prefer something that will give them a good cry. We men want to laugh mostly.''

''Yes,'' said I; ''I would rather laugh myself, I think.''

''You'd know you'd rather if you had to live in Sharon. The laugh is one of the big differences between women and men, and I would give you my views about it, only my Sunday-off time is up, and I've got to go to telegraphing.''

''Our ways are together,'' said I. ''I'm going back to the railroad hotel.''

''There's Guy,'' continued Stuart. ''He

took the prize on 'The Jumping Frog.' Spoke
better than Leola, anyhow. She spoke 'The
Wreck of the Hesperus.' But Guy had the
back benches—that's where the men sit—
pretty well useless. Guess if there had been a
fire, some of the fellows would have been
scorched before they'd have got strength sufficient to run out. But the ladies did not
laugh much. Said they saw nothing much in
jumping a frog. And if Leola had made 'em
cry good and hard that night, the committee's
decision would have kicked up more of a fuss
than it did. As it was, Mrs. Mattern got me
alone; but I worked us around to where Mrs.
Jeffries was having her ice-cream, and I left
them to argue it out.''

"Let us adhere to that policy," I said to
Stuart; and he replied nothing, but into the
corner of his eye wandered that lurking smile
which revealed that life brought him compensations.

He went to telegraphing, and I to reverie
concerning strawberry night. I found myself
wishing now that there could have been two
prizes; I desired both Leola and Guy to be
happy; and presently I found the matter
would be very close, so far at least as my
judgment went. For boy and girl both

brought me their selections, begging I would
coach them, and this I had plenty of leisure to
do. I preferred Guy's choice—the story of
that blue-jay who dropped nuts through the
hole in a roof, expecting to fill it, and his
friends came to look on and discovered the
hole went into the entire house. It is better
even than "The Jumping Frog"—better than
anything, I think—and young Guy told it well.
But Leola brought a potent rival on the tear-
ful side of things. "The Death of Paul Dombey" is plated pathos, not wholly sterling; but
Sharon could not know this; and while Leola
most prettily recited it to me I would lose my
recent opinion in favor of Guy, and acknowl-
edge the value of her performance. Guy
might have the men strong for him, but this
time the women were going to cry. I got also
a certain other sort of entertainment out of
the competing mothers. Mrs. Jeffries and
Mrs. Mattern had a way of being in the hotel
office at hours when I passed through to meals.
They never came together, and always were
taken by surprise at meeting me.

"Leola is ever so grateful to you," Mrs.
Mattern would say.

"Oh," I would answer, "do not speak of it.

Have you ever heard Guy's 'Blue-Jay' story?''

"Well, if it's anything like that frog business, I don't want to." And the lady would leave me.

"Guy tells me you are helping him so kindly," said Mrs. Jeffries.

"Oh, yes, I'm severe," I answered, brightly. "I let nothing pass. I only wish I was as careful with Leola. But as soon as she begins 'Paul had never risen from his little bed,' I just lose myself listening to her."

On the whole, there were also compensations for me in these mothers, and I thought it as well to secure them in advance.

When the train arrived from El Paso, and I saw our strawberries and our ice-cream taken out, I felt the hour to be at hand, and that whatever our decision, no bias could be laid to me. According to his prudent habit, Eastman had the speakers follow each other alphabetically. This happened to place Leola after Guy, and perhaps might give her the last word, as it were, with the people; but our committee was there, and superior to such accidents. The flags and the bunting hung gay around the draped stage. While the audience rustled or resoundingly trod to its chairs, and seated neighbors conferred solemnly together over the programme, Stuart, behind the bunting, played "Silver Threads among the Gold" upon a melodeon.

"Pretty good this," he said to me, pumping his feet.

"What?" I said.

"Tune. Sharon is for free silver."

"Do you think they will catch your allusion?" I asked him.

"No. But I have a way of enjoying a thing by myself." And he pumped away, playing with tasteful variations until the hall was full and the singing-class assembled in gloves and ribbons.

They opened the ceremonies for us by rendering "Sweet and Low" very happily; and I trusted it was an omen.

Sharon was hearty, and we had "Sweet and Low" twice. Then the speaking began, and the speakers were welcomed, coming and going, with mild and friendly demonstrations. Nothing that one would especially mark went wrong until Reuben Gadsden. He strode to the middle of the boards, and they creaked beneath his tread. He stood a moment in large glittering boots and with hair flat and prominently watered. As he straightened from his bow his suspender-buttons came into view, and remained so for some singular internal reason, while he sent his right hand down into the nearest pocket and began his oratory:

"It is sixteen or seventeen years since I saw the Queen of France," he said, impressively, and stopped.

We waited, and presently he resumed:

"It is sixteen or seventeen years since I saw the Queen of France." He took the right hand out and put the left hand in.

"It is sixteen or seventeen years," said he, and stared frowning at his boots.

I found the silence was getting on my nerves. I felt as if it were myself who was drifting to idiocy, and tremulous empty sensations began to occur in my stomach. Had I been able to recall the next sentence, I should have prompted him.

"It is sixteen or seventeen years since I saw the Queen of France," said the orator, rapidly.

And down deep back among the men came a voice, "Well, I guess it must be, Reub."

This snapped the tension. I saw Reuben's boots march away; Mr. Eastman came from behind the bunting and spoke (I suppose) words of protest. I could not hear them, but in a minute, or perhaps two, we grew calm, and the speaking continued.

There was no question what they thought of Guy and Leola. He conquered the back of the room. They called his name, they blessed him with endearing audible oaths, and even the ladies smiled at his pleasant, honest face— the ladies, except Mrs. Mattern. She sat near Mrs. Jeffries, and throughout Guy's "Blue-Jay" fanned herself, exhibiting a well-sustained inattention. She might have foreseen that Mrs. Jeffries would have her turn. When "The Death of Paul Dombey" came, and handkerchiefs began to twinkle out among the audience, and various noises of grief were rising around us, and the men themselves murmured in sympathy, Mrs. Jeffries not only preserved a suppressed-hilarity countenance, but managed to cough twice with a cough that visibly bit into Mrs. Mattern's soul.

But Leola's appealing cadences moved me also. When Paul was dead, she made her pretty little bow, and we sat spellbound, then gave her applause surpassing Guy's. Unexpectedly I found embarrassment of choice dazing me, and I sat without attending to the later speakers. Was not successful humor

more difficult than pathos? Were not tears
more cheaply raised than laughter? Yet, on
the other hand, Guy had one prize, and where
merit was so even—I sat, I say, forgetful of
the rest of the speakers, when suddenly I was
aware of louder shouts of welcome, and I
awaked to Joseph Yeatts bowing at us.

"Spit it out, Josey!" a large encouraging
voice was crying in the back of the hall.
"We'll see you through."

"Don't be scared, Josey!" yelled another.

Then Josey opened his mouth and rhythmi-
cally rattled the following:

> "I love little pussy her coat is so warm
> And if I don't hurt her she'll do me no harm
> I'll sit by the fi-yer and give her some food
> And pussy will love me because I am good."

That was all. It had come without falter or
pause, even for breath. Josey stood, and the
room rose to him.

"Again! again!" they roared. "He ain't a
bit scared!" "Go it, Josey!" "You don't
forgit yer piece!" And a great deal more,
while they pounded with their boots.

> "I love little pussy,"

began Josey.

"Poor darling!" said a lady next me. "No
mother."

"I'll sit by the fi-yer,"

Josey was continuing. But nobody heard him finish. The room was a babel.

"Look at his little hand!" "Only three fingers inside them rags!" "Nobody to mend his clothes any more." They all talked to each other, and clapped and cheered, while Josey stood, one leg slightly advanced and proudly stiff, somewhat after the manner of those military engravings where some general is seen erect upon an eminence at the moment of victory.

Mr. Eastman again appeared from the bunting, and was telling us, I have no doubt, something of importance; but the giant barkeeper now shouted above the din, "Who says Josey Yeatts ain't the speaker for this night?"

At that striking of the common chord I saw them heave, promiscuous and unanimous, up the steps to the stage. Josey was set upon Abe Hanson's shoulder, while ladies wept around him. What the literary committee might have done I do not know, for we had not the time even to resign. Guy and Leola now appeared, bearing the prize between them—a picture of Washington handing the Bible out of clouds to Abraham Lincoln—and very im-

mediately I found myself part of a procession.
Men and women we were, marching about
Sharon. The barkeeper led; four of Sharon's
fathers followed him, escorting Josey borne
aloft on Abe Hanson's shoulder, and rigid and
military in his bearing. Leola and Guy followed with the picture; Stuart walked with
me, whistling melodies of the war—Dixie and
others. Eastman was not with us. When the
ladies found themselves conducted to the
saloon, they discreetly withdrew back to the
entertainment we had broken out from. Josey
saw them go, and shrilly spoke his first word:
"Ain't I going to have any ice-cream?"
This presently caused us to return to the
ladies, and we finished the evening with entire
unity of sentiment. Eastman alone took the
incident to heart; inquired how he was to accomplish anything with hands tied, and murmured his constant burden once more: "One
is not appreciated, not appreciated."
I do not stop over in Sharon any more. My
ranch friend, whose presence there brought
me to visit him, is gone away. But such was
my virgin experience of the place; and in later
days fate led me to be concerned with two
more local competitions—one military and one
civil—which greatly stirred the population.

So that I never pass Sharon on my long travels without affectionately surveying the sandy, quivering, bleached town, unshaded by its twinkling forest of wind-wheels. Surely the heart always remembers a spot where it has been merry! And one thing I should like to know—shall know, perhaps: what sort of citizen in our republic Josey will grow to be. For whom will he vote? May he not himself come to sit in Washington and make laws for us? Universal suffrage holds so many possibilities.

Napoleon Shave-Tail

AUGUSTUS ALBUMBLATT, young and new and sleek with the latest book-knowledge of war, reported to his first troop commander at Fort Brown. The ladies had watched for him, because he would increase the number of men, the officers because he would lessen the number of duties; and he joined at a crisis favorable to becoming speedily known by them all. Upon that same day had household servants become an extinct race. The last one, the commanding officer's cook, had told the commanding officer's wife that she was used to living where she could see the cars. She added that there was no society here "fit for man or baste at all." This opinion was formed on the preceding afternoon when Casey, a sergeant of roguish attractions in G troop, had told her that he was not a marrying man. Three hours later she wedded a gambler, and this morning at six they had taken the stage for Green River, two hundred miles south, the nearest point where the bride could see the cars.

"Frank," said the commanding officer's wife, "send over to H troop for York."

171

"Catherine," he answered, "my dear, our statesmen at Washington say it's wicked to hire the free American soldier to cook for you. It's too menial for his manhood."

"Frank, stuff!"

"Hush, my love. Therefore York must be spared the insult of twenty more dollars a month, our statesmen must be re-elected, and you and I, Catherine, being cookless, must join the general mess."

Thus did all separate housekeeping end, and the garrison began unitedly to eat three times a day what a Chinaman set before them, when the long-expected Albumblatt stepped into their midst, just in time for supper.

This youth was spick-and-span from the Military Academy, with a top-dressing of three months' thoughtful travel in Germany. "I was deeply impressed with the modernity of their scientific attitude," he pleasantly remarked to the commanding officer. For Captain Duane, silent usually, talked at this first meal to make the boy welcome in this forlorn two-company post.

"We're cut off from all that sort of thing here," said he. "I've not been east of the Missouri since '69. But we've got the railroad across, and we've killed some Indians, and we've had some fun, and we're glad we're alive—eh, Mrs. Starr?"

"I should think so," said the lady.

"Especially now we've got a bachelor at the post!" said Mrs. Bainbridge. "That has been the one drawback, Mr. Albumblatt."

"I thank you for the compliment," said Augustus, bending solemnly from his hips; and Mrs. Starr looked at him and then at Mrs. Bainbridge.

"We're not over-gay, I fear," the Captain continued; "but the flat's full of antelope, and there's good shooting up both cañons."

"Have you followed the recent target experiments at Metz?" inquired the traveller. "I refer to the flattened trajectory and the obus controversy."

"We have not heard the reports," answered the commandant, with becoming gravity. "But we own a mountain howitzer."

"The modernity of German ordnance—" began Augustus.

"Do you dance, Mr. Albumblatt?" asked Mrs. Starr.

"For we'll have a hop and all be your partners," Mrs. Bainbridge exclaimed.

"I will be pleased to accommodate you, ladies."

"It's anything for variety's sake with us, you see," said Mrs. Starr, smoothly smiling; and once again Augustus bent blandly from his hips.

But the commanding officer still felt kindly. "You see us all," he hastened to say. "Commissioned officers and dancing-men. Pretty shabby—"

"Oh, Captain!" said a lady.

"And pretty old."

"*Captain!*" said another lady.

"But alive and kicking. Captain Starr, Mr. Bainbridge, the Doctor and me. We are seven."

Augustus looked accurately about him. "Do I understand seven, Captain?"

"We are seven," the senior officer repeated.

Again Mr. Albumblatt counted heads. "I imagine you include the ladies, Captain? Ha! ha!"

"Seven commissioned males, sir. Our Major is on sick-leave, and two of our Lieutenants are related to the President's wife. She can't bear them to be exposed. None of us in the church-yard lie—but we are seven."

"Ha! ha, Captain! That's an elegant double-entendre on Wordsworth's poem and the War Department. Only, if I may correct your addition—ha! ha!—our total, including myself, is eight.'' And Augustus grew as hilarious as a wooden nutmeg.

The commanding officer rolled an intimate eye at his wife.

The lady was sitting big with rage, but her words were cordial still: "Indeed, Mr. Albumblatt, the way officers who have influence in Washington shirk duty here and get details East is something I can't laugh about. At one time the Captain was his own adjutant and quartermaster. There are more officers at this table to-night than I've seen in three years. So we are doubly glad to welcome you at Fort Brown.''

"I am fortunate to be on duty where my services are so required, though I could object to calling it Fort Brown.'' And Augustus exhaled a new smile.

"Prefer Smith?" said Captain Starr.

"You misunderstand me. When we say *Fort* Brown, *Fort* Russell, *Fort* Et Cetera, we are inexact. They are not fortified.''

"Cantonment Et Cetera would be a trifle lengthy, wouldn't it?" put in the Doctor, his endurance on the wane.

"Perhaps; but technically descriptive of our Western posts. The Germans criticize these military laxities.''

Captain Duane now ceased talking, but

urbanely listened; and from time to time his eye would scan Augustus, and then a certain sublimated laugh, to his wife well known, would seize him for a single voiceless spasm, and pass. The experienced Albumblatt meanwhile continued, "By-the-way, Doctor, you know the Charité, of course?"

Doctor Guild had visited that great hospital, but being now a goaded man he stuck his nose in his plate, and said, unwisely: "Sharrity? What's that?" For then Augustus told him what and where it was, and that Krankenhaus is German for hospital, and that he had been deeply impressed with the modernity of the ventilation. "Thirty-five cubic metres to a bed in new wards," he stated. "How many do you allow, Doctor?"

"None," answered the surgeon.

"Do I understand none, Doctor?"

"You do, sir. My patients breathe in cubic feet, and swallow their doses in grains, and have their inflation measured in inches."

"Now there again!" exclaimed Augustus, cheerily. "More antiquity to be swept away! And people say we young officers have no work cut out for us!"

"Patients don't die then under the metric system?" said the Doctor.

"No wonder Europe's overcrowded," said Starr.

But the student's mind inhabited heights above such trifling. "Death," he said, "occurs in ratios not differentiated from our statistics." And he told them much more while they looked at him over their plates. He managed to say 'modernity' and 'differentiate' again, for he came from our Middle West, where they encounter education too suddenly, and it would take three generations of him to speak clean English. But with all his polysyllabic wallowing, he showed himself keen-minded, pat with authorities, a spruce young graduate among these dingy Rocky Mountain campaigners. They had fought and thirsted and frozen; the books that he knew were not written when they went to school; and so far as war is to be mastered on paper, his equipment was full and polished while theirs was meagre and rusty.

And yet, if you know things that other and older men do not, it is as well not to mention them too hastily. These soldiers wished that they could have been taught what he knew; but they watched young Augustus unfolding himself with a gaze that might have seemed chill to a less highly abstract thinker. He, however, rose from the table pleasantly edified by himself, and hopeful for them. And as he left them, "Good-night, ladies and gentlemen," he said; "we shall meet again."

"Oh, yes," said the Doctor. "Again and again."

"He's given me indigestion," said Bainbridge.

"Take some metric system," said Starr.

"And lie flat on your trajectory," said the Doctor.

"I hate hair parted in the middle for a man," said Mrs. Guild.

"And his superior eye-glasses," said Mrs. Bainbridge.

"His staring conceited teeth," hissed Mrs. Starr.

"I don't like children slopping their knowledge all over me," said the Doctor's wife.

"He's well brushed, though," said Mrs. Duane, seeking the bright side. "He'll wipe his feet on the mat when he comes to call."

"I'd rather have mud on my carpet than that bandbox in any of my chairs," said Mrs. Starr.

"He's no fool," mused the Doctor. "But, kingdom come, what an ass!"

"Well, gentlemen," said the commanding

officer (and they perceived a flavor of the official in his tone), "Mr. Albumblatt is just twenty-one. I don't know about you; but I'll never have that excuse again."

"Very well, Captain, we'll be good," said Mrs. Bainbridge.

"And gr-r-ateful," said Mrs. Starr, rolling her "r" piously. "I prophesy he'll entertain us."

The Captain's demeanor remained slightly official; but walking home, his Catherine by his side in the dark was twice aware of that laugh of his, twinkling in the recesses of his opinions. And later, going to bed, a little joke took him so unready that it got out before he could suppress it. "My love," said he, "my Second Lieutenant is grievously mislaid in the cavalry. Providence designed him for the artillery."

It was wifely but not right in Catherine to repeat this strict confidence in strictest confidence to her neighbor, Mrs. Bainbridge, over the fence next morning before breakfast. At breakfast Mrs. Bainbridge spoke of artillery reinforcing the post, and her husband giggled girlishly and looked at the puzzled Duane; and at dinner Mrs. Starr asked Albumblatt, would not artillery strengthen the garrison?

"Even a light battery," pronounced Augustus, promptly, "would be absurd and useless."

Whereupon the mess rattled knives, sneezed, and became variously disturbed. So they called him Albumbattery, and then Blattery, which is more condensed; and Captain Duane's official tone availed him nothing in this matter. But he made no more little military jokes; he disliked garrison personalities. Civilized by birth and ripe from weatherbeaten years of men and observing, he looked his Second Lieutenant over, and remembered to have seen worse than this. He had no quarrel with the metric system (truly the most sensible), and thinking to leaven it with a little rule of thumb, he made Augustus his acting quartermaster. But he presently indulged his wife with the soldier-cook she wanted at home, so they no longer had to eat their meals in Albumblatt's society; and Mrs. Starr said that this showed her husband dreaded his quartermaster worse than the Secretary of War.

Alas for the quartermaster's sergeant, Johannes Schmoll, that routined and clock-work German! He found Augustus so much more German than he had ever been himself, that he went speechless for three days. Upon his lists, his red ink, and his ciphering, Augustus swooped like a bird of prey, and all his fond red-tape devices were shredded to the winds. Augustus set going new quadratic ones of his own, with an index and cross-references. It was then that Schmoll recovered his speech and walked alone, saying, "Mein Gott!" And often thereafter, wandering among the piled stores and apparel, he would fling both arms heavenwards and repeat the exclamation. He had rated himself the unique human soul at Fort Brown able to count and arrange under-clothing. Augustus rejected his laborious tally, and together they vigiled after hours, verifying socks and drawers. Next, Augustus found more horseshoes than his papers called for.

"That man gif me der stomach pain efry day," wailed Schmoll to Sergeant Casey. "I tell him, 'Lieutenant, dose horseshoes is expendable. We don't acgount for efry shoe like they was men's shoes, und oder dings dot is issued.' 'I prefer to dake them oop!' says Baby Bismarck. Und he smile mit his two beaver teeth."

"Baby Bismarck!" cried, joyfully, the rosy-faced Casey. "Yo-hanny, take a drink."

"Und so," continued the outraged Schmoll, "he haf a Board of Soorvey on dree-pound horseshoes, und I haf der stomach pain."

It was buckles the next month. The allowance exceeded the expenditure, Augustus's arithmetic came out wrong, and another board sat on buckles.

"Yo-hanny, you're lookin' jaded under Colonel Safetypin," said Casey. "Have something."

"Safetypin is my treat," said Schmoll; "und very apt."

But Augustus found leisure to pervade the post with his modernity. He set himself military problems, and solved them; he wrote an essay on "The Contact Squadron"; he corrected Bainbridge for saying "throw back the left flank" instead of "refuse the left flank"; he had reading-room ideas, canteen ideas, ideas for the Indians and the Agency, and recruit-drill ideas, which he presented to Sergeant Casey. Casey gave him, in exchange, the name of Napoleon Shave-Tail, and had his whisky again paid for by the sympathetic Schmoll.

"But bless his educated heart," said Casey, "he don't learn me nothing that'll soil my innercence!"

Thus did the sunny-humored Sergeant take

it, but not thus the mess. Had Augustus seen
himself as they saw him, could he have heard
Mrs. Starr— But he did not; the youth was
impervious, and to remove his complacency
would require (so Mrs. Starr said) an opera-
tion, probably fatal. The commanding officer
held always aloof from gibing, yet often when
Augustus passed him his gray eye would dwell
upon the Lieutenant's back, and his voiceless
laugh would possess him. That is the picture
I retain of these days—the unending golden
sun, the wide, gentle-colored plain, the splendid mountains, the Indians ambling through
the flat, clear distance; and here, close along
the parade-ground, eye-glassed Augustus,
neatly hastening, with the Captain on his
porch, asleep you might suppose.

One early morning the agent, with two Indian chiefs, waited on the commanding officer,
and after their departure his wife found him
breakfasting in solitary mirth.

"Without me," she chided, sitting down.
"And I know you've had some good news."

"The best, my love. Providence has been
tempted at last. The wholesome irony of life
is about to function."

"Frank, don't tease so! And where are you
rushing now before the cakes?"

"To set our Augustus a little military problem, dearest. Plain living for to-day, and high thinking be jolly well—''

"Frank, you're going to swear, and I *must* know!''

But Frank had sworn and hurried out to the right to the Adjutant's office, while his Catherine flew to the left to the fence.

"Ella!'' she cried. "Oh, Ella!''

Mrs. Bainbridge, instantly on the other side of the fence, brought scanty light. A telegram had come, she knew, from the Crow Agency in Montana. Her husband had admitted this three nights ago; and Captain Duane (she knew) had given him some orders about something; and could it be the Crows? "Ella, I don't know,'' said Catherine. "Frank talked all about Providence in his incurable way, and it may be anything.'' So the two ladies wondered together over the fence, until Mrs. Duane, seeing the Captain return, ran to him and asked, were the Crows on the war-path? Then her Frank told her yes, and that he had detailed Albumblatt to vanquish them and escort them to Carlisle School to learn German and Beethoven's sonatas.

"Stuff, stuff, stuff! Why, there he *does* go!'' cried the unsettled Catherine. "It's something at the Agency!'' But Captain Duane was gone into the house for a cigar.

Albumblatt, with Sergeant Casey and a detail of six men, was in truth hastening over that broad mile which opens between Fort Brown and the Agency. On either side of them the level plain stretched, gray with its sage, buff with intervening grass, hay-cocked with the smoky, mellow-stained, meerschaum-like canvas tepees of the Indians, quiet as a painting; far eastward lay long, low, rose-red hills, half dissolved in the trembling mystery of sun and distance; and westward, close at hand and high, shone the great pale-blue serene mountains through the vaster serenity of the air. The sounding hoofs of the troops brought the Indians out of their tepees to see. When Albumblatt reached the Agency, there waited the agent and his two chiefs, who pointed to one lodge standing apart some three hundred yards, and said, ''He is there.'' So then Augustus beheld his problem, the military duty fallen to him from Providence and Captain Duane.

It seems elementary for him who has written of ''The Contact Squadron.'' It was to arrest one Indian. This man, Ute Jack, had done a murder among the Crows, and fled south for shelter. The telegram heralded him, but with boundless miles for hiding he had stolen in under the cover of night. No wel-

come met him. These Fort Brown Indians
were not his friends at any time, and less so
now, when he arrived wild drunk among their
families. Hounded out, he sought this empty
lodge, and here he was, at bay, his hand
against every man's, counting his own life
worthless except for destroying others before
he must himself die.

"Is he armed?" Albumblatt inquired, and
was told, yes.

Augustus considered the peaked cone tent.
The opening was on this side, but a canvas
drop closed it. Not much of a problem—one
man inside a sack with eight outside to catch
him! But the books gave no rule for this
combination, and Augustus had met with
nothing of the sort in Germany. He considered at some length. Smoke began to rise
through the meeting poles of the tepee, leisurely and natural, and one of the chiefs
said:

"Maybe Ute Jack cooking. He hungry."

"This is not a laughing matter," said Augustus to the by-standers, who were swiftly
gathering. "Tell him that I command him to
surrender," he added to the agent, who
shouted this forthwith; and silence followed.

"Tell him I say he must come out at once,"

said Augustus then; and received further silence.

"He eat now," observed the chief. "Can't talk much."

"Sergeant Casey," bellowed Albumblatt, "go over there and take him out!"

"The Lootenant understands," said Casey, slowly, "that Ute Jack has got the drop on us, and there ain't no getting any drop on him."

"Sergeant, you will execute your orders without further comment."

At this amazing step the silence fell cold indeed; but Augustus was in command.

"Shall I take any men along, sir?" said Casey in his soldier's machine voice.

"Er—yes. Er—no. Er—do as you please."

The six troopers stepped forward to go, for they loved Casey; but he ordered them sharply to fall back. Then, looking in their eyes, he whispered, "Good-bye, boys, if it's to be that way," and walked to the lodge, lifted the flap, and fell, shot instantly dead through the heart. "Two bullets into him," muttered a trooper, heavily breathing as the sounds rang. "He's down," another spoke to himself with fixed eyes; and a sigh they did not know of passed among them. The two chiefs looked at Augustus and grunted short talk together;

and one, with a sweeping lift of his hand out towards the tepee and the dead man by it, said, ''Maybe Ute Jack only got three—four—cartridges—so!'' (his fingers counted it). ''After he kill three—four—men, you get him pretty good.'' The Indian took the white man's death thus; but the white men could not yet be even saturnine.

''This will require reinforcement,'' said Augustus to the audience. ''The place must be attacked by a front and flank movement. It must be knocked down. I tell you I must have it knocked down. How are you to see where he is, I'd like to know, if it's not knocked down?'' Augustus's voice was getting high. ''I want the howitzer,'' he screeched generally.

A soldier saluted, and Augustus chattered at him.

''The howitzer, the mountain howitzer, I tell you. Don't you hear me? To knock the cursed thing he's in down. Go to Captain Duane and give him my compliments, and—no, I'll go myself. Where's my horse? My horse, I tell you! It's got to be knocked down.''

''If you please, Lieutenant,'' said the trooper, ''may we have the Red Cross ambulance?''

"Red Cross? What's that for? What's that?"

"Sergeant Casey, sir. He's a-lyin' there."

"Ambulance? Certainly. The howitzer—perhaps they're only flesh wounds. I hope they are only flesh wounds. I must have more men—you'll come with me."

From his porch Duane viewed both Augustus approach and the man stop at the hospital, and having expected a bungle, sat to hear; but at Albumblatt's mottled face he stood up quickly and said, "What's the matter?" And hearing, burst out: "Casey! Why, he was worth fifty of— Go on, Mr. Albumblatt. What next did you achieve, sir?" And as the tale was told he cooled, bitter, but official.

"Reinforcements is it, Mr. Albumblatt?"

"The howitzer, Captain."

"Good. And G Troop?"

"For my double flank movement I—"

"Perhaps you'd like H troop as reserve?"

"Not reserve, Captain. I should establish—"

"This is your duty, Mr. Albumblatt. Perform it as you can, with what force you need."

"Thank you, sir. It is not exactly a battle, but with a, so-to-speak, intrenched—"

"Take your troops and go, sir, and report to me when you have arrested your man."

Then Duane went to the hospital, and out with the ambulance, hoping that the soldier might not be dead. But the wholesome irony of life reckons beyond our calculations; and the unreproachful, sunny face of his Sergeant evoked in Duane's memory many marches through long heat and cold, back in the rough, good times.

"Hit twice, I thought they told me," said he; and the steward surmised that one had missed.

"Perhaps," mused Duane. "And perhaps it went as intended, too. What's all that fuss?"

He turned sharply, having lost Augustus among his sadder thoughts; and here were the operations going briskly. Powder-smoke in three directions at once! Here were pickets far out-lying, and a double line of skirmishers deployed in extended order, and a mounted reserve, and men standing to horse— a command of near a hundred, a pudding of pompous, incompetent, callow bosh, with Augustus by his howitzer, scientifically raising and lowering it to bear on the lone white tepee that shone in the plain. Four races were assembled to look on—the mess Chinaman, two black laundresses, all the whites in the place (on horse and foot, some with their hats left behind), and several hundred Indians in blankets. Duane had a thought to go away and leave this galling farce under the eye of Starr, for the officers were at hand also. But his second thought bade him remain; and looking at Augustus and the howitzer, his laugh would have returned to him; but his heart was sore for Casey.

It was an hour of strategy and cannonade, a humiliating hour, which Fort Brown tells of to this day; and the tepee lived through it all. For it stood upon fifteen slender poles, not speedily to be chopped down by shooting lead from afar. When low bullets drilled the canvas, the chief suggested to Augustus that Ute Jack had climbed up; and when the bullets flew high, then Ute Jack was doubtless in a hole. Nor did Augustus contrive to drop a shell from the howitzer upon Ute Jack and explode him—a shrewd and deadly conception; the shells went beyond, except one, that ripped through the canvas, somewhat near the ground; and Augustus, dripping, turned at length, and saying, "It won't go down," stood vacantly wiping his white face. Then the two chiefs got his leave to stretch a rope between their horses and ride hard against the tepee.

It was military neither in essence nor to see, but it prevailed. The tepee sank, a huge umbrella wreck along the earth, and there lay Ute Jack across the fire's slight hollow, his knee-cap gone with the howitzer shell. But no blood had flowed from that; blood will not run, you know, when a man has been dead some time. One single other shot had struck him—one through his own heart. It had singed the flesh.

"You see, Mr. Albumblatt," said Duane, in the whole crowd's hearing, "he killed himself directly after killing Casey. A very rare act for an Indian, as you are doubtless aware. But if your manœuvres with his corpse have taught you anything you did not know before, we shall all be gainers."

"Captain," said Mrs. Starr, on a later day, "you and Ute Jack have ended our fun. Since the Court of Inquiry let Mr. Albumblatt off, he has not said Germany once—and that's three months to-morrow."

Twenty Minutes for
Refreshments

UPON turning over again my diary of
that excursion to the Pacific, I find that
I set out from Atlantic waters on the
30th day of a backward and forlorn April,
which had come and done nothing towards
making its share of spring, but had gone,
missing its chance, leaving the trees as bare
as it had received them from the winds of
March. It was not bleak weather alone, but
care, that I sought to escape by a change of
sky; and I hoped for some fellow-traveller
who might begin to interest my thoughts at
once. No such person met me in the several
Pullmans which I inhabited from that afternoon until the forenoon of the following Friday. Through that long distance, though I
had slanted southwestward across a multitude
of States and vegetations, and the Mississippi
lay eleven hundred miles to my rear, the single event is my purchasing some cat's-eyes of
the news-agent at Sierra Blanca. Save this,
my diary contains only neat additions of daily

expenses, and moral reflections of a delicate
and restrained melancholy. They were Pecos
cat's-eyes, he told me, obtained in the rocky
cañons of that stream, and destined to be
worth little until fashion turned from foreign
jewels to become aware of these fine native
stones. And I, glad to possess the jewels of
my country, chose two bracelets and a necklace of them, paying but twenty dollars for
fifteen or sixteen cat's-eyes, and resolved to
give them a setting worthy of their beauty.
The diary continues with moral reflections
upon the servility of our taste before anything
European, and the handwriting is clear and
deliberate. It abruptly becomes hurried, and
at length well-nigh illegible. It is best, I think,
that you should have this portion as it comes,
unpolished, unamended, unarranged—hot, so
to speak, from my immediate pencil, instead
of cold from my subsequent pen. I shall dis-
guise certain names, but that is all.

Friday forenoon, May 5.—I don't have to
gaze at my cat's-eyes to kill time any more.
I'm not the only passenger any more. There's
a lady. She got in at El Paso. She has taken
the drawing-room, but sits outside reading
newspaper cuttings and writing letters. She
is sixty, I should say, and has a cap and one

gray curl. This comes down over her left ear
as far as a purple ribbon which suspends a
medallion at her throat. She came in wearing
a sage-green duster of pongee silk, pretty
nice, only the buttons are as big as those largest mint-drops. ''You porter,'' she said,
''brush this.'' He put down her many things
and received it. Her dress was sage-green,
and pretty nice, too. ''You porter,'' said she,
''open every window. Why, they are open, I
declare! What's the thermometer in this
car?'' ''Ninety-five, ma'am. Folks mostly
travelling—'' ''That will do, porter. Now
you go make me a pitcher of lemonade right
quick.'' She went into the state-room and
shut the door. When she came out she was
dressed in what appeared to be chintz bed-
room curtains. They hang and flow loosely
about her, and are covered with a pattern of
pink peonies. She has slippers—Turkish—
that stare up in the air, pretty handsome and
comfortable. But I never before saw any one
travel with fly-paper. It must be hard to pack.
But it's quite an idea in this train. Fully a
dozen flies have stuck to it already; and she
reads her clippings, and writes away, and sips
another glass of lemonade, all with the most
extreme appearance of leisure, not to say

sloth. I can't imagine how she manages to produce this atmosphere of indolence when in reality she is steadily occupied. Possibly it's the way she sits. But I think it's partly the bedroom curtains.

These notes were interrupted by the entrance of the new conductor. "If you folks have chartered a private car, just say so," he shouted instantly at the sight of us. He stood still at the extreme end and removed his hat, which was acknowledged by the lady. "Travel is surely very light, Gadsden," she assented, and went on with her writing. But he remained standing still, and shouting like an orator: "Sprinkle the floor of this car, Julius, and let the pore passengers get a breath of cool. My lands!" He fanned himself sweepingly with his hat. He seemed but little larger than a red squirrel, and precisely that color. Sorrel hair, sorrel eyebrows, sorrel freckles, light sorrel mustache, thin aggressive nose, receding chin, and black, attentive, prominent eyes. He approached, and I gave him my ticket, which is as long as a neck-tie, and has my height, the color of my eyes and hair, and my general description, punched in the margin. "Why, you ain't middle-aged!" he shouted, and a singular croak sounded behind me. But the lady was writing. "I have been growing younger since I bought that ticket," I explained. "That's it, that's it," he sang; "a man's always as old as he feels, and a woman—is ever young," he finished. "I see you are true to the old teachings and the old-time chivalry, Gadsden,'" said the lady, continuously busy. "Yes, ma'am. Jacob served seven years for Leah and seven more for Rachel." "Such men are raised to-day in every worthy Louisiana home, Gadsden, be it ever so humble." "Yes, ma'am. Give a fresh sprinkle to the floor, Julius, soon as it goes to get dry. Excuse me, but do you shave yourself, sir?" I told him that I did, but without excusing him. "You will see that I have a reason for asking," he consequently pursued, and took out of his coat-tails a round tin box handsomely labelled "Nat. Fly Paper Co.," so that I supposed it was thus, of course, that the lady came by her fly-paper. But this was pure coincidence, and the conductor explained: "That company's me and a man at Shreveport, but he dissatisfies me right frequently. You know what heaven a good razor is for a man, and what you feel about a bad one. Vaseline and ground shells," he said, opening the box, "and I'm not saying anything except it will last your lifetime and never hardens. Rub the size of a pea on the fine side of your strop, spread it to an inch with your thumb. May I beg a favor on so short a meeting? Join me in the gentlemen's lavatory with your razor-strop in five minutes. I have to attend to a corpse in the baggage-car, and will return at once." "Anybody's corpse I know, Gadsden?" said the lady. "No, ma'am. Just a corpse."

When I joined him, for I was now willing to do anything, he was apologetic again. " 'Tis a short acquaintance," he said, "but may I also beg your razor? Quick as I get out of the National Fly I am going to register my new label. First there will be Uncle Sam embracing the world, signifying this mixture is universal, then my name, then the word *Stropine,* which is a novelty and carries copyright, and I shall win comfort and doubtless luxury. The post barber at Fort Bayard took a dozen off me at sight to retail to the niggers of the Twenty-fourth, and as he did not happen to have the requisite cash on his person I charged him two roosters and fifty cents, and both of us done well. He's after more Stropine, and I got Pullman prices for my roosters, the buffet-car being out of chicken a la Marengo. There is your razor, sir, and I appreciate your courtesy." It was beautifully sharpened, and I bought a box of the Stropine and asked him who the lady was. "Mrs. Sedalia Preene!" he exclaimed. "Have you never met her socially? Why she—why she is the most intellectual lady in Bee Bayou." "Indeed!" I said. "Why she visits N' Yawlans, and Mobeel, and all the principal centres of refinement, and is welcomed in Baltimo'. She converses freely with our statesmen, and is considered a queen of learning. Why, she writes po'try, sir, and is strong-minded. But a man wouldn't want to pick her up for a fool, all the samey." "I shouldn't; I don't," said I. "Don't you do it, sir. She's run her plantation all alone since the Colonel was killed in sixty-two. She taught me Sunday-school when I was a lad, and she used to catch me at her pecan-trees 'most every time in Bee Bayou."

He went forward, and I went back with the Stropine in my pocket. The lady was sipping the last of the lemonade and looking haughtily over the top of her glass into (I suppose) the world of her thoughts. Her eyes met mine, however. "Has Gadsden—yes, I perceive he has been telling about me," she said, in her languid, formidable voice. She set her glass down and reclined among the folds of the bed-room curtains, considering me. "Gadsden has always been lavish," she mused, caressingly. "He seems destined to succeed in life," I hazarded. "O—h n—o!" she sighed, with decision. "He will fail." As she said no more and as I began to resent the manner in which she surveyed me, I remarked, "You seem rather sure of his failure." "I am old enough to be his mother, and yours," said Mrs. Sedalia Preene among her curtains. "He is a noble-hearted fellow, and would have been a high-souled Southern gentleman if born to that station. But what should a conductor earning $103.50 a month be dispersing his attention on silly patents for? Many's the time I've told him what I think; but Gadsden will always be flighty." No further observations occurring to me, I took up my necklace and bracelets from the seat and put them in my pocket. "Will you permit a meddlesome old woman to inquire what made you buy those cat's-eyes?" said Mrs. Preene. "Why—" I dubiously began. "Never mind," she cried, archly. "If you were thinking of some one in your Northern home, they will be prized because the thought, at any rate, was beautiful and genuine. 'Where'er I roam, whatever realms to see, my heart, untravelled, fondly

turns to thee.' Now don't you be embarrassed
by an old woman!" I desired to inform her
that I disliked her, but one can never do those
things; and, anxious to learn what was the
matter with the cat's-eyes, I spoke amiably
and politely to her. "Twenty dollars!" she
murmured. "And he told you they came from
the Pecos!" She gave that single melodious
croak I had heard once before. Then she sat
up with her back as straight as if she was
twenty. "My dear young fellow, never do you
buy trash in these trains. Here you are with
your coat full of—what's Gadsden's absurd
razor concoction? — strut — strup — bother!
And Chinese paste buttons. Last summer, on
the Northern Pacific, the man offered your
cat's-eyes to me as native gems found exclusively in Dakota. But I just sat and mentioned
to him that I was on my way home from a
holiday in China, and he went right out of the
car. The last day I was in Canton I bought a
box of those cat's-eyes at eight cents a dozen."
After this we spoke a little on other subjects,
and now she's busy writing again. She's on
business in California, but will read a paper
at Los Angeles at the annual meeting of the
Golden Daughters of the West. The meal station is coming, but we have agreed to—

Later, Friday afternoon.—I have been in-

terrupted again. Gadsden entered, removed
his hat, and shouted: "Sharon. Twenty minutes for dinner." I was calling the porter to
order a buffet lunch in the car when there
tramped in upon us three large men of such
appearance that a flash of thankfulness went
through me at having so little ready-money
and only a silver watch. Mrs. Preene looked
at them and said, "Well, gentlemen?" and
they took off their embroidered Mexican hats.
"We've got a baby show here," said one of
them, slowly, looking at me, "and we'd be kind
of obliged if you'd hold the box." "There's
lunch put up in a basket for you to take
along," said the next, "and a bottle of wine—
champagne. So losing your dinner won't lose
you nothing." "We're looking for somebody
raised East and without local prejudice," said
the third. "So we come to the Pullman." I
now saw that so far from purposing to rob us
they were in a great and honest distress of
mind. "But I am no judge of a baby," said I;
"not being mar—" "You don't have to be,"
broke in the first, more slowly and earnestly.
"It's a fair and secret ballot we're striving
for. The votes is wrote out and ready, and all
we're shy of is a stranger without family ties
or business interests to hold the box and count

fair." His deep tones ceased, and he wiped heavy drops from his forehead with his shirt sleeve. "We'd be kind of awful obliged to you," he urged. "The town would be liable to make it two bottles," said the second. The third brought his fist down on the back of a seat and said, "I'll make it that now." "But, gentlemen," said I, "five, six, and seven years ago I was not a stranger in Sharon. If my friend Dean Drake was still here—" "But he ain't. Now you might as well help folks, and eat later. This town will trust you. And if you quit us—" Once more he wiped the heavy drops away, while in a voice full of appeal his friend finished his thought: "If we lose you, we'll likely have to wait till this train comes in to-morrow for a man satisfactory to this town. And the show is costing us a heap." A light hand tapped my arm, and here was Mrs. Preene saying: "For shame! Show your enterprise." "I'll hold this yere train," shouted Gadsden, "if necessary." Mrs. Preene rose alertly, and they all hurried me out. "My slippers will stay right on when I'm down the steps," said Mrs. Preene, and Gadsden helped her descend into the blazing dust and sun of Sharon. "Gracious!" said she, "what a place! But I make it a point to see

everything as I go." Nothing had changed.
There, as of old, lay the flat litter of the town
—sheds, stores, and dwellings, a shapeless
congregation in the desert, gaping wide everywhere to the glassy, quivering immensity; and
there, above the roofs, turned the slatted
wind-wheels. But close to the tracks, opposite
the hotel, was an edifice, a sort of tent of bunting, whence whifts of brass music and the
wailing of infants issued, while about a hundred pink and blue sun-bonnets moved and
mixed near the entrance. Little black Mexicans, like charred toys, lounged and lay staring among the ungraded dunes of sand.
"Gracious!" said Mrs. Preene again. Her
eye lost nothing; and as she made for the tent
the chintz peonies flowed around her, and her
step was surprisingly light. We passed
through the sun-bonnets and entered where
the music played. "The precious blessed dar-
lings!" she exclaimed, clasping her hands.
"This will do for the Golden Daughters," she
rapidly added; "yes, this will distinctly do."
And she hastened away from me into the
throng.

I had no time to look at much this first general minute. I could see there were booths,
each containing a separate baby. I passed a

whole section of naked babies, and one baby farther along had on golden wings and a crown, and was bawling frightfully. Their names were over the booths, and I noticed Lucille, Erskine Wales, Banquo Lick Nolin, Cuba, Manilla, Ellabelle, Bosco Grady, James J. Corbett Nash, and Aqua Marine. There was a great sign at the end, painted "Mrs. Eden's Manna in the Wilderness," and another sign, labelled "Shot-gun Smith's twins." In the midst of these first few impressions I found myself seated behind a bare table raised three feet or so, with two boxes on it, and a quantity of blank paper and pencils, while one of the men was explaining me the rules and facts. I can't remember them all now, because I couldn't understand them all then, and Mrs. Preene was distant among the sun-bonnets, talking to a gathering crowd and feeling in the mouths of babies that were being snatched out of the booths and brought to her. The man was instructing me steadily all the while, and it occurred to me to nod silently and coldly now and then, as if I was judging herds of the new-born every day. But I insisted that some one should help me count, and they gave me Gadsden.

Now these facts I do remember very clearly,

and shall never forget them. The babies came from two towns—Sharon, and Rincon its neighbor. Alone, neither had enough for a good show, though in both it was every family's pride to have a baby every year. The babies were in three classes: Six months and under, one prize offered; eighteen months, two prizes; three years, two prizes. A three-fourths vote of all cast was necessary to a choice. No one entitled to vote unless of immediate family of a competing baby. No one entitled to cast more than one vote. There were rules of entry and fees, but I forget them, except that no one could have two exhibits in the same class. When I read this I asked, how about twins? "Well, we didn't kind of foresee that," muttered my instructor, painfully; "what would be your idea?" "Look here, you sir," interposed Mrs. Preene, "he came in to count votes." I was very glad to have her back. "That's right, ma'am," admitted the man; "he needn't to say a thing. We've only got one twins entered," he pursued, "which we're glad of. Shot-gun—" "Where is this Mr. Smith?" interrupted Mrs. Preene. "Uptown, drinking, ma'am." "And who may Mr. Smith be?" "Most popular citizen of Rincon, ma'am. We had to accept his twins because—well, he come down here himself, and most of Rincon come with him, and as we aimed to have everything pass off pleasant-like—'' ''I quite comprehend,'' said Mrs. Preene. ''And I should consider twins within the rule; or any number born at one time. But little Aqua Marine is the finest single child in that 6-months class. I told her mother she ought to take that splurgy ring off the poor little thing's thumb. It's most unsafe. But I should vote for that child myself.'' ''Thank you for your valuable endorsement,'' said a spruce, slim young man. ''But the public is not allowed to vote here,'' he added. He was standing on the floor and resting his elbows on the table. Mrs. Preene stared down at him. ''Are you the father of the child?'' she inquired. ''Well, that's a good one! I am the agent. I—'' ''Aqua Marine's agent?'' said Mrs. Preene, sharply. ''Ha, ha!'' went the young man. ''Ha, ha! Well, that's good, too. She's part of our exhibit. I'm in charge of the manna-feds, don't you know?'' ''I don't know,'' said Mrs. Preene. ''Why, Mrs. Eden's Manna in the Wilderness! Nourishes, strengthens, and makes no unhealthy fat. Take a circular, and welcome. I'm travelling for the manna. I organized this show. I've conducted twenty-eight similar shows in two years. We hold them in every State and Territory. Second of last March I gave Denver—you heard of it, probably?'' ''I did not,'' said Mrs. Preene. ''Well! Ha, ha! I thought every person up to date had heard of Denver's Olympic Off-spring Olio.'' ''Is it up to date to loll your elbows on the table when you're speaking to a lady?'' inquired Mrs. Preene. He jumped, and then grew scarlet with rage. ''I didn't expect to learn manners in New Mexico,'' said he. ''I doubt if you will,'' said Mrs. Preene, and turned her back on him. He was white now; but better instincts, or else business, prevailed in his injured bosom. ''Well,'' said he, ''I had no bad intentions. I was going to say you'd have seen ten thousand people and five hundred babies at Denver. And our manna-feds won out to beat the band. Three first medals, and all exclusively manna-fed. We took the costume prize also. Of course here in Sharon I've simplified. No special medal for weight, beauty, costume, or decorated per-ambulator. Well, I must go back to our ex-hibit. Glad to have you give us a call up there and see the medals we're offering, and our

fifteen manna-feds, and take a package away
with you." He was gone.

The voters had been now voting in my two
boxes for some time, and I found myself hoping the manna would not win, whoever did;
but it seemed this agent was a very capable
person. To begin with, every family entering
a baby drew a package of the manna free, and
one package contained a diamond ring. Then,
he had managed to have the finest babies of
all classes in his own exhibit. This was incon-
testable, Mrs. Preene admitted, after returning from a general inspection; and it seemed
to us extraordinary. "That's easy, ma'am,"
said Gadsden; "he came around here a month
ago. Don't you see?" I did not see, but Mrs.
Preene saw at once. He had made a quiet
selection of babies beforehand, and then introduced the manna into those homes. And
everybody in the room was remarking that his
show was very superior, taken as a whole—
they all added, "taken as a whole"; I heard
them as they came up to vote for the 3-year
and the 18-month classes. The 6-month was
to wait till last, because the third box had been
accidentally smashed by Mr. Smith. Gadsden
caught several trying to vote twice. "No, you

don't!'' he would shout. "I know faces. I'm
not a conductor for nothing.'' And the victim
would fall back amid jeers from the sun-
bonnets. Once the passengers sent over to
know when the train was going. "Tell them
to step over here and they'll not feel so lonesome!'' shouted Gadsden; and I think a good
many came. The band was playing "White
Wings,'' with quite a number singing it, when
Gadsden noticed the voting had ceased, and
announced this ballot closed. The music
paused for him, and again we could suddenly
hear how many babies were in distress; but
for a moment only; as we began our counting,
"White Wings'' resumed, and the sun-bonnets outsang their progeny. There was something quite singular in the way they had
voted. Here are some of the 3-year-old
tickets: "First choice, "Ulysses Grant Blum;
2d choice, Lewis Hendricks.'' "First choice,
James Redfield; 2d, Lewis Hendricks.''
"First, Elk Chester; 2d, Lewis Hendricks.''
"Can it be?'' said the excited Gadsden.
"Finish these quick. I'll open the 18-month-
ers.'' But he swung round to me at once.
"See there!'' he cried. "Read that! and
that!'' He plunged among more, and I read:
"First choice, Lawrence Nepton Ford, Jr.;

2d, Iona Judd." "First choice, Mary Louise Kenton; 2d, Iona Judd." "Hurry up!" said Gadsden; "that's it!" And as we counted, Mrs. Preene looked over my shoulder and uttered her melodious croak, for which I saw no reason. "That young whipper-snapper will go far," she observed; nor did I understand this. But when they stopped the band for me to announce the returns, one fact did dawn on me even while I was reading: "Three-year-olds: Whole number of votes cast, 300; necessary to a choice, 225. Second prize, Lewis Hendricks, receiving 300. First prize, largest number of votes cast, 11, for Salvisa van Meter. No award. Eighteen-month class: Whole number of votes cast, 300; necessary to a choice, 225. Second prize, Iona Judd, receiving 300. Lillian Brown gets 15 for 1st prize. None awarded." There was a very feeble applause, and then silence for a second, and then the sun-bonnets rushed together, rushed away to others, rushed back; and talk swept like hail through the place. Yes, that is what they had done. They had all voted for Lewis Hendricks and Iona Judd for second prize, and every family had voted the first prize to its own baby. The Browns and van Meters happened to be the largest families present. "He'll go far! he'll go far!" repeated Mrs. Preene. Sport glittered in her eye. She gathered her curtains, and was among the sun-bonnets in a moment. Then it fully dawned on me. The agent for Mrs. Eden's Manna in the Wilderness was indeed a shrewd strategist, and knew his people to the roots of the grass. They had never seen a baby-show. They were innocent. He came among them. He gave away packages of manna and a diamond ring. He offered the prizes. But he proposed to win some. Therefore he made that rule about only the immediate families voting. He foresaw what they would do; and now they had done it. Whatever happened, two prizes went to his manna-feds. "They don't see through it in the least, which is just as well," said Mrs. Preene, returning. "And it's little matter that only second prizes go to the best babies. But what's to be done now?" I had no idea; but it was not necessary that I should.

"You folks of Rincon and Sharon," spoke a deep voice. It was the first man in the Pullman, and drops were rolling from his forehead, and his eyes were the eyes of a beleaguered ox. "You fathers and mothers," he said, and took another breath. They grew

quiet. "I'm a father myself, as is well
known." They applauded this. "Salvisa is
mine, and she got my vote. The father that
will not support his own child is not—does
not—is worse than if they were orphans."
He breathed again, while they loudly applauded. "But, folks, I've got to get home to
Rincon. I've got to. And I'll give up Salvisa
if I'm met fair." "Yes, yes, you'll be met,"
said voices of men. "Well, here's my proposition: Mrs. Eden's Manna has took two, and
I'm satisfied it should. We voted, and we'll
stay voted." "Yes, yes!" "Well, now, here's
Sharon and Rincon, two of the finest towns in
this section, and I say Sharon and Rincon has
equal rights to get something out of this, and
drop private feelings, and everybody back
their town. And I say let this lady and gentleman, who will act elegant and on the square,
take a view and nominate the finest Rincon 3-
year-old and the finest Sharon 18-month they
can cut out of the herd. And I say let's vote
unanimous on their pick, and let each town
hold a first prize and go home in friendship,
feeling that it has been treated right."

Universal cheers endorsed him, and he got
down panting. The band played "Union Forever," and I accompanied Mrs. Preene to the

booths. "You'll remember!" shouted the orator urgently after us; "one apiece." We nodded. "Don't get mixed," he appealingly insisted. We shook our heads, and out of the booths rushed two women, and simultaneously dashed their infants in our faces. "You'll never pass Cuba by!" entreated one. "This is Bosco Grady," said the other. Cuba wore an immense garment made of the American flag, but her mother whirled her out of it in a second. "See them dimples; see them knees!" she said. "See them feet! Only feel of her toes!" "Look at his arms!" screamed the mother of Bosco. "Doubled his weight in four months." "Did he indeed, ma'am?" said Cuba's mother; "well, he hadn't much to double." "Didn't he, then? Didn't he, indeed?" "No at you; he didn't indeed and indeed! I guess Cuba is known to Sharon. I guess Sharon 'll not let Cuba be slighted." "Well, and I guess Rincon 'll see that Bosco Grady gets his rights." "Ladies," said Mrs. Preene, towering but poetical with her curl, "I am a mother myself, and raised five noble boys and two sweet peerless girls." This stopped them immediately; they stared at her and her chintz peonies as she put the curl gently away from her medallion and pro-

ceeded: "But never did I think of myself in
those dark weary days of the long ago. I
thought of my country and the Lost Cause."
They stared at her, fascinated. "Yes, m'm,"
whispered they, quite humbly. "Now," said
Mrs. Preene, "what is more sacred than an
American mother's love? Therefore let her
not shame it with anger and strife. All little
boys and girls are precious gems to me and to
you. What is a cold, lifeless medal compared
to one of them? Though I would that all could
get the prize! But they can't, you know."
"No, m'm." Many mothers, with their children in their arms, were now dumbly watching Mrs. Preene, who held them with a
honeyed, convincing smile. "If I choose only
one in this beautiful and encouraging harvest,
it is because I have no other choice. Thank
you so much for letting me see that little hero
and that lovely angel," she added, with a yet
sweeter glance to the mothers of Bosco and
Cuba. "And I wish them all luck when their
turn comes. I've no say about the 6-month
class, you know. And now a little room,
please."

The mothers fell back. But my head swam
slightly. The 6-month class, to be sure! The
orator had forgotten all about it. In the

general joy over his wise and fair proposition, nobody had thought of it. But they would pretty soon. Cuba and Bosco were likely to remind them. Then we should still be face to face with a state of things that—I cast a glance behind at those two mothers of Sharon and Rincon following us, and I asked Mrs. Preene to look at them. "Don't think about it now," said she, "it will only mix you. I always like to take a thing when it comes, and not before." We now reached the 18-month class. They were the naked ones. The 6-month had stayed nicely in people's arms; these were crawling hastily everywhere, like crabs upset in the market, and they screamed fiercely when taken upon the lap. The mother of Thomas Jefferson Brayin Lucas showed us a framed letter from the statesman for whom her child was called. The letter reeked with gratitude, and said that offspring was man's proudest privilege; that a souvenir sixteen-to-one spoon would have been cheerfully sent, but 428 babies had been named after Mr. Brayin since January. It congratulated the swelling army of the People's Cause. But there was nothing eminent about little Thomas except the letter; and we selected Reese Moran, a vigorous Sharon baby, who, when they attempted to set him down and pacify him, stiffened his legs, dashed his candy to the floor, and burst into lamentation. We were soon on our way to the 3-year class, for Mrs. Preene was rapid and thorough. As we went by the Manna Exhibit, the agent among his packages and babies invited us in. He was loudly declaring that he would vote for Bosco if he could. But when he examined Cuba, he became sure that Denver had nothing finer than that. Mrs. Preene took no notice of him, but bade me admire Aqua Marine as far surpassing any other 6-month child. I proclaimed her splendid (she was a wide-eyed, contented thing, with a head shaped like a croquet mallet), and the agent smiled modestly and told the mothers that as for his babies two prizes was luck enough for them; they didn't want the earth. "If that thing happened to be brass," said Mrs. Preene, bending over the ring that Aqua was still sucking; and again remonstrating with the mother for this imprudence, she passed on. The 3-year-olds were, many of them, in costume, with extraordinary arrangements of hair; and here was the child with gold wings and a crown I had seen on arriving. Her name was Verbena M., and she personated Faith. She had colored slippers, and was drinking green tea from her mother's cup. Another child, named Broderick McGowan, represented Columbus, and joyfully shouted "Ki-yi!" every half-minute. One child was attired as a prominent admiral; another as a prominent general; and one stood in a boat and was Washington. As Mrs. Preene examined them and dealt with the mothers, the names struck me afresh—not so much the boys; Ulysses Grant and James J. Corbett explained themselves; but I read the names of five adjacent girls—Lula, Ocilla, Nila, Cusseta, and Maylene. And I asked Mrs. Preene how they got them. "From romances," she told me, "in papers that we of the upper classes never see." In choosing Horace Boyd, of Rincon, for his hair, his full set of front teeth well cared for, and his general beauty, I think both of us were also influenced by his good sensible name, and his good clean sensible clothes. With both our selections, once they were settled, were Sharon and Rincon satisfied. We were turning back to the table to announce our choice when a sudden clamor arose behind us, and we saw confusion in the Manna Department. Women were running and shrieking, and I hastened after Mrs. Preene to see what was the matter. Aqua Marine had swallowed the ring on her thumb. "It was gold! it was pure gold!" wailed the mother, clutching Mrs. Preene. "It cost a whole dollar in El Paso." "She must have white of egg instantly," said Mrs. Preene, handing me her purse. "Run to the hotel—" "Save your money," said the agent, springing forward with some eggs in a bowl. "Lord! you don't catch us without all the appliances handy. We'd run behind the trade in no time. There, now, there," he added, comfortingly to the mother. "Will you make her swallow it? Better let me—better let me— And here's the emetic. Lord! why, we had three swallowed rings at the Denver Olio, and I got 'em all safe back within ten minutes after time of swallowing." "You go away," said Mrs. Preene to me, "and tell them our nominations." The mothers sympathetically surrounded poor little Aqua, saying to each other: "She's a beautiful child!" "Sure indeed she is!" "But the manna-feds has had their turn." "Sure indeed they've been recognized," and so forth, while I was glad to retire to the voting table. The music paused for me, and as the crowd cheered my small speech, some one said, "And now what are you going to do about me?" It was Bosco

Grady back again, and close behind him Cuba.
They had escaped from Mrs. Preene's eye and
had got me alone. But I pretended in the
noise and cheering not to see these mothers.
I noticed a woman hurrying out of the tent,
and hoped Aqua was not in further trouble—
she was still surrounded, I could see. Then
the orator made some silence, thanked us in
the names of Sharon and Rincon, and proposed our candidates be voted on by acclama-
tion. This was done. Rincon voted for Sharon
and Reese Moran in a solid roar, and Sharon
voted for Rincon and Horace Boyd in a roar
equally solid. So now each had a prize, and
the whole place was applauding happily, and
the band was beginning again, when the
mothers with Cuba and Bosco jumped up beside me on the platform, and the sight of them
produced immediate silence.

"There's a good many here has a right to
feel satisfied," said Mrs. Grady, looking
about, "and they're welcome to their feelings.
But if this meeting thinks it is through with
its business, I can tell it that it ain't—not if it
acts honorable, it ain't. Does those that have
had their chance and those that can take home
their prizes expect us 6-month mothers come
here for nothing? Do they expect I brought

my Bosco from Rincon to be insulted, and him the pride of the town?" "Cuba is known to Sharon," spoke the other lady. "I'll say no more." "Jumping Jeans!" murmured the orator to himself. "I can't hold this train much longer," said Gadsden; "she's due at Lordsburg now." "You'll have made it up by Tucson, Gadsden," spoke Mrs. Preene, quietly, across the whole assembly from the Manna Department. "As for towns," continued Mrs. Grady, "that think anything of a baby that's only got three teeth—" "Ha! Ha!" laughed Cuba's mother, shrilly. "Teeth! Well, we're not proud of bald babies in Sharon." Bosco was certainly bald. All the men were looking wretched, and all the women were growing more and more like eagles. Moreover, they were separating into two bands and taking their husbands with them—Sharon and Rincon drawing to opposite parts of the tent —and what was coming I cannot say; for we all had to think of something else. A third woman, bringing a man, mounted the platform. It was she I had seen hurry out. "My name's Shot-gun Smith," said the man, very carefully, "and I'm told you've reached my case." He was extremely good-looking, with a blue eye and a blond mustache, not above thirty, and was trying hard to be sober, holding himself with dignity. "Are you the judge?" said he to me. "Well—" I began. "N-not guilty, your honor," said he. At this his wife looked anxious. "S-self-defence," he slowly continued; "told you once already." "Why, Rolfe!" exclaimed his wife, touching his elbow. "Don't you cry, little woman," said he; "this 'll come out all right. Where 're the witnesses?" "Why, Rolfe! *Rolfe!*" She shook him as you shake a sleepy child. "Now see here," said he, and wagged a finger at her affectionately, "you promised me you'd not cry if I let you come." "Rolfe, dear, it's not that to-day; it's the twins." "It's your twins, Shot-gun, this time," said many men's voices. "We acquitted you all right last month." "Justifiable homicide," said Gadsden. "Don't you remember?" "Twins?" said Shot-gun, drowsily. "Oh, yes, mine. Why—" He opened on us his blue eyes that looked about as innocent as Aqua Marine's, and he grew more awake. Then he blushed deeply, face and forehead. "I was not coming to this kind of thing," he explained. "But she wanted the twins to get something." He put his hand on her shoulder and straightened himself. "I done a heap of prospecting before

I struck this claim,'' said he, patting her shoulder. "We got married last March a year. It's our first—first—first"—he turned to me with a confiding smile—"it's our first dividend, judge.'' "Rolfe! I never! You come right down.'' "And now let's go get a prize,'' he declared, with his confiding pleasantness. "I remember now! I remember! They claimed twins was barred. And I kicked down the bars. Take me to those twins. They're not named yet, judge. After they get the prize we'll name them fine names, as good as any they got anywhere—Europe, Asia, Africa—anywhere. My gracious! I wish they was boys. Come on, judge! You and me'll go give 'em a prize, and then we'll drink to 'em.'' He hugged me suddenly and affectionately, and we half fell down the steps. But Gadsden as suddenly caught him and righted him, and we proceeded to the twins. Mrs. Smith looked at me helplessly, saying: "I'm that sorry, sir! I had no idea he was going to be that gamesome.'' "Not at all,'' I said; "not at all!'' Under many circumstances I should have delighted in Shot-gun's society. He seemed so utterly sure that, now he had explained himself, everybody would rejoice to give the remaining medal to his little girls.

But Bosco and Cuba had not been idle. Shot-gun did not notice the spread of whispers, nor feel the divided and jealous currents in the air as he sat, and, in expanding good-will, talked himself almost sober. To entice him out there was no way. Several of his friends had tried it. But beneath his innocence there seemed to lurk something wary, and I grew apprehensive about holding the box this last time. But Gadsden relieved me as our count began. "Shot-gun is a splendid man," said he, "and he has trailed more train-robbers than any deputy in New Mexico. But he has seen too many friends to-day, and is not quite him-self. So when he fell down that time I just took this off him." He opened the drawer, and there lay a six-shooter. "It was touch and go," said Gadsden; "but he's thinking that hard about his twins that he's not missed it yet. 'Twould have been the act of an enemy to leave that on him to-day.—Well, d'you say!" he broke off. "Well, well, well!" It was the tickets we took out of the box that set him exclaiming. I began to read them, and saw that the agent was no mere politician, but a statesman. His Aqua Marine had a solid vote. I remembered his extreme praise of both Bosco and Cuba. This had set Rincon and

Sharon bitterly against each other. I remembered his modesty about Aqua Marine. Of course. Each town, unable to bear the idea of the other's beating it, had voted for the manna-fed, who had 299 votes. Shot-gun and his wife had voted for their twins. I looked towards the Manna Department, and could see that Aqua Marine was placid once more, and Mrs. Preene was dancing the ring before her eyes. I hope I announced the returns in a firm voice. "What!" said Shot-gun Smith; and at that sound Mrs. Preene stopped dancing the ring. He strode to our table. "There's the winner," said Gadsden, quickly pointing to the Manna Exhibit. "What!" said Smith again, but this time very, very softly, almost singing his words, "and they threw me down for that hammer-headed, medicated, patent-stomached inflation?" He whirled around. The men stood ready, and the women fled shrieking and cowering to their infants in the booths. "Gentlemen! Gentlemen!" cried Gadsden, "don't hurt him! Look here!" And from the drawer he displayed Shot-gun's weapon. They understood in a second, and calmly watched the enraged and disappointed Shot-gun. But he was a man. He saw how he had frightened the women, and he stood in the middle of the floor with eyes that did not at all resemble Aqua Marine's at present. "I'm all right now, boys," he said. "I hope I've harmed no one. Ladies, will you try and forget about me making such a break? It got ahead of me, I guess; for I had promised the little woman—" He stopped himself; and then his eye fell upon the Manna Department. "I guess I don't like one thing much now. I'm not after prizes. I'd not accept one from a gold-bug-combine-trust that comes sneaking around stuffing wholesale concoctions into our children's systems. My twins are not manna-fed. My twins are raised as nature intended. Perhaps if they were swelled out with trash that acts like baking-powder, they would have a medal, too—for I notice he has made you vote his way pretty often this afternoon." I saw the agent at the end of the room look very queer. "That's so!" said several. "I think I'll clear out his boxes," said Shot-gun, with rising joy. "I feel like I've got to do something before I go home. Come on, judge!" He swooped towards the manna with a joyous yell, and the men swooped with him, and Gadsden and I were swooped with them. Again the women shrieked. But Mrs. Preene stood out before the boxes with her curl and her chintz.

"Mr. Smith," said she, "you are not going to do anything like that. You are going to behave yourself like the gentleman you are, and not like the wild beast that's inside you." Never in his life before, probably, had Shotgun been addressed in such a manner, and he, too, became hypnotized, fixing his blue eyes upon the strange lady. "I do not believe in patent foods for children," said Mrs. Preene. "We agree on that, Mr. Smith, and I am a grandmother, and I attend to what my grandchildren eat. But this highly adroit young man has done you no harm. If he has the prizes, whose doing is that, please? And who paid for them? Will you tell me, please? Ah, you are all silent!" And she croaked melodiously. "Now let him and his manna go along. But I have enjoyed meeting you all, and I shall not forget you soon. And, Mr. Smith, I want you to remember me. Will you, please?" She walked to Mrs. Smith and the twins, and Shot-gun followed her, entirely hypnotized. She beckoned to me. "Your judge and I," she said, "consider not only your beautiful twins worthy of a prize, but also the mother and father that can so proudly claim them." She put her hand in my pocket. "These cat's-eyes," she said, "you will wear, and think of me and the judge who presents them." She placed a bracelet on each twin, and the necklace upon Mrs. Smith's neck. "Give him Gadsden's stuff," she whispered to me. "Do you shave yourself, sir?" said I, taking out the Stropine. "Vaseline and ground shells, and will last your life. Rub the size of a pea on your strop and spread it to an inch." I placed the box in Shot-gun's motionless hand. "And now, Gadsden, we'll take the train," said Mrs. Preene. "Here's your lunch! Here's your wine!" said the orator, forcing a basket upon me. "I don't know what we'd have done without you and your mother." A flash of indignation crossed Mrs. Preene's face, but changed to a smile. "You've forgot to name my girls!" exclaimed Shot-gun, suddenly finding his voice. "Suppose *you* try that," said Mrs. Preene to me, a trifle viciously. "Thank you," I said to Smith. "Thank you. I—" "Something handsome," he urged. "How would Cynthia do for one?" I suggested. "Shucks, no! I've known two Cynthias. You don't want that?" he asked Mrs. Smith; and she did not at all. "Something extra, something fine, something not stale," said he. I looked about the room. There was no time for thought, but my eye fell once more upon Cuba. This reminded me of

Spain, and the Spanish; and my brain leaped. "I have them!" I cried. "'Armada' and 'Loyola.'" "That's what they're named!" said Shot-gun; "write it for us." And I did. Once more the band played, and we left them, all calling, "Good-bye, ma'am. Good-bye, judge," happy as possible. The train was soon going sixty miles an hour through the desert. We had passed Lordsburg, San Simon, and were nearly at Benson before Mrs. Preene and Gadsden (whom she made sit down with us) and I finished the lunch and champagne. "I wonder how long he'll remember me?" mused Mrs. Preene at Tucson, where we were on time. "That woman is not worth one of his boots."

The Promised Land

PERHAPS there were ten of them—these galloping dots were hard to count—down in the distant bottom across the river. Their swiftly moving dust hung with them close, thinning to a yellow veil when they halted short. They clustered a moment, then parted like beads, and went wide asunder on the plain. They veered singly over the level, merged in twos and threes, apparently racing, shrank together like elastic, and broke ranks again to swerve over the stretching waste. From this visioned pantomime presently came a sound, a tiny shot. The figures were too far for discerning which fired it. It evidently did no harm, and was repeated at once. A babel of diminutive explosions followed, while the horsemen galloped on in unexpected circles. Soon, for no visible reason, the dots ran together, bunching compactly. The shooting stopped, the dust rose thick again from the crowded hoofs, cloaking the group, and so passed back and was lost among the silent barren hills.

Four emigrants had watched this from the

high bleak rim of the Big Bend. They stood
where the flat of the desert broke and tilted
down in grooves and bulges deep to the lurking Columbia. Empty levels lay opposite, nar-
rowing up into the high country.

"That's the Colville Reservation across the
river from us," said the man.

"Another!" sighed his wife.

"The last Indians we'll strike. Our trail
to the Okanagon goes over a corner of it."

"We're going to those hills?" The mother
looked at her little girl and back where the
cloud had gone.

"Only a corner, Liza. The ferry puts us
over on it, and we've got to go by the ferry or
stay this side of the Columbia. You wouldn't
want to start a home here?"

They had driven twenty-one hundred miles
at a walk. Standing by them were the six
horses with the wagon, and its tunnelled roof
of canvas shone duskily on the empty verge
of the wilderness. A dry windless air hung
over the table-land of the Big Bend, but a
sound rose from somewhere, floating volumi-
nous upon the silence, and sank again.

"Rapids!" The man pointed far up the
giant rut of the stream to where a streak
of white water twinkled at the foot of the

hills. "We've struck the river too high," he added.

"Then we don't cross here?" said the woman quickly.

"No. By what they told me the cabin and the ferry ought to be five miles down."

Her face fell. "Only five miles! I was wondering, John— Wouldn't there be a way round for the children to—"

"Now, mother," interrupted the husband, "that ain't like you. We've crossed plenty Indian reservations this trip a'ready."

"I don't want to go round," the little girl said. "Father, don't make me go round."

Mart, the boy, with a loose hook of hair hanging down to his eyes from his hat, did not trouble to speak. He had been disappointed in the westward journey to find all the Indians peaceful. He knew which way he should go now, and he went to the wagon to look once again down the clean barrel of his rifle.

"Why, Nancy, you don't like Indians?" said her mother.

"Yes, I do. I like chiefs."

Mrs. Clallam looked across the river. "It was so strange, John, the way they acted. It seems to get stranger, thinking about it."

"They didn't see us. They didn't have a notion—"

"But if we're going right over?"

"We're not going over there, Liza. That quick water's the Mahkin Rapids, and our ferry's clear down below from this place."

"What could they have been after, do you think?"

"Those chaps? Oh, nothing, I guess. They weren't killing anybody."

"Playing cross-tag," said Mart.

"I'd like to know, John, how you know they weren't killing anybody. They might have been trying to."

"Then we're perfectly safe, Liza. We can set and let 'em kill us all day."

"Well, I don't think it's any kind of way to behave, running around shooting right off your horse."

"And Fourth of July over, too," said Mart from the wagon. He was putting cartridges into the magazine of his Winchester. His common-sense told him that those horsemen would not cross the river, but the notion of a night attack pleased the imagination of young sixteen.

"It was the children," said Mrs. Clallam. "And nobody's getting me any wood. How am I going to cook supper? Stir yourselves!"

They had carried water in the wagon, and

father and son went for wood. Some way
down the hill they came upon a gully with
some dead brush, and climbed back with this.
Supper was eaten on the ground, the horses
were watered, given grain, and turned loose
to find what pickings they might in the lean
growth; and dusk had not turned to dark
when the emigrants were in their beds on the
soft dust. The noise of the rapids dominated
the air with distant sonority, and the children
slept at once, the boy with his rifle along his
blanket's edge. John Clallam lay till the moon
rose hard and brilliant, and then quietly, lest
his wife should hear from her bed by the
wagon, went to look across the river. Where
the downward slope began he came upon her.
She had been watching for some time. They
were the only objects in that bald moonlight.
No shrub grew anywhere that reached to the
waist, and the two figures drew together on
the lonely hill. They stood hand in hand and
motionless, except that the man bent over the
woman and kissed her. When she spoke of
Iowa they had left, he talked of the new region
of their hopes, the country that lay behind the
void hills opposite, where it would not be a
struggle to live. He dwelt on the home they
would make, and her mood followed his at

last, till husband and wife were building distant plans together. The Dipper had swung
low when he remarked that they were a couple
of fools, and they went back to their beds.
Cold came over the ground, and their musings
turned to dreams. Next morning both were
ashamed of their fears.

By four the wagon was on the move. Inside, Nancy's voice was heard discussing with
her mother whether the school-teacher where
they were going to live now would have a
black dog with a white tail, that could swim
with a basket in his mouth. They crawled
along the edge of the vast descent, making
slow progress, for at times the valley widened
and they receded far from the river, and then
circuitously drew close again where the slant
sank abruptly. When the ferryman's cabin
came in sight, the canvas interior of the wagon
was hot in the long-risen sun. The lay of
the land had brought them close above the
stream, but no one seemed to be at the cabin
on the other side, nor was there any sign of a
ferry. Groves of trees lay in the narrow folds
of the valley, and the sinister Columbia swept
black and swift between untenanted shores.
Nothing living could be seen along the scant
levels of the bottom-land. Yet there stood the

cabin as they had been told, the only one between the rapids and the Okanagon; and
bright in the sun the Colville Reservation con-
fronted them. They came upon tracks going
down over the hill, marks of wagons and
horses, plain in the soil, and charred sticks,
with empty cans, lying where camps had been.
Heartened by this proof that they were on the
right road, John Clallam turned his horses
over the brink. The slant steepened suddenly
in a hundred yards, tilting the wagon so no
brake or shoe would hold it if it moved
farther.

"All out!" said Clallam. "Either folks
travel light in this country or they unpack."
He went down a little way. "That's the trail,
too," he said. "Wheel marks down there, and
the little bushes are snapped off."

Nancy slipped out. "I'm unpacked," said
she. "Oh, what a splendid hill to go down!
We'll go like anything."

"Yes, that surely is the trail," Clallam pursued. "I can see away down where somebody's left a wheel among them big stones.
But where does he keep his ferry-boat? And
where does he keep himself?"

"Now, John, if it's here we're to go down,
don't you get to studying over something else.

It'll be time enough after we're at the bottom. Nancy, here's your chair.'' Mrs. Clallam began lifting the lighter things from the wagon.

"Mart," said the father, "we'll have to chain-lock the wheels after we're empty. I guess we'll start with the worst. You and me'll take the stove apart and get her down somehow. We're in luck to have open country and no timber to work through. Drop that bedding, mother! Yourself is all you're going to carry. We'll pack that truck on the horses.''

"Then pack it now and let me start first. I'll make two trips while you're at the stove.''

"There's the man!" said Nancy.

A man—a white man—was riding up the other side of the river. Near the cabin he leaned to see something on the ground. Ten yards more and he was off the horse and picked up something and threw it away. He loitered along, picking up and throwing till he was at the door. He pushed it open and took a survey of the interior. Then he went to his horse, and when they saw him going away on the road he had come, they set up a shouting, and Mart fired a signal. The rider dived from his saddle and made headlong into the cabin, where the door clapped to like a trap. Nothing happened further, and the horse stood on the bank.

"That's the funniest man I ever saw," said Nancy.

"They're all funny over there," said Mart. "I'll signal him again." But the cabin remained shut, and the deserted horse turned, took a few first steps of freedom, then trotted briskly down the river.

"Why, then, he don't belong there at all," said Nancy.

"Wait, child, till we know something about it."

"She's liable to be right, Liza. The horse, anyway, don't belong, or he'd not run off. That's good judgment, Nancy. Right good for a little girl."

"I am six years old," said Nancy, "and I know lots more than that."

"Well, let's get mother and the bedding started down. It'll be noon before we know it."

There were two pack-saddles in the wagon, ready against such straits as this. The rolls were made, balanced as side packs, and circled with the swing-ropes, loose cloths, clothes, frying-pans, the lantern, and the axe tossed in to fill the gap in the middle, canvas flung over the whole, and the diamond-hitch hauled taut on the first pack, when a second rider appeared across the river. He came out of a space between the opposite hills, into which the trail seemed to turn, and he was leading the first man's horse. The heavy work before them was forgotten, and the Clallams sat down in a row to watch.

"He's stealing it," said Mrs. Clallam.

"Then the other man will come out and catch him," said Nancy.

Mart corrected them. "A man never steals horses that way. He drives them up in the mountains, where the owner don't travel much."

The new rider had arrived at the bank and came steadily along till opposite the door, where he paused and looked up and down the river.

"See him stoop," said Clallam the father. "He's seen the tracks don't go further."

"I guess he's after the other one," added Clallam the son.

"Which of them is the ferry-man?" said Mrs. Clallam.

The man had got off and gone straight inside the cabin. In the black of the doorway appeared immediately the first man, dangling in the grip of the other, who kicked him along to the horse. There the victim mounted his own animal and rode back down the river. The chastiser was returning to the cabin, when Mart fired his rifle. The man stopped short, saw the emigrants, and waved his hand. He dismounted and came to the edge of the water. They could hear he was shouting to them, but it was too far for the words to carry. From a certain reiterated cadence, he seemed to be saying one thing. John and Mart tried to show they did not understand, and indicated their wagon, walking to it and getting aboard. On that the stranger redoubled his signs and shoutings, ran to the cabin, where he opened and shut the door several times, came back, and pointed to the hills.

"He's going away, and can't ferry us over," said Mrs. Clallam.

"And the other man thought he'd gone," said Nancy, "and he came and caught him in his house."

"This don't suit me," Clallam remarked. "Mart, we'll go to the shore and talk to him."

When the man saw them descending the hill, he got on his horse and swam the stream. It carried him below, but he was waiting for them when they reached the level. He was tall, shambling, and bony, with a pleasant, restless eye.

"Good-morning," said he. "Fine weather. I was baptized Edward Wilson, but you inquire for Wild-Goose Jake. Them other names are retired and pensioned. I expect you seen me kick him?"

"Couldn't help seeing."

"Oh, I ain't blamin' you, son, not a bit, I ain't. He can't bile water without burnin' it, and his toes turns in, and he's blurry round the finger-nails. He's jest kultus, he is. Hev some?" With a furtive smile that often ran across his lips, he pulled out a flat bottle, and all took an acquaintanceship swallow, while the Clallams explained their journey. "How many air there of yu' slidin' down the hill?" he inquired, shifting his eye to the wagon.

"I've got my wife and little girl up there. That's all of us."

"Ladies along! Then I'll step behind this bush." He was dragging his feet from his waterlogged boots. "Hear them suck now?" he commented. "Didn't hev to think about a wetting wunst. But I ain't young any more. There, I guess I ain't caught a chill." He had whipped his breeches off and spread them on the sand. "Now you arrive down this here

hill from Ioway, and says you: 'Where's that
ferry? Ain't we hit the right spot?' Well,
that's what you hev hit. You're all right, and
the spot is hunky-dory, and it's the durned old
boat hez made the mistake, begosh! A cloud
busted in this country, and she tore out fer the
coast, and the joke's on her! You'd ought to
hev heerd her cable snap! Whoosh, if that
wire didn't screech! Jest last week it was,
and the river come round the corner on us in
a wave four feet high, same as a wall. I was
up here on business, and seen the whole thing.
So the ferry she up and bid us good-bye, and
lit out for Astoria with her cargo. Beggin'
pardon, hev you tobacco, for mine's in my
wet pants? Twenty-four hogs and the driver,
and two Sheeny drummers bound to the mines
with brass jew'lry, all gone to hell, for they
didn't near git to Astoria. They sank in the
sight of all, as we run along the bank. I seen
their arms wave, and them hogs rolling over
like 'taters bilin' round in the kettle.'' Wild-
Goose Jake's words came slow and went more
slowly as he looked at the river and spoke, but
rather to himself. "It warn't long, though. I
expect it warn't three minutes till the water
was all there was left there. My stars, what
a lot of it! And I might hev been part of that

cargo, easy as not. Freight behind time was all that come between me and them that went. So, we'd hev gone bobbin' down that flood, me and my piah-chuck.''

''Your piah-chuck?'' Mart inquired.

The man faced the boy like a rat, but the alertness faded instantly from his eye, and his lip slackened into a slipshod smile. ''Why, yes, sonny, me and my grub-stake. You've been to school, I'll bet, but they didn't learn yu' Chinook, now, did they? Chinook's the lingo us white folks trade in with the Siwashes, and we kinder falls into it, talking along. I was thinkin' how but for delay me and my grub-stake—provisions, ye know— that was consigned to me clear away at Spokane, might hev been drownded along with them hogs and Hebrews. That's what the good folks calls a dispensation of the Sauklee Tyee! —Providence, ye know, in Chinook. 'One shall be taken and the other left.' And that's what beats me—they got left; and I'm a bigger sinner than them drummers, for I'm ten years older than they was. And the poor hogs was better than any of us. That can't be gainsaid. Oh no! oh no!''

Mart laughed.

''I mean it, son. Some day such thoughts

will come to you.'' He stared at the river unsteadily with his light gray eyes.

"Well, if the ferry's gone," said John Clallam, getting on his legs, "we'll go on down to the next one."

"Hold on! hold on! Did you never hear tell of a raft? I'll put you folks over this river. Wait till I git my pants on," said he, stalking nimbly to where they lay.

"It's just this way," Clallam continued; "we're bound for the upper Okanagon country, and we must get in there to build our cabin before cold weather."

"Don't you worry about that. It'll take you three days to the next ferry, while you and me and the boy kin build a raft right here by to-morrow noon. You hev an axe, I expect? Well, here is timber close, and your trail takes over to my place on the Okanagon, where you've got another crossin' to make. And all this time we're keeping the ladies waitin' up the hill! We'll talk business as we go along; and, see here, if I don't suit yu', or fail in my bargain, you needn't to pay me a cent."

He began climbing, and on the way they came to an agreement. Wild-Goose Jake bowed low to Mrs. Clallam, and as low to Nancy, who held her mother's dress and said

nothing, keeping one finger in her mouth. All
began emptying the wagon quickly, and tins
of baking-powder, with rocking-chairs and
flowered quilts, lay on the hill. Wild-Goose
Jake worked hard, and sustained a pleasant
talk by himself. His fluency was of an eagerness that parried interruption or inquiry.

"So you've come acrosst the Big Bend!
Ain't it a cosey place? Reminds me of them
medicine pictures, 'Before and After Using.'
The Big Bend's the way this world looked before using—before the Bible fixed it up, ye
know. Ever seen specimens of Big Bend
produce, ma'am? They send 'em East. Grain
and plums and such. The feller that gathered
them curiosities hed to hunt forty square
miles apiece for 'em. But it's good-payin'
policy, and it fetches lots of settlers to the
Territory. They come here hummin' and
walks around the wilderness, and 'Where's the
plums?' says they. 'Can't you see I'm busy?'
says the land agent; and out they goes. But
you needn't to worry, ma'am. The country
where you're goin' ain't like that. There's
water and timber and rich soil and mines.
Billy Moon has gone there—he's the man run
the ferry. When she wrecked, he pulled his
freight for the new mines at Loop Loop."

"Did the man live in the little house?" said Nancy.

"Right there, miss. And nobody lives there any more, so you take it if you're wantin' a place of your own."

"What made you kick the other man if it wasn't your house?"

"Well, now, if it ain't a good one on him to hev you see that! I'll tell him a little girl seen that, and maybe he'll feel the disgrace. Only he's no account, and don't take any experience the reg'lar way. He's nigh onto thirty, and you'll not believe me, I know, but he ain't never even learned to spit right."

"Is he yours?" inquired Nancy.

"Gosh! no, miss—beggin' pardon. He's jest workin' for me."

"Did he know you were coming to kick him when he hid?"

"Hid? What's that?" The man's eyes narrowed again into points. "You folks seen him hide?" he said to Clallam.

"Why, of course; didn't he say anything?"

"He didn't get much chance," muttered Jake. "What did he hide at?"

"Us."

"You, begosh!"

"I guess so," said Mart. "We took him for

the ferry-man, and when he couldn't hear us—''

''What was he doin'?''

''Just riding along. And so I fired to signal him, and he flew into the door.''

''So you fired, and he flew into the door. Oh, h'm.'' Jake continued to pack the second horse, attending carefully to the ropes. ''I never knowed he was that weak in the upper story,'' he said, in about five minutes. ''Knew his brains was tenas, but didn't suspect he were that weak in the upper story. You're sure he didn't go in till he heerd your gun?''

''He'd taken a look and was going away,'' said Mart.

''Now ain't some people jest odd! Now you follow me, and I'll tell you folks what I'd figured he'd been at. Billy Moon he lived in that cabin, yu' see. And he had his stuff there, yu' see, and run the ferry, and a kind of a store. He kept coffee and canned goods and star-plug and this and that to supply the prospectin' outfits that come acrosst on his ferry on the trail to the mines. Then a cloud-burst hits his boat and his job's sp'iled on the river, and he quits for the mines, takin' his stuff along —do you follow me? But he hed to leave some, and he give me the key, and I was to send the balance after him next freight team that come along my way. Leander—that's him I was kickin'—he knowed about it, and he'll steal a hot stove he's that dumb. He knowed there was stuff here of Billy Moon's. Well, last night we hed some horses stray, and I says to him, 'Andy, you get up by daylight and find them.' And he gits. But by seven the horses come in all right of theirselves, and Mr. Leander he was missin'; and says I to myself, 'I'll ketch you, yu' blamed hobo.' And I thought I had ketched him, yu' see. Weren't that reasonable of me? Wouldn't any of you folks hev drawed that conclusion?" The man had fallen into a wheedling tone as he studied their faces. "Jest put yourselves in my place," he said.

"Then what was he after?" said Mart.

"Stealin'. But he figured he'd come again."

"He didn't like my gun much."

"Guns always skeers him when he don't know the parties shootin'. That's his dumbness. Maybe he thought I was after him; he's jest that distrustful. Begosh! we'll have the laugh on him when he finds he run from a little girl."

"He didn't wait to see who he was running from," said Mart.

"Of course he didn't. Andy hears your gun
and he don't inquire further, but hits the first
hole he kin crawl into. That's Andy! That's
the kind of boy I hev to work for me. All the
good ones goes where you're goin', where the
grain grows without irrigation and the black-
tail deer comes out on the hill and asks yu' to
shoot 'em for dinner. Who's ready for the
bottom? If I stay talkin' the sun 'll go down
on us. Don't yu' let me get started agin. Just
you shet me off twiced anyway each twenty-
four hours."

He began to descend with his pack-horse
and the first load. All afternoon they went
up and down over the hot bare face of the hill,
until the baggage, heavy and light, was trans-
ported and dropped piecemeal on the shore.
The torn-out insides of their home littered the
stones with familiar shapes and colors, and
Nancy played among them, visiting each par-
cel and folded thing.

"There's the red table-cover!" she exclaimed, "and the big coffee-grinder. And
there's our table, and the hole Mart burned
in it." She took a long look at this. "Oh,
how I wish I could see our pump!" she said,
and began to cry.

"You talk to her, mother," said Clallam.
"She's tuckered out."

The men returned to bring the wagon.
With chain-locked wheels, and tilted half over
by the cross slant of the mountain, it came
heavily down, reeling and sliding on the slip-
pery yellow weeds, and grinding deep ruts
across the faces of the shelving beds of gravel.
Jake guided it as he could, straining back on
the bits of the two hunched horses when their
hoofs glanced from the stones that rolled to
the bottom; and the others leaned their weight
on a pole lodged between the spokes, making
a balance to the wagon, for it leaned the other
way so far that at any jolt the two wheels left
the ground. When it was safe at the level of
the stream, dusk had come and a white flat of
mist lay along the river, striping its course
among the gaunt hills. They slept without
moving, and rose early to cut logs, which the
horses dragged to the shore. The outside
trunks were nailed and lashed with ropes, and
sank almost below the surface with the weight
of the wood fastened crosswise on top. But
the whole floated dry with its cargo, and
crossed clumsily on the quick-wrinkled current. Then it brought the wagon; and the six
horses swam. The force of the river had
landed them below the cabin, and when they
had repacked there was too little left of day

to go on. Clallam suggested it was a good time to take Moon's leavings over to the Okanagon, but Wild-Goose Jake said at once that their load was heavy enough; and about this they could not change his mind. He made a journey to the cabin by himself, and returned saying that he had managed to lock the door.

"Father," said Mart, as they were harnessing next day, "I've been up there. I went awful early. There's no lock to the door, and the cabin's empty."

"I guessed that might be."

"There has been a lock pried off pretty lately. There was a lot of broken bottles around everywheres, inside and out."

"Part of what he says is all right," said Clallam. "You can see where the ferry's cable used to be fastened on this side. And yonder goes the trail."

"What do you make out of it?" said Mart.

"Nothing yet. He wants to get us away, and I'm with him there. I want to get up the Okanagon as soon as we can."

"Well, I'm takin' yu' the soonest way," said Wild-Goose Jake, behind them. From his casual smile there was no telling what he had heard. "I'll put your stuff acrosst the

Okanagon to-morrow mornin'. But to-night yourselves 'll all be over, and the ladies kin sleep in my room.''

The wagon made good time. The trail crossed easy valleys and over the yellow grass of the hills, while now and then their guide took a short-cut. He wished to get home, he said, since there could be no estimating what Leander might be doing. While the sun was still well up in the sky they came over a round knob and saw the Okanagon, blue in the bright afternoon, and the cabin on its further bank. This was a roomier building to see than common, and a hay-field was by it, and a bit of green pasture, fenced in. Saddle-horses were tied in front, heads hanging and feet knuckled askew with long waiting, and from inside an uneven, riotous din whiffled lightly across the river and intervening meadow to the hill.

''If you'll excuse me,'' said Jake, ''I'll jest git along ahead, and see what game them folks is puttin' up on Andy. Likely as not he's weighin' 'em out flour at two cents, with it costin' me two and a half on freightin' alone. I'll hev supper ready time you ketch up.''

He was gone at once, getting away at a sharp pace, till presently they could see him swimming the stream. When he was in the cabin the sounds changed, dropping off to one at a time, and expired. But when the riders came out into the air, they leaned and collided at random, whirled their arms, and, screaming till they gathered heart, charged with wavering menace at the door. The foremost was flung from the sill, and he shot along toppling and scraped his length in the dust, while the owner of the cabin stood in the entrance. The Indian picked himself up, and at some word of Jake's which the emigrants could half follow by the fierce lift of his arm, all got on their horses and set up a wailing, like spirits of ill omen. They went up the river a little and crossed, but did not come down this side, and Mrs. Clallam was thankful when their evil noise had died away up the valley. They had seen the wagon coming, but gave it no attention. A man soon came over the river from the cabin, and was lounging against a tree when the emigrants drew up at the margin.

"I don't know what you know," he whined defiantly from the tree, "but I'm goin' to Cornwall, Connecticut, and I don't care who knows it." He sent a cowed look at the cabin across the river.

"Get out of the wagon, Nancy," said Clallam. "Mart, help her down."

"I'm going back," said the man, blinking like a scolded dog. "I ain't stayin' here for nobody. You can tell him I said so, too." Again his eye slunk sidewise towards the cabin, and instantly back.

"While you're staying," said Mart, "you might as well give a hand here."

He came with alacrity, and made a shift of unhitching the horses. "I was better off coupling freight cars on the Housatonic," he soon remarked. His voice came shallow, from no deeper than his throat, and a peevish apprehension rattled through it. "That was a good job. And I've had better, too; forty, fifty, sixty dollars better."

"Shall we unpack the wagon?" Clallam inquired.

"I don't know. You ever been to New Milford? I sold shoes there. Thirty-five dollars and board."

The emigrants attended to their affairs, watering the horses and driving picket stakes. Leander uselessly followed behind them with conversation, blinking and with lower lip sagged, showing a couple of teeth. "My brother's in business in Pittsfield, Massachusetts," said he, "and I can get a salary in Bridgeport any day I say so. That a Marlin?"

"No," said Mart. "It's a Winchester."

"I had a Marlin. He's took it from me. I'll bet you never got shot at."

"Anybody want to shoot you?" Mart inquired.

"Well and I guess you'll believe they did day before yesterday."

"If you're talking about up at that cabin, it was me."

Leander gave Mart a leer. "That won't do," said he. "He's put you up to telling me that, and I'm going to Cornwall, Connecticut. I know what's good for me, I guess."

"I tell you we were looking for the ferry, and I signalled you across the river."

"No, no," said Leander. "I never seen you in my life. Don't you be like him and take me for a fool."

"All right. Why did they want to murder you?"

"Why?" said the man, shrilly. "Why? Hadn't they broke in and filled themselves up on his piah-chuck till they were crazy-drunk? And when I came along didn't they—"

"When you came along they were nowhere near there," said Mart.

"Now you're going to claim it was me drunk it and scattered all them bottles of his," screamed Leander, backing away. "I tell you I didn't. I told him I didn't, and he knowed it well, too. But he's just that mean when he's mad he likes to put a thing on me whether or no, when he never seen me touch a drop of whisky, nor any one else, neither. They were riding and shooting loose over the country like they always do on a drunk. And I'm glad they stole his stuff. What business had he to keep it at Billy Moon's old cabin and send me away up there to see it was all right? Let him do his own dirty work. I ain't going to break the laws on the salary he pays me.''

The Clallam family had gathered round Leander, who was stricken with volubility. "It ain't once in a while, but it's every day and every week," he went on, always in a woolly scream. "And the longer he ain't caught the bolder he gets, and puts everything that goes wrong on to me. Was it me traded them for that liquor this afternoon? It was his squaw, Big Tracks, and he knowed it well. He lets that mud-faced baboon run the house when he's off, and I don't have the keys nor nothing, and never did have. But of course he had to come in and say it was me just because he was mad about having you see them Siwashes hollering around. And he come and shook me where I was sittin', and oh, my, he

knowed well the lie he was acting. I bet I've
got the marks on my neck now. See any red
marks?'' Leander exhibited the back of his
head, but the violence done him had evidently
been fleeting. ''He'll be awful good to you,
for he's that scared—''

Leander stood tremulously straight in silence, his lip sagging, as Wild-Goose Jake
called pleasantly from the other bank. ''Come
to supper, you folks,'' said he. ''Why, Andy,
I told you to bring them acrosst, and you've
let them picket their horses. Was you ex-
pectin' Mrs. Clallam to take your arm and
ford six feet of water?'' For some reason
his voice sounded kind as he spoke to his
assistant.

''Well, mother?'' said Clallam.

''If it was not for Nancy, John—''

''I know, I know. Out on the shore here on
this side would be a pleasanter bedroom for
you, but'' (he looked up the valley) ''I guess
our friend's plan is more sensible to-night.''

So they decided to leave the wagon behind
and cross to the cabin. The horses put them
with not much wetting to the other bank,
where Jake, most eager and friendly, hovered
to meet his party, and when they were safe
ashore pervaded his premises in their behalf.

"Turn them horses into the pasture, Andy," said he, "and first feed 'em a couple of quarts." It may have been hearing himself say this, but tone and voice dropped to the confidential and his sentences came with a chuckle. "Quarts to the horses and quarts to the Siwashes and a skookum pack of trouble all round, Mrs. Clallam! If I hedn't a-came to stop it a while ago, why, about all the spirits that's in stock jest now was bein' traded off for some blamed ponies the bears hev let hobble on the range unswallered ever since I settled here. A store on a trail like this here, ye see, it hez to keep spirits, of course; and—well, well! here's my room; you ladies 'll excuse, and make yourselves at home as well as you can."

It was of a surprising neatness, due all to him, they presently saw; the log walls covered with a sort of bunting that was also stretched across to make a ceiling below the shingles of the roof; fresh soap and towels, china service, a clean floor and bed, on the wall a print of some white and red village among elms, with a covered bridge and the water running over an apron-dam just above; and a rich smell of whisky everywhere. "Fix up as comfortable as yu' can," the host repeated, "and I'll see

how Mrs. Jake's tossin' the flapjacks. She's
Injun, yu' know, and five years of married life
hain't learned her to toss flapjacks. Now if I
was you'' (he was lingering in the doorway)
''I wouldn't shet that winder so quick. It
don't smell nice yet for ladies in here, and I'd
hev liked to git the time to do better for ye;
but them Siwashes—well, of course, you folks
see how it is. Maybe it ain't always and only
white men that patronizes our goods. Uncle
Sam is a long way off, and I don't say we'd
ought to, but when the cat's away, why the
mice *will*, ye know—they most always *will!*''

There was a rattle of boards outside, at
which he shut the door quickly, and they
heard him run. A light muttering came in at
the window, and the mother, peeping out, saw
Andy fallen among a rubbish of crates and
empty cans, where he lay staring, while his
two fists beat up and down like a disordered
toy. Wild-Goose Jake came, and having lifted
him with great tenderness, was laying him flat
as Elizabeth Clallam hurried to his help.

''No, ma'am,'' he sighed, ''you can't do
nothing, I guess.''

''Just let me go over and get our medicines.''

''Thank you, ma'am,'' said Jake, and the

pain on his face was miserable to see; ''there ain't no medicine. We're kind o' used to this, Andy and me. Maybe, if you wouldn't mind stayin' till he comes to— Why, a sick man takes comfort at the sight of a lady.''

When the fit had passed they helped him to his feet, and Jake led him away.

Mrs. Jake made her first appearance upon the guests sitting down to their meal, when she waited on table, passing busily forth from the kitchen with her dishes. She had but three or four English words, and her best years were plainly behind her; but her cooking was good, fried and boiled with sticks of her own chopping, and she served with industry. Indeed, a squaw is one of the few species of the domestic wife that survive to-day upon our continent. Andy seemed now to keep all his dislike for her, and followed her with a scowling eye, while he frequented Jake, drawing a chair to sit next him when he smoked by the wall after supper, and sometimes watching him with a sort of clouded affection upon his face. He did not talk, and the seizure had evidently jarred his mind as well as his frame. When the squaw was about lighting a lamp he brushed her arm in a childish way so that the match went out, and set him laughing.

She poured out a harangue in Chinook, showing the dead match to Jake, who rose and
gravely lighted the lamp himself, Andy laughing more than ever. When Mrs. Clallam had
taken Nancy with her to bed, Jake walked
John Clallam to the river-bank, and looking
up and down, spoke a little of his real mind.

"I guess you see how it is with me. Anyway, I don't commonly hev use for stranger-
folks in this house. But that little girl of
yourn started cryin' about not havin' the
pump along that she'd been used to seein' in
the yard at home. And I says to myself, 'Look
a-here, Jake, I don't care if they do ketch on
to you and yer blamed whisky business.
They're not the sort to tell on you.' Gee! but
that about the pump got me! And I says,
'Jake, you're goin' to give them the best you
hev got.' Why, that Big Bend desert and lonesome valley of the Columbia hez chilled my
heart in the days that are gone when I weren't
used to things; and the little girl hed came so
fur! And I knowed how she was a-feelin'.''

He stopped, and seemed to be turning matters over.

"I'm much obliged to you,'' said Clallam.

"And your wife was jest beautiful about
Andy. You've saw me wicked to Andy. I am,

and often, for I rile turruble quick, and God forgive me! But when that boy gits at his meanness—yu've seen jest a touch of it— there's scarcely livin' with him. It seems like he got reg'lar inspired. Some days he'll lie —make up big lies to the fust man comes in at the door. They ain't harmless, his lies ain't. Then he'll trick my woman, that's real good to him; and I believe he'd lick whisky up off the dirt. And every drop is poison for him with his complaint. But I'd ought to remember. You'd surely think I could remember, and forbear. Most likely he made a big talk to you about that cabin.''

John Clallam told him.

"Well, that's all true, for wunst. I did think he'd been up to stealin' that whisky gradual, 'stead of fishin', the times he was out all day. And the salary I give him''—Jake laughed a little—''ain't enough to justify a man's breaking the law. I did take his rifle away when he tried to shoot my woman. I guess it was Siwashes bruck into that cabin.''

"I'm pretty certain of it,'' said Clallam.

"You? What makes you?''

John began the tale of the galloping dots, and Jake stopped walking to listen the harder. "Yes,'' he said; ''that's bad. That's jest bad.

They hev carried a lot off to drink. That's the worst.''

He had little to say after this, but talked under his tongue as they went to the house, where he offered a bed to Clallam and Mart. They would not turn him out, so he showed them over to a haystack, where they crawled in and went to sleep.

Most white men know when they have had enough whisky. Most Indians do not. This is a difference between the races of which government has taken notice. Government says that "no ardent spirits shall be introduced under any pretence into the Indian country.'' It also says that the white man who attempts to break this law "shall be punished by imprisonment for not more than two years and by a fine of not more than three hundred dollars.'' It further says that if any superintendent of Indian affairs has reason to suspect a man, he may cause the "boats, stores, packages, wagons, sleds, and places of deposit'' of such person to be searched, and if ardent spirits be found it shall be forfeit, together with the boats and all other substances with it connected, one half to the informer and the other half to the use of the United States. The courts and all legal machines necessary for trial and punishment of offenders are oiled and ready; two years is a long while in jail; three hundred dollars and confiscation sounds heavy; altogether the penalty looks severe on the printed page—and all the while there's no brisker success in our far West than selling whisky to Indians. Very few people know what the whisky is made of, and the Indian does not care. He drinks till he drops senseless. If he has killed nobody and nobody him during the process, it is a good thing, for then the matter ends with his getting sober and going home to his tent till such happy time when he can put his hand on some further possession to trade away. The white offender is caught now and then; but Okanagon County lies pretty snug from the arms of the law. It's against Canada to the north, and the empty county of Stevens to the east; south of it rushes the Columbia, with the naked horrible Big Bend beyond, and to its west rises a domain of unfooted mountains. There is law up in the top of it at Conconully sometimes, but not much even to-day, for that is still a new country, where flow the Methow, the Ashinola, and the Similikameen.

Consequently a cabin like Wild-Goose Jake's was a holiday place. The blanketed denizens of the reservation crossed to it, and the citizens who had neighboring cabins along the trail repaired here to spend what money they had. As Mrs. Clallam lay in her bed she heard customers arrive. Two or three loud voices spoke in English, and several Indians and squaws seemed to be with the party, bantering in Chinook. The visitors were in too strong force for Jake's word about coming some other night to be of any avail. .

"Open your cellar and quit your talk," Elizabeth heard, and next she heard some door that stuck, pulled open with a shriek of the warped timber. Next they were gambling, and made not much noise over it at first; but the Indians in due time began to lose to the soberer whites, becoming quarrelsome, and raising a clumsy disturbance, though it was plain the whites had their own way and were feared. The voices rose, and soon there was no moment that several were not shouting curses at once, till Mrs. Clallam stopped her ears. She was still for a time, hearing only in a muffled way, when all at once the smell of drink and tobacco, that had sifted only a little through the cracks, grew heavy in the room, and she felt Nancy shrink close to her side.

"Mother, mother," the child whispered, "what's that?"

It had gone beyond card-playing with the company in the saloon; they seemed now to be having a savage horse-play, those on their feet tramping in their scuffles upon others on the floor, who bellowed incoherently. Elizabeth Clallam took Nancy in her arms and told her that nobody would come where they were.

But the child was shaking. "Yes, they will," she whispered, in terror. "They are!" And she began a tearless sobbing, holding her mother with her whole strength.

A little sound came close by the bed, and Elizabeth's senses stopped so that for half a minute she could not stir. She stayed rigid beneath the quilt, and Nancy clung to her. Something was moving over the floor. It came quite near, but turned, and its slight rustle crawled away towards the window.

"Who is that?" demanded Mrs. Clallam, sitting up.

There was no answer, but the slow creeping continued, always close along the floor, like the folds of stuff rubbing, and hands feeling their way in short slides against the boards. She had no way to find where her husband was sleeping, and while she thought of this and whether or not to rush out at the door, the table was gently shaken, there was a drawer opened, and some object fell.

"Only a thief," she said to herself, and in a sort of sharp joy cried out her question again.

The singular broken voice of a woman answered, seemingly in fear. "Match-es," it said; and "Match-es" said a second voice, pronouncing with difficulty, like the first. She knew it was some of the squaws, and sprang from the bed, asking what they were doing there. "Match-es," they murmured; and when she had struck a light she saw how the two were cringing, their blankets huddled round them. Their motionless black eyes looked up at her from the floor where they lay sprawled, making no offer to get up. It was clear to her from the pleading fear in the one word they answered to whatever she said, that they had come here to hide from the fury of the next room; and as she stood listening to this she would have let them remain, but their escape had been noticed. A man burst into the room, and at sight of her and Nancy stopped, and was blundering excuses, when Jake caught his arm and had dragged him almost out, but he saw the two on the floor; at this, getting himself free, he half swept the crouching figures with his boot as they fled out of the room, and the door was swung shut. Mrs. Clallam heard his violent words to the squaws for daring to disturb the strangers, and there followed the heavy lashing of a quirt, with screams and lamenting. No trouble came from the Indian husbands, for they were stupefied on the ground, and when their intelligences quickened enough for them to move, the punishment was long over and no one in the house awake but Elizabeth and Nancy, seated together in their bed, watching for the day. Mother and daughter heard them rise to go out one by one, and the hoof-beats of their horses grew distant up and down the river. As the rustling trees lighted and turned transparent in the rising sun, Jake roused those that remained and got them away. Later he knocked at the door.

"I hev a little raft fixed this morning," said he, "and I guess we can swim the wagon over here."

"Whatever's quickest to take us from this place," Elizabeth answered.

"Breakfast 'll be ready, ma'am, whenever you say."

"I am ready now. I shall want to start fer-

rying our things— Where's Mr. Clallam?
Tell him to come here."

"I will, ma'am. I'm sorry—"

"Tell Mr. Clallam to come here please."

John had slept sound in his haystack, and
heard nothing. "Well," he said, after com-
forting his wife and Nancy, "you were better
off in the room, anyway. I'd not blame him
so, Liza. How was he going to help it?"

But Elizabeth was a woman, and just now
saw one thing alone: if selling whisky led to
such things in this country, the man who sold
it was much worse than any mere law-breaker.
John Clallam, being now a long time married,
made no argument. He was looking absently
at the open drawer of a table. "That's
queer," he said, and picked up a tintype.

She had no curiosity for anything in that
room, and he laid it in the drawer again, his
thoughts being taken up with the next step
of their journey, and what might be coming
to them all.

During breakfast Jake was humble about
the fright the ladies had received in his house,
explaining how he thought he had acted for
the best; at which Clallam and Mart said that
in a rough country folks must look for rough

doings, and get along as well as they can; but Elizabeth said nothing. The little raft took all but Nancy over the river to the wagon, where they set about dividing their belongings in loads that could be floated back, one at a time, and Jake returned to repair some of the disorder that remained from the night at the cabin. John and Mart poled the first cargo across, and while they were on the other side, Elizabeth looked out of the wagon, where she was working alone, and saw five Indian riders coming down the valley. The dust hung in the air they had rushed through, and they swung apart and closed again as she had seen before; so she looked for a rifle; but the fire-arms had gone over the Okanagon with the first load. She got down and stood at the front wheel of the wagon, confronting the riders when they pulled up their horses. One climbed unsteadily from his saddle and swayed towards her.

"Drink!" said he, half friendly, and held out a bottle.

Elizabeth shook her head.

"Drink," he grunted again, pushing the bottle at her. "Piah-chuck! Skookum!" He had a sluggish animal grin, and when she drew back, tipped the bottle into his mouth, and directly choked, so that his friends on their horses laughed loud as he stood coughing. "Heap good," he remarked, looking at Elizabeth, who watched his eyes swim with the glut of the drink. "Where you come back?" he inquired, touching the wagon. "You cross Okanagon? Me cross you; cross horses; cross all. Heap cheap. What yes?"

The others nodded. "Heap cheap," they said.

"We don't want you," said Elizabeth.

"No cross? Maybe he going cross you? What yes?"

Again Elizabeth nodded.

"Maybe he Jake?" pursued the Indian.

"Yes, he is. We don't want you."

"We cross you all same. He not."

The Indian spoke loud and thick, and Elizabeth looked over the river where her husband was running with a rifle, and Jake behind him, holding a warning hand on his arm. Jake called across to the Indians, who listened sullenly, but got on their horses and went up the river.

"Now," said Jake to Clallam, "they ain't gone. Get your wife over here so she kin set in my room till I see what kin be done."

John left him at once, and crossed on the

raft. His wife was stepping on it, when the noise and flight of riders descended along the other bank, where Jake was waiting. They went in a circle, with hoarse shouts, round the cabin as Mart with Nancy came from the pasture. The boy no sooner saw them than he caught his sister up and carried her quickly away among the corrals and sheds, where the two went out of sight.

"You stay here, Liza," her husband said. "I'll go back over."

But Mrs. Clallam laughed.

"Get ashore," he cried to her. "Quick!"

"Where you go, I go, John."

"What good, what good, in the name—"

"Then I'll get myself over," said she. And he seized her as she would have jumped into the stream.

While they crossed, the Indians had tied their horses and rambled into the cabin. Jake came from it to stop the Clallams.

"They're after your contract," said he, quietly. "They say they're going to have the job of takin' the balance of your stuff that's left acrosst the Okanagon over to this side."

"What did you say?" asked Mrs. Clallam.

"I set 'em up drinks to gain time."

"Do you want me there?" said Clallam.

"Begosh, no! That would mix things worse."

"Can't you make tnem go away?" Elizabeth inquired.

"Me and them, ye see, ma'am, we hev a sort of bargain they're to git certain ferryin'. I can't make 'em savvy how I took charge of you. If you want them—" He paused.

"We want them!" exclaimed Elizabeth. "If you're joking, it's a poor joke."

"It ain't no joke at all, ma'am." Jake's face grew brooding. "Of course folks kin say who they'll be ferried by. And you may believe I'd rather do it. I didn't look for jest this complication; but maybe I kin steer through; and it's myself I've got to thank. Of course, if them Siwashes did git your job, they'd sober up gittin' ready. And—"

The emigrants waited, but he did not go on with what was in his mind. "It's all right," said he, in a brisk tone. "Whatever's a-comin's a-comin'." He turned abruptly towards the door. "Keep yerselves away jest now," he added, and went inside.

The parents sought their children, finding Mart had concealed Nancy in the haystack. They put Mrs. Clallam also in a protected place, as a loud altercation seemed to be rising

at the cabin; this grew as they listened, and
Jake's squaw came running to hide herself.
She could tell them nothing, nor make them
understand more than they knew; but she
touched John's rifle, signing to know if it were
loaded, and was greatly relieved when he
showed her the magazine full of cartridges.
The quarrelling had fallen silent, but rose in
a new gust of fierceness, sounding as if in the
open air and coming their way. No Indian
appeared, however, and the noise passed to
the river, where the emigrants soon could hear
wood being split in pieces.

John risked a survey. "It's the raft," he
said. "They're smashing it. Now they're
going back. Stay with the children, Liza."

"You're never going to that cabin?" she
said.

"He's in a scrape, mother."

John started away, heedless of his wife's
despair. At his coming the Indians shouted
and surrounded him, while he heard Jake say,
"Drop your gun and drink with them."

"Drink!" said Andy, laughing with the
same screech he had made at the match going
out. "We're all going to Canaan, Connecticut."

Each Indian held a tin cup, and at the instant these were emptied they were thrust towards Jake, who filled them again, going and coming through a door that led a step or two down into a dark place which was half underground. Once he was not quick, or was imagined to be refusing, for an Indian raised his cup and drunkenly dashed it on Jake's head. Jake laughed good-humoredly, and filled the cup.

"It's our one chance," said he to John as the Indian, propping himself by a hand on the wall, offered the whisky to Clallam.

"We cross you Okanagon," he said. "What yes?"

"Maybe you say no?" said another, pressing the emigrant to the wall.

A third interfered, saying something in their language, at which the other two disagreed. They talked a moment with threatening rage till suddenly all drew pistols. At this the two remaining stumbled among the group, and a shot went into the roof. Jake was there in one step with a keg, that they no sooner saw than they fell upon it, and the liquor jetted out as they climbed, wrestling over the room till one lay on his back with his mouth at the open bung. It was wrenched from him, and directly there was not a drop more in it. They tilted it, and when none ran out, flung the keg out of doors and crowded to the door of the dark place, where Jake barred the way. "Don't take to that yet!" he said to Clallam, for John was lifting his rifle.

"Piah-chuck!" yelled the Indians, scarcely able to stand. All other thought had left them, and a new thought came to Jake. He reached for a fresh keg, while they held their tin cups in the left hand and pistols in the right, pushing so it was a slow matter to get the keg opened. They were fast nearing the sodden stage, and one sank on the floor. Jake glanced in at the door behind him, and filled the cups once again. While all were drinking he went in the store-room and set more liquor open, beckoning them to come as they looked up from the rims to which their lips had been glued. They moved round behind the table, grasping it to keep on their feet, with the one on the floor crawling among the legs of the rest. When they were all inside, Jake leaped out and locked the door.

"They kin sleep now," said he. "Gunpowder won't be needed. Keep wide away from in front."

There was a minute of stillness within, and then a grovelling noise and struggle. A couple of bullets came harmless through the door. Those inside fought together as well as they could, while those outside listened as it grew less, the bodies falling stupefied without further sound of rising. One or two, still active, began striking at the boards with what heavy thing they could find, until suddenly the blade of an axe crashed through.

"Keep away!" cried Jake. But Andy had leaped insanely in front of the door, and fell dead with a bullet through him. With a terrible scream, Jake flung himself at the place, and poured six shots through the panel; then, as Clallam caught him, wrenched at the lock, and they saw inside. Whisky and blood dripped together, and no one was moving there. It was liquor with some, and death with others, and all of it lay upon the guilty soul of Jake.

"You deserve killing yourself," said Clallam.

"That's been attended to," replied Jake, and he reeled, for during his fire some Indian had shot once more.

Clallam supported him to the room where his wife and Nancy had passed the night, and laid him on the bed. "I'll get Mrs. Clallam," said he.

"If she'll be willin' to see me," said the wounded man, humbly.

She came, dazed beyond feeling any horror, or even any joy, and she did what she could. "It was seein' 'em hit Andy," said Jake. "Is Andy gone? Yes, I kin tell he's gone from your face." He shut his eyes, and lay still so long a time that they thought he might be dying now; but he moved at length, and looked slowly round the wall till he saw the print of the village among the elms and the covered bridge. His hand lifted to show them this. "That's the road," said he. "Andy and me used to go fishin' acrosst that bridge. Did you ever see the Housatonic River? I've fished a lot there. Cornwall, Connecticut. The hills are pretty there. Then Andy got worse. You look in that drawer." John remembered, and when he got out the tintype, Jake stretched for it eagerly. "His mother and him, age ten," he explained to Elizabeth, and held it for her to see, then studied the faces in silence. "You kin tell it's Andy, can't yu'?" She told him yes. "That was before we knowed he weren't—weren't goin' to grow up like the other boys he played with. So after a while, when she was gone, I got ashamed seein' Andy's friends makin' their

way when he couldn't seem to, and so I took
him away where nobody hed ever been acquainted with us. I was layin' money by to
get him the best doctor in Europe. I ain't
been a good man.''

A faintness mastered him, and Elizabeth
would have put the picture on the table, but
his hand closed round it. They let him lie so,
and Elizabeth sat there, while John, with
Mart, kept Nancy away till the horror in the
outer room was made invisible. They came
and went quietly, and Jake seemed in a deep-
ening torpor, once only rousing suddenly to
call his son's name, and then, upon looking
from one to the other, he recollected, and his
eyes closed again. His mind wandered, but
very little, for torpor seemed to be overcom-
ing him. The squaw had stolen in, and sat
cowering and useless. Towards sundown
John's heart sickened at the sound of more
horsemen; but it was only two white men, a
sheriff and his deputy.

"Go easy," said John. "He's not going to
resist."

"What's up here, anyway? Who are you?"

Clallam explained, and was evidently not so
much as half believed.

"If there are Indians killed," said the

sheriff, "there's still another matter for the law to settle with him. We're sent to search for whisky. The county's about tired of him."

"You'll find him pretty sick," said John.

"People I find always are pretty sick," said the sheriff, and pushed his way in, stopping at sight of Mrs. Clallam and the figure on the bed. "I'm arresting that man, madam," he said, with a shade of apology. "The county court wants him."

Jake sat up and knew the sheriff. "You're a little late, Proctor," said he. "The Supreme Court's a-goin' to call my case." Then he fell back, for his case had been called.

Padre Ignacio

I

AT Santa Ysabel del Mar the season was at one of those moments when the air rests quiet over land and sea. The old breezes were gone; the new ones were not yet risen. The flowers in the mission garden opened wide; no wind came by day or night to shake the loose petals from their stems. Along the basking, silent, many-colored shore gathered and lingered the crisp odors of the mountains. The dust hung golden and motionless long after the rider was behind the hill, and the Pacific lay like a floor of sapphire, whereon to walk beyond the setting sun into the East. One white sail shone there. Instead of an hour, it had been from dawn till afternoon in sight between the short headlands; and the Padre had hoped that it might be the ship his homesick heart awaited. But it had slowly passed. From an arch in his garden cloisters he was now watching the last of it. Presently it was gone, and the great ocean lay empty. The Padre put his glasses in his lap. For a short while he read in his breviary, but soon forgot it again. He looked at the flowers and sunny ridges, then at the huge blue triangle of sea which the opening of the hills let into sight. "Paradise," he murmured, "need not hold more beauty and peace. But I think I would exchange all my remaining years of this for one sight again of Paris or Seville. May God forgive me such a thought!"

Across the unstirred fragrance of oleanders the bell for vespers began to ring. Its tones passed over the Padre as he watched the sea in his garden. They reached his parishioners in their adobe dwellings near by. The gentle circles of sound floated outward upon the smooth, immense silence—over the vines and pear-trees; down the avenues of the olives; into the planted fields, whence women and children began to return; then out of the lap of the valley along the yellow uplands, where the men that rode among the cattle paused, looking down like birds at the map of their home. Then the sound widened, faint, un-broken, until it met Temptation in the guise of a youth, riding toward the Padre from the South, and cheered the steps of Temptation's jaded horse.

"For a day, one single day of Paris!" repeated the Padre, gazing through his cloisters
at the empty sea.

Once in the year the mother-world remembered him. Once in the year, from Spain,
tokens and home-tidings came to him, sent
by certain beloved friends of his youth. A
barkentine brought him these messages.
Whenever thus the mother-world remembered him, it was like the touch of a warm
hand, a dear and tender caress; a distant life,
by him long left behind, seemed to be drawing the exile home-ward from these alien
shores. As the time for his letters and packets
drew near, the eyes of Padre Ignacio would
be often fixed wistfully upon the harbor,
watching for the barkentine. Sometimes, as
to-day, he mistook other sails for hers, but
hers he mistook never. That Pacific Ocean,
which, for all its hues and jeweled mists, he
could not learn to love, had, since long before
his day, been furrowed by the keels of Spain.
Traders, and adventurers, and men of God
had passed along this coast, planting their
colonies and cloisters; but it was not his
ocean. In the year that we, a thin strip of
patriots away over on the Atlantic edge of
the continent, declared ourselves an inde-

pendent nation, a Spanish ship, in the name
of Saint Francis, was unloading the centuries
of her own civilization at the Golden Gate.
San Diego had come earlier. Then, slowly, as
mission after mission was built along the soft
coast wilderness, new ports were established
—at Santa Barbara, and by Point San Luis
for San Luis Obispo, which lay inland a little
way up the gorge where it opened among the
hills. Thus the world reached these missions
by water; while on land, through the mountains, a road led to them, and also to many
more that were too distant behind the hills
for ships to serve—a rough road, long and
lonely, punctuated with church towers and
gardens. For the Fathers gradually so stationed their settlements that the traveller
might each morning ride out from one mission
and by evening of a day's fair journey ride
into the next. A lonely, rough, dangerous
road, but lovely, too, with a name like music
—El Camino Real. Like music also were the
names of the missions—San Juan Capistrano,
San Luis Rey de Francia, San Miguel, Santa
Ynez—their very list is a song.

So there, by-and-by, was our continent, with
the locomotive whistling from Savannah to
Boston along its eastern edge, and on the

western the scattered chimes of Spain, ringing among the unpeopled mountains. Thus grew the two sorts of civilization—not equally. We know what has happened since. To-day the locomotive is whistling also from the Golden Gate to San Diego—but still the old mission-road goes through the mountains, and along it the footsteps of vanished Spain are marked with roses, and broken cloisters, and the crucifix.

But this was 1855. Only the barkentine brought to Padre Ignacio the signs from the world that he once had known and loved so dearly. As for the new world making a rude noise to the northward, he trusted that it might keep away from Santa Ysabel, and he waited for the vessel that was overdue with its package containing his single worldly luxury.

As the little, ancient bronze bell continued swinging in the tower, its plaintive call reached something in the Padre's memory. Softly, absently, he began to sing. He took up the slow strain not quite correctly, and dropped it, and took it up again, always in cadence with the bell:

At length he heard himself, and, glancing
at the belfry, smiled a little. "It is a pretty
tune," he said, "and it always made me sorry
for poor Fra Diavolo. Auber himself con-
fessed to me that he had made it sad and put
the hermitage bell to go with it, because he,
too, was grieved at having to kill his villain,
and wanted him, if possible, to die in a re-
ligious frame of mind. And Auber touched
glasses with me and said—how well I remember it!—'Is it the good Lord, or is it merely
the devil, that makes me always have a weakness for rascals?' I told him it was the devil.
I was not a priest then. I could not be so sure
with my answer now." And then Padre
Ignacio repeated Auber's remark in French:
" 'Est-ce le bon Dieu, ou est-ce bien le diable,
qui veut toujours que j'aime les coquins?' I
don't know! I don't know! I wonder if Auber
has composed anything lately? I wonder who
is singing 'Zerlina' now?"

He cast a farewell look at the ocean, and
took his steps between the monastic herbs, the
jasmines and the oleanders to the sacristy.
"At least," he said, "if we cannot carry with
us into exile the friends and the places we
have loved, music will go whither we go, even
to an end of the world such as this.—Felipe!"

he called to his organist. "Can they sing the
music I taught them for the Dixit Dominus
to-night?"

"Yes, father, surely."

"Then we will have that. And, Felipe—"
The Padre crossed the chancel to the small,
shabby organ. "Rise, my child, and listen.
Here is something you can learn. Why, see
now if you cannot learn it from a single
hearing."

The swarthy boy of sixteen stood watching
his master's fingers delicate and white, as
they played. Thus, of his own accord, he had
begun to watch them when a child of six; and
the Padre had taken the wild, half-scared,
spellbound creature and made a musician of
him.

"There, Felipe!" he said now. "Can you
do it? Slower, and more softly, muchacho
mio. It is about the death of a man, and it
should go with our bell."

The boy listened. "Then the father has
played it a tone too low," said he, "for our
bell rings the note of sol, or something very
near it, as the father must surely know." He
placed the melody in the right key—an easy
thing for him; and the Padre was delighted.

"Ah, my Felipe," he exclaimed, "what

could you and I not do if we had a better
organ! Only a little better! See! above this
row of keys would be a second row, and many
more stops. Then we would make such music
as has never yet been heard in California. But
my people are so poor and so few! And some
day I shall have passed from them, and it will
be too late."

"Perhaps," ventured Felipe, "the Amer-
icanos—"

"They care nothing for us, Felipe. They
are not our religion—or of any religion, from
what I can hear. Don't forget my Dixit
Dominus."

The Padre retired once more to the sacristy,
while the horse that brought Temptation came
over the hill.

The hour of service drew near; and as the
Padre waited he once again stepped out for
a look at the ocean; but the blue triangle of
water lay like a picture in its frame of land,
bare as the sky. "I think, from the color,
though," said he, "that a little more wind
must have begun out there."

The bell rang a last short summons to
prayer. Along the road from the south a
young rider, leading a pack-animal, ambled
into the mission and dismounted. Church was

not so much in his thoughts as food and, after
due digestion, a bed; but the doors stood open,
and, as everybody was passing within them,
more variety was to be gained by joining this
company than by waiting outside alone until
they should return from their devotions. So
he seated himself in a corner near the entrance, and after a brief, jaunty glance at the
sunburned, shaggy congregation, made himself as comfortable as might be. He had not
seen a face worth keeping his eyes open for.
The simple choir and simple fold, gathered
for even-song, paid him no attention—a rough
American bound for the mines was but an
object of aversion to them.

The Padre, of course, had been instantly
aware of the stranger's presence. To be
aware of unaccustomed presences is the sixth
sense with vicars of every creed and heresy;
and if the parish is lonely and the worshippers
few and seldom varying, a newcomer will
gleam out like a new book to be read. And a
trained priest learns to read keenly the faces
of those who assemble to worship under his
guidance. But American vagrants with no
thoughts save of gold-digging, and an over-
weening illiterate jargon for speech, had long
ceased to interest this priest, even in his star-

vation for company and talk from the outside
world; and therefore after the intoning he
sat with his homeside thoughts unchanged, to
draw both pain and enjoyment from the music
that he had set to the Dixit Dominus. He listened to the tender chorus that opens William
Tell; and, as the Latin psalm proceeded, pictures of the past rose between him and the
altar. One after another came these strains
he had taken from operas famous in their day,
until at length the Padre was murmuring to
some music seldom long out of his heart—
not the Latin verse which the choir sang, but
the original French words:

> "Ah, voilà mon envie,
>   Voilà mon seul désir:
> Rendez moi ma patrie,
>   Ou laissez moi mourir."

Which may be rendered:

> But one wish I implore,
>   One wish in all my cry:
> Give back my native land once more,
>   Give back, or let me die.

Then it happened that his eye fell again
upon the stranger near the door, and he
straightway forgot his Dixit Dominus. The
face of the young man was no longer hidden
by the slouching position he had at first taken.

"I only noticed his clothes at first," thought the Padre. Restlessness was plain upon the handsome brow, and violence was in the mouth; but Padre Ignacio liked the eyes. "He is not saying any prayers," he surmised, presently. "I doubt if he has said any for a long while. And he knows my music. He is of educated people. He cannot be American. And now—yes, he has taken—I think it must be a flower, from his pocket. I shall have him to dine with me." And vespers ended with rosy clouds of eagerness drifting across the Padre's brain.

II

But the stranger made his own beginning. As the priest came from the church, the rebellious young figure was awaiting. "Your organist tells me," he said, impetuously, "that it is you who—"

"May I ask with whom I have the great pleasure of speaking?" said the Padre, putting formality to the front and his pleasure out of sight.

The stranger's face reddened beneath its sun-beaten bronze, and he became aware of the Padre's pale features, molded by refinement and the world. "I beg your lenience," said he, with a graceful and confident utterance, as of equal to equal. "My name is Gaston Villeré, and it was time I should be reminded of my manners."

The Padre's hand waved a polite negative.

"Indeed, yes, Padre. But your music has amazed me. If you carried such associations as—Ah! the days and the nights!"—he broke off. "To come down a California mountain and find Paris at the bottom! The Huguenots, Rossini, Hérold—I was waiting for Il Trovatore."

"Is that something new?" inquired the Padre, eagerly.

The young man gave an exclamation. "The whole world is ringing with it!" he cried.

"But Santa Ysabel del Mar is a long way from the whole world," murmured Padre Ignacio.

"Indeed, it would not appear to be so," returned young Gaston. "I think the Comédie Francaise must be round the corner."

A thrill went through the priest at the theater's name. "And have you been long in America?" he asked.

"Why, always—except two years of foreign travel after college."

"An American!" exclaimed the surprised

Padre, with perhaps a tone of disappointment in his voice. "But no Americans who are yet come this way have been—have been"—he veiled the too-blunt expression of this thought —"have been familiar with The Huguenots," he finished, making a slight bow.

Villeré took his under-meaning. "I come from New Orleans," he returned. "And in New Orleans there live many of us who can recognize a—who can recognize good music wherever we hear it." And he made a slight bow in his turn.

The Padre laughed outright with pleasure and laid his hand upon the young man's arm. "You have no intention of going away tomorrow, I trust?"

"With your leave," answered Gaston, "I will have such an intention no longer."

It was with the air and gait of mutual understanding that the two now walked on together toward the Padre's door. The guest was twenty-five, the host sixty.

"And have you been in America long?" inquired Gaston.

"Twenty years."

"And at Santa Ysabel how long?"

"Twenty years."

"I should have thought," said Gaston, looking lightly at the desert and unpeopled mountains, "that now and again you might have wished to travel."

"Were I your age," murmured Padre Ignacio, "it might be so."

The evening had now ripened to the long after-glow of sunset. The sea was the purple of grapes, and wine-colored hues flowed among the high shoulders of the mountains.

"I have seen a sight like this," said Gaston, "between Granada and Malaga."

"So you know Spain!" said the Padre.

Often he had thought of this resemblance, but never till now met any one to share his thought. The courtly proprietor of San Fernando and the other patriarchal rancheros with whom he occasionally exchanged visits across the wilderness knew hospitality and inherited gentle manners, sending to Europe for silks and laces to give their daughters; but their eyes had not looked upon Granada, and their ears had never listened to William Tell.

"It is quite singular," pursued Gaston, "how one nook in the world will suddenly remind you of another nook that may be thousands of miles away. One morning, behind the Quai Voltaire, an old, yellow house with rusty balconies made me almost homesick for New Orleans.''

''The Quai Voltaire!'' said the Padre.

''I heard Rachel in Valérie that night,'' the young man went on. ''Did you know that she could sing, too? She sang several verses by an astonishing little Jew violoncellist that is come up over there.''

The Padre gazed down at his blithe guest. ''To see somebody, somebody, once again, is very pleasant to a hermit!''

''It cannot be more pleasant than arriving at an oasis,'' returned Gaston.

They had delayed on the threshold to look at the beauty of the evening, and now the priest watched his parishioners come and go. ''How can one make companions—'' he began; then, checking himself, he said: ''Their souls are as sacred and immortal as mine, and God helps me to help them. But in this world it is not immortal souls that we choose for companions; it is kindred tastes, intelligences, and—and so I and my books are growing old together, you see,'' he added, more lightly. ''You will find my volumes as behind the times as myself.''

He had fallen into talk more intimate than he wished; and while the guest was uttering something polite about the nobility of missionary work, he placed him in an easy-chair and sought aquardiente for his immediate refreshment. Since the year's beginning there had been no guest for him to bring into his rooms, or to sit beside him in the high seats at table, set apart for the *gente fina*.

Such another library was not then in California; and though Gaston Villeré, in leaving Harvard College, had shut Horace and Sophocles forever at the earliest instant possible under academic requirements, he knew the Greek and Latin names that he now saw as well as he knew those of Shakespeare, Dante, Molière, and Cervantes. These were here also; but it could not be precisely said of them, either, that they made a part of the young man's daily reading. As he surveyed the Padre's august shelves, it was with a touch of the histrionic southern gravity which his northern education had not wholly schooled out of him that he said:

"I fear I am no scholar, sir. But I know what writers every gentleman ought to respect."

The polished Padre bowed gravely to this compliment.

It was when his eyes caught sight of the music that the young man felt again at ease, and his vivacity returned to him. Leaving his chair, he began enthusiastically to examine the tall piles that filled one side of the room. The volumes lay piled and scattered everywhere, making a pleasant disorder; and, as perfume comes from a flower, memories of singers and chandeliers rose bright from the printed names. Norma, Tancredi, Don Pasquale, La Vestale, dim lights in the fashions of to-day, sparkled upon the exploring Gaston, conjuring the radiant halls of Europe before him. "The Barber of Seville!" he presently exclaimed. "And I happened to hear it in Seville."

But Seville's name brought over the Padre a new rush of home thoughts. "Is not Andalusia beautiful?" he said. "Did you see it in April, when the flowers come?"

"Yes," said Gaston, among the music. "I was at Cordova then."

"Ah, Cordova!" murmured the Padre.

"Semiramide!" cried Gaston, lighting upon that opera. "That was a week! I should like to live it over, every day and night of it!"

"Did you reach Malaga from Marseilles or Gibraltar?" asked the Padre, wistfully.

"From Marseilles. Down from Paris through the Rhone Valley, you know."

"Then you saw Provence! And did you

go, perhaps, from Avignon to Nismes by the
Pont du Gard? There is a place I have made
here—a little, little place—with olive-trees.
And now they have grown, and it looks something like that country, if you stand in a particular position. I will take you there to-
morrow. I think you will understand what I
mean.''

''Another resemblance!'' said the volatile
and happy Gaston. ''We both seem to have
an eye for them. But, believe me, Padre, I
could never stay here planting olives. I
should go back and see the original ones—
and then I'd hasten on to Paris.'' And, with
a volume of Meyerbeer open in his hand,
Gaston hummed: '' 'Robert, Robert, toi que
j'aime.' Why, Padre, I think that your library contains none of the masses, and all of
the operas in the world!''

''I will make you a little confession,'' said
Padre Ignacio, ''and then you shall give me a
little absolution.''

''For a penance,'' said Gaston; ''you must
play over some of these things to me.''

''I suppose I could not permit myself this
luxury,'' began the Padre, pointing to his
operas, ''and teach these to my choir, if the
people had any worldly associations with the

music. But I have reasoned that the music cannot do them harm—''

The ringing of a bell here interrupted him. ''In fifteen minutes,'' he said, ''our poor meal will be ready for you.'' The good Padre was not quite sincere when he spoke of a ''poor meal.'' While getting the aquardiente for his guest he had given orders, and he knew how well such orders would be carried out. He lived alone, and generally supped simply enough, but not even the ample table at San Fernando could surpass his own on occasions. And this was for him indeed an occasion!

''Your half-breeds will think I am one of themselves,'' said Gaston, showing his dusty clothes. ''I am not fit to be seated with you.'' But he did not mean this any more than his host had meant his remark about the food. In his pack, which an Indian had brought from his horse, he carried some garments of civilization. And presently, after fresh water and not a little painstaking with brush and scarf, there came back to the Padre a young guest whose elegance and bearing and ease of the great world were to the exiled priest as sweet as was his travelled conversation.

They repaired to the hall and took their seats at the head of the long table. For the

Spanish centuries of stately custom lived at
Santa Ysabel del Mar, inviolate, feudal, remote.

They were the only persons of quality present; and between themselves and the *gente de
razon* a space intervened. Behind the Padre's
chair stood an Indian to wait upon him, and
another stood behind the chair of Gaston
Villeré. Each of these servants wore one single white garment and offered the many
dishes to the *gente fina* and refilled their
glasses. At the lower end of the table a general attendant waited upon *mesclados*—the
half-breeds. There was meat with spices, and
roasted quail, with various cakes and other
preparations of grain; also the brown fresh
olives and grapes, with several sorts of figs
and plums, and preserved fruits, and white
and red wine—the white fifty years old. Beneath the quiet shining of candles, fresh-cut
flowers leaned from vessels of old Mexican
and Spanish make.

There at one end of this feast sat the wild,
pastoral, gaudy company, speaking little over
their food; and there at the other the pale
Padre, questioning his visitor about Rachel.
The mere name of a street would bring memories crowding to his lips; and when his guest

told him of a new play he was ready with old
quotations from the same author. Alfred de
Vigny they spoke of, and Victor Hugo, whom
the Padre disliked. Long after the *dulce,* or
sweet dish, when it was the custom for the
vaqueros and the rest of the retainers to rise
and leave the *gente fina* to themselves, the
host sat on in the empty hall, fondly talking
to his guest of his bygone Paris and fondly
learning of the later Paris that the guest had
seen. And thus the two lingered, exchanging
their enthusiasms, while the candles waned,
and the long-haired Indians stood silent behind the chairs.

"But we must go to my piano," the host
exclaimed. For at length they had come to a
lusty difference of opinion. The Padre, with
ears critically deaf, and with smiling, uncon-
vinced eyes, was shaking his head, while
young Gaston sang Trovatore to him, and
beat upon the table with a fork.

"Come and convert me, then," said Padre
Ignacio, and he led the way. "Donizetti I
have always admitted. There, at least, is refinement. If the world has taken to this Verdi,
with his street-band music—But there, now!
Sit down and convert me. Only don't crush
my poor little Erard with Verdi's hoofs. I

brought it when I came. It is behind the times, too. And, oh, my dear boy, our organ is still worse. So old, so old! To get a proper one I would sacrifice even this piano of mine in a moment—only the tinkling thing is not worth a sou to anybody except its master. But there! Are you quite comfortable?" And having seen to his guest's needs, and placed spirits and cigars and an ash-tray within his reach, the Padre sat himself comfortably in his chair to hear and expose the false doctrine of Il Trovatore.

By midnight all of the opera that Gaston could recall had been played and sung twice. The convert sat in his chair no longer, but stood singing by the piano. The potent swing and flow of rhythms, the torrid, copious inspiration of the South, mastered him. "Verdi has grown," he cried. "Verdi is become a giant." And he swayed to the beat of the melodies, and waved an enthusiastic arm. He demanded every note. Why did not Gaston remember it all? But if the barkentine would arrive and bring the whole music then they would have it right! And he made Gaston teach him what words he knew. " 'Non ti scordar, ' " he sang—" 'non ti scordar di me.'

That is genius. But one sees how the world moves when one is out of it. 'A nostri monti ritorneremo'; home to our mountains. Ah, yes, there is genius again.'' And the exile sighed and his spirit voyaged to distant places while Gaston continued brilliantly with the music of the final scene.

Then the host remembered his guest. "I am ashamed of my selfishness," he said. "It is already to-morrow."

"I have sat later in less good company," answered the pleasant Gaston. "And I shall sleep all the sounder for making a convert."

"You have dispensed roadside alms," said the Padre, smiling. "And that should win excellent dreams."

Thus, with courtesies more elaborate than the world has time for at the present day, they bade each other good-night and parted, bearing their late candles along the quiet halls of the mission. To young Gaston in his bed easy sleep came without waiting, and no dreams at all. Outside his open window was the quiet, serene darkness, where the stars shone clear, and tranquil perfumes hung in the cloisters. But while the guest lay sleeping all night in unchanged position like a child, up and down

between the oleanders went Padre Ignacio,
walking until dawn. Temptation indeed had
come over the hill and entered the cloisters.

III

Day showed the ocean's surface no longer
glassy, but lying like a mirror breathed upon;
and there between the short headlands came
a sail, gray and plain against the flat water.
The priest watched through his glasses, and
saw the gradual sun grow strong upon the
canvas of the barkentine. The message from
his world was at hand, yet to-day he scarcely
cared so much. Sitting in his garden yesterday, he could never have imagined such a
change. But his heart did not hail the barkentine as usual. Books, music, pale paper,
and print—this was all that was coming to
him, and some of its savor had gone; for the
siren voice of Life had been speaking with him
face to face, and in his spirit, deep down, the
love of the world was restlessly answering it.
Young Gaston showed more eagerness than
the Padre over this arrival of the vessel that
might be bringing Trovatore in the nick of
time. Now he would have the chance, before
he took his leave, to help rehearse the new

music with the choir. He would be a missionary, too: a perfectly new experience.

"And you still forgive Verdi the sins of
his youth?" he said to his host. "I wonder
if you could forgive mine?"

"Verdi has left his behind him," retorted
the Padre.

"But I am only twenty-five!" exclaimed
Gaston, pathetically.

"Ah, don't go away soon!" pleaded the
exile. It was the first unconcealed complaint
that had escaped him, and he felt instant
shame.

But Gaston was too much elated with the
enjoyment of each new day to comprehend
the Padre's soul. The shafts of another's
pain might hardly pierce the bright armor
of his gaiety. He mistook the priest's en-
treaty, for anxiety about his own happy spirit.

"Stay here under your care?" he asked.
"It would do me no good, Padre. Temptation
sticks closer to me than a brother!" and he
gave that laugh of his which had disarmed
severer judges than his host. "By next week
I should have introduced some sin or other
into your beautiful Garden of Ignorance here.
It will be much safer for your flock if I go and
join the other serpents at San Francisco."

Soon after breakfast the Padre had his two mules saddled, and he and his guest set forth down the hills together to the shore. And, beneath the spell and confidence of pleasant, slow riding and the loveliness of everything, the young man talked freely of himself.

"And, seriously," said he, "if I missed nothing else at Santa Ysabel, I should long for—how shall I say it?—for insecurity, for danger, and of all kinds—not merely danger to the body. Within these walls, beneath these sacred bells, you live too safe for a man like me."

"Too safe!" These echoed words upon the lips of the pale Padre were a whisper too light, too deep, for Gaston's heedless ear.

"Why," the young man pursued in a spirit that was but half levity, "though I yield often to temptation, at times I have resisted it, and here I should miss the very chance to resist. Your garden could never be Eden for me, because temptation is absent from it."

"Absent!" Still lighter, still deeper, was this whisper that the Padre breathed.

"I must find life!" exclaimed Gaston. "And my fortune at the mines, I hope. I am not a bad fellow, Father. You can easily guess all the things I do. I have never, to my knowledge, harmed any one. I didn't even try to kill my adversary in an affair of honor. I gave him a mere flesh-wound, and by this time he must be quite recovered. He was my friend. But as he came between me—''

Gaston stopped, and the Padre, looking keenly at him, saw the violence that he had noticed in church pass like a flame over the young man's handsome face.

''There's nothing dishonorable,'' said Gaston, answering the priest's look. And then, because this look made him not quite at his ease: ''Perhaps a priest might feel obliged to say it was dishonorable. She and her father were—a man owes no fidelity before he is— but you might say that had been dishonorable.''

''I have not said so, my son.''

''I did what every gentleman would do,'' insisted Gaston.

''And that is often wrong!'' said the Padre, gently and gravely. ''But I'm not your confessor.''

''No,'' said Gaston, looking down. ''And it is all over. It will not begin again. Since leaving New Orleans I have travelled an innocent journey straight to you. And when I make my fortune I shall be in a position to return and—''

''Claim the pressed flower?'' suggested the Padre. He did not smile.

''Ah, you remember how those things are!'' said Gaston; and he laughed and blushed.

''Yes,'' said the Padre, looking at the anchored barkentine, ''I remember how those things are.''

For a while the vessel and its cargo and the landed men and various business and conversations occupied them. But the freight for the mission once seen to, there was not much else to detain them.

The barkentine was only a coaster like many others which had begun to fill the sea a little more of late years, and presently host and guest were riding homeward. Side by side they rode, companions to the eye, but wide apart in mood; within the turbulent young figure of Gaston dwelt a spirit that could not be more at ease, while revolt was steadily kindling beneath the schooled and placid mask of the Padre.

Yet still the strangeness of his situation in such a remote, resourceless place came back as a marvel into the young man's lively mind.

Twenty years in prison, he thought, and hardly aware of it! And he glanced at the silent priest. A man so evidently fond of music, of theaters, of the world, to whom pressed flowers had meant something once—and now contented to bleach upon these wastes! Not even desirous of a brief holiday, but finding an old organ and some old operas enough recreation! "It is his age, I suppose," thought Gaston. And then the notion of himself when he should be sixty occurred to him, and he spoke.

"Do you know, I do not believe," said he, "that I should ever reach such contentment as yours."

"Perhaps you will," said Padre Ignacio, in a low voice.

"Never!" declared the youth. "It comes only to the few, I am sure."

"Yes. Only to the few," murmured the Padre.

"I am certain that it must be a great possession," Gaston continued; "and yet—and yet—dear me! life is a splendid thing!"

"There are several ways to live it," said the Padre.

"Only one for me!" cried Gaston. "Action, men, women, things—to be there, to be known,

to play a part, to sit in the front seats; to
have people tell one another, 'There goes
Gaston Villeré!' and to deserve one's prom-
inence. Why, if I were Padre of Santa Ysabel
del Mar for twenty years—no! for one year
—do you know what I should have done?
Some day it would have been too much for
me. I should have left these savages to a
pastor nearer their own level, and I should
have ridden down this cañon upon my mule,
and stepped on board the barkentine, and
gone back to my proper sphere. You will understand, sir, that I am far from venturing to
make any personal comment. I am only thinking what a world of difference lies between na-
tures that can feel as alike as we do upon so
many subjects. Why, not since leaving New
Orleans have I met any one with whom I
could talk, except of the weather and the brute
interests common to us all. That such a one
as you should be here is like a dream.''

"But it is not a dream," said the Padre.

"And, sir—pardon me if I do say this—are
you not wasted at Santa Ysabel del Mar? I
have seen the priests at the other missions.
They are—the sort of good men that I expected. But are you needed to save such souls
as these?''

"There is no aristocracy of souls," said the Padre, again whispering.

"But the body and the mind!" cried Gaston. "My God, are they nothing? Do you think that they are given to us for nothing but a trap? You cannot teach such a doctrine with your library there. And how about all the cultivated men and women away from whose quickening society the brightest of us grow numb? You have held out. But will it be for long? Are you never to save any souls of your own kind? Are not twenty years of *mesclados* enough? No, no!" finished young Gaston, hot with his unforeseen eloquence; "I should ride down some morning and take the barkentine."

Padre Ignacio was silent for a space.

"I have not offended you?" asked the young man.

"No. Anything but that. You are surprised that I should—choose—to stay here. Perhaps you may have wondered how I came to be here at all?"

"I had not intended any impertinent—"

"Oh, no. Put such an idea out of your head, my son. You may remember that I was going to make you a confession about my operas. Let us sit down in this shade."

So they picketed the mules near the stream
and sat down.

IV

"You have seen," began Padre Ignacio,
"what sort of a man I—was once. Indeed, it
seems very strange to myself that you should
have been here not twenty-four hours yet, and
know so much of me. For there has come no
one else at all"—the Padre paused a moment
and mastered the unsteadiness that he had
felt approaching in his voice—"there has
been no one else to whom I have talked so
freely. In my early days I had no thought of
being a priest. My parents destined me for a
diplomatic career. There was plenty of money
and—and all the rest of it; for by inheri-
tance came to me the acquaintance of many
people whose names you would be likely to
have heard of. Cities, people of fashion, art-
ists—the whole of it was my element and my
choice; and by-and-by I married, not only
where it was desirable, but where I loved.
Then for the first time Death laid his staff
upon my enchantment, and I understood
many things that had been only words to me
hitherto. To have been a husband for a year,
and a father for a moment, and in that mo-

ment to lose all—this unblinded me. Looking
back, it seemed to me that I had never done
anything except for myself all my days. I left
the world. In due time I became a priest and
lived in my own country. But my worldly experience and my secular education had given
to my opinions a turn too liberal for the place
where my work was laid. I was soon advised
concerning this by those in authority over me.
And since they could not change me and I
could not change them, yet wished to work and
to teach, the New World was suggested, and I
volunteered to give the rest of my life to missions. It was soon found that some one was
needed here, and for this little place I sailed,
and to these humble people I have dedicated
my service. They are pastoral creatures of
the soil. Their vineyard and cattle days are
apt to be like the sun and storm around them
—strong alike in their evil and in their good.
All their years they live as children—children
with men's passions given to them like deadly
weapons, unable to measure the harm their
impulses may bring. Hence, even in their
crimes, their hearts will generally open soon
to the one great key of love, while civilization
makes locks which that key cannot always fit
at the first turn. And coming to know this,''

said Padre Ignacio, fixing his eyes steadily upon Gaston, "you will understand how great a privilege it is to help such people, and how the sense of something accomplished—under God—should bring Contentment with Renunciation."

"Yes," said Gaston Villeré. Then, thinking of himself, "I can understand it in a man like you."

"Do not speak of me at all!" exclaimed the Padre, almost passionately. "But pray Heaven that you may find the thing yourself some day—Contentment with Renunciation—and never let it go."

"Amen!" said Gaston, strangely moved.

"That is the whole of my story," the priest continued, with no more of the recent stress in his voice. "And now I have talked to you about myself quite enough. But you must have my confession." He had now resumed entirely his half-playful tone. "I was just a little mistaken, you see—too self-reliant, perhaps—when I supposed, in my first missionary ardor, that I could get on without any remembrance of the world at all. I found that I could not. And so I have taught the old operas to my choir—such parts of them as are within our compass and suitable for worship.

And certain of my friends still alive at home
are good enough to remember this taste of
mine and to send me each year some of the
new music that I should never hear of otherwise. Then we study these things also. And
although our organ is a miserable affair,
Felipe manages very cleverly to make it do.
And while the voices are singing these operas,
especially the old ones, what harm is there
if sometimes the priest is thinking of something else? So there's my confession! And
now, whether Trovatore is come or not, I
shall not allow you to leave us until you have
taught all you know of it to Felipe.''

The new opera, however, had duly arrived.
And as he turned its pages Padre Ignacio was
quick to seize at once upon the music that
could be taken into his church. Some of it was
ready fitted. By that afternoon Felipe and
his choir could have rendered ''Ah! se l' error
t' ingombra'' without slip or falter.

Those were strange rehearsals of Il Trovatore upon this California shore. For the
Padre looked to Gaston to say when they went
too fast or too slow, and to correct their emphasis. And since it was hot, the little Erard
piano was carried each day out into the mission garden. There, in the cloisters among

the jessamine, the orange blossoms, the
oleanders, in the presence of the round yellow
hills and the blue triangle of sea, the Miserere
was slowly learned. The Mexicans and Indians gathered, swarthy and black-haired,
around the tinkling instrument that Felipe
played; presiding over them were young Gaston and the pale Padre, walking up and down
the paths, beating time or singing now one
part and now another. And so it was that
the wild cattle on the uplands would hear
Trovatore hummed by a passing vaquero,
while the same melody was filling the streets
of the far-off world.

For three days Gaston Villeré remained at
Santa Ysabel del Mar; and though not a word
of restlessness came from him, his host could
read San Francisco and the gold-mines in his
countenance. No, the young man could not
have stayed here for twenty years! And the
Padre forebore urging his guest to extend
his visit.

"But the world is small," the guest declared at parting. "Some day it will not be
able to spare you any longer. And then we are
sure to meet. But you shall hear from me
soon, at any rate."

Again, as upon the first evening, the two

exchanged a few courtesies, more graceful
and particular than we, who have not time,
and fight no duels, find worth a man's while
at the present day. For duels are gone, which
is a very good thing, and with them a certain
careful politeness, which is a pity; but that
is the way in the eternal profit and loss. So
young Gaston rode northward out of the mission, back to the world and his fortune; and
the Padre stood watching the dust after the
rider had passed from sight. Then he went
into his room with a drawn face. But appearances at least had been kept up to the end;
the youth would never know of the elder
man's unrest.

V.

Temptation had arrived with Gaston, but
was destined to make a longer stay at Santa
Ysabel del Mar. Yet it was perhaps a week
before the priest knew this guest was come to
abide with him. The guest could be discreet,
could withdraw, was not at first importunate.

Sail away on the barkentine? A wild notion, to be sure! although fit enough to enter
the brain of such a young scapegrace. The
Padre shook his head and smiled affectionately when he thought of Gaston Villeré. The

youth's handsome, reckless countenance
would shine out, smiling, in his memory, and
he repeated Auber's old remark, "Is it the
good Lord, or is it merely the devil, that always makes me have a weakness for rascals?"

Sail away on the barkentine! Imagine taking leave of the people here—of Felipe! In
what words should he tell the boy to go on in-
dustriously with his music? No, this was not
imaginable! The mere parting alone would
make it forever impossible to think of such
a thing. "And then," he said to himself each
new morning, when he looked out at the ocean,
"I have given to them my life. One does not
take back a gift."

. Pictures of his departure began to shine
and melt in his drifting fancy. He saw himself explaining to Felipe that now his presence was wanted elsewhere; that there would
come a successor to take care of Santa Ysabel
—a younger man, more useful, and able to
visit sick people at a distance. "For I am old
now. I should not be long here in any case."
He stopped and pressed his hands together;
he had caught his Temptation in the very act.
Now he sat staring at his Temptation's face;
close to him, while there in the triangle two
ships went sailing by.

One morning Felipe told him that the barkentine was here on its return voyage south. "Indeed?" said the Padre, coldly. "The things are ready to go, I think." For the vessel called for mail and certain boxes that the mission sent away. Felipe left the room in wonder at the Padre's manner. But the priest was laughing secretly to see how little it was to him where the barkentine was, or whether it should be coming or going. But in the afternoon, at his piano, he found himself saying, "Other ships call here, at any rate." And then for the first time he prayed to be delivered from his thoughts. Yet presently he left his seat and looked out of the window for a sight of the barkentine; but it was gone.

The season of the wine-making passed, and the preserving of all the fruits that the mission fields grew. Lotions and medicines were distilled from garden herbs. Perfume was manufactured from the petals of flowers and certain spices, and presents of it despatched to San Fernando and Ventura, and to friends at other places; for the Padre had a special receipt. As the time ran on, two or three visitors passed a night with him; and presently there was a word at various missions that Padre Ignacio had begun to show his years.

At Santa Ysabel del Mar they whispered,
"The Padre is not well." Yet he rode a great
deal over the hills by himself, and down the
cañon very often, stopping where he had sat
with Gaston, to sit alone and look up and
down, now at the hills above, and now at the
ocean below. Among his parishioners he had
certain troubles to soothe, certain wounds to
heal; a home from which he was able to drive
jealousy; a girl whom he bade her lover set
right. But all said, "The Padre is unwell."
And Felipe told them that the music seemed
nothing to him any more; he never asked for
his Dixit Dominus nowadays. Then for a
short time he was really in bed, feverish with
the two voices that spoke to him without ceas-
ing. "You have given your life," said one
voice. "And, therefore," said the other,
"have earned the right to go home and die."
"You are winning better rewards in the service of God," said the first voice. "God can be
better served in other places," answered the
second. As he lay listening he saw Seville
again, and the trees of Aranhal, where he had
been born. The wind was blowing through
them, and in their branches he could hear the
nightingales. "Empty! Empty!" he said,
aloud. And he lay for two days and nights

hearing the wind and the nightingales in the far trees of Aranhal. But Felipe, watching, only heard the Padre crying through the hours, "Empty! Empty!"

Then the wind in the trees died down, and the Padre could get out of bed, and soon be in the garden. But the voices within him still talked all the while as he sat watching the sails when they passed between the headlands. Their words, falling forever the same way, beat his spirit sore, like blows upon flesh already bruised. If he could only change what they said, he would rest.

"Has the Padre any mail for Santa Barbara?" asked Felipe. "The ship bound southward should be here to-morrow."

"I will attend to it," said the priest, not moving. And Felipe stole away.

At Felipe's words the voices had stopped as a clock finished striking. Silence, strained like expectation, filled the Padre's soul. But in place of the voices came old sights of home again, the waving trees at Aranhal; then it would be Rachel for a moment, declaiming tragedy while a houseful of faces that he knew by name watched her; and through all the panorama rang the pleasant laugh of Gaston. For a while in the evening the Padre

sat at his Erard playing Trovatore. Later, in
his sleepless bed he lay, saying now and then:
"To die at home! Surely I may be granted
at least this." And he listened for the inner
voices. But they were not speaking any more,
and the black hole of silence grew more dread-
ful to him than their arguments. Then the
dawn came in at his window, and he lay watching its gray grow warm into color, until suddenly he sprang from his bed and looked at
the sea. Blue it lay, sapphire-hued and dancing with points of gold, lovely and luring as a
charm; and over its triangle the south-bound
ship was approaching. People were on board
who in a few weeks would be sailing the Atlantic, while he would stand here looking out
of this same window. "Merciful God!" he
cried, sinking on his knees. "Heavenly Father, Thou seest this evil in my heart! Thou
knowest that my weak hand cannot pluck it
out! My strength is breaking, and still Thou
makest my burden heavier than I can bear."
He stopped, breathless and trembling. The
same visions were flitting across his closed
eyes; the same silence gaped like a dry crater
in his soul. "There is no help in earth or
heaven," he said, very quietly; and he dressed
himself.

VI

It was still so early that few of the Indians were stirring, and one of these saddled the Padre's mule. Felipe was not yet awake, and for a moment it came in the priest's mind to open the boy's door softly, look at him once more, and come away. But this he did not, nor even take a farewell glance at the church and organ. He bade nothing farewell, but, turning his back upon his room and his garden, rode down the cañon.

The vessel lay at anchor, and some one had landed from her and was talking with other men on the shore. Seeing the priest slowly coming, this stranger approached to meet him.

"You are connected with the mission here?" he inquired.

"I—am."

"Perhaps it is with you that Gaston Villeré stopped?"

"The young man from New Orleans? Yes. I am Padre Ignacio."

"Then you'll save me a journey. I promised him to deliver these into your own hands."

The stranger gave them to him.

"A bag of gold-dust," he explained, "and a

letter. I wrote it at his dictation while he was dying. He lived hardly an hour afterward.''

The stranger bowed his head at the stricken cry which his news elicited from the priest, who, after a few moments' vain effort to speak, opened the letter and read:

"My dear Friend,—It is through no man's fault but mine that I have come to this. I have had plenty of luck, and lately have been counting the days until I should return home. But last night heavy news from New Orleans reached me, and I tore the pressed flower to pieces. Under the first smart and humiliation of broken faith I was rendered desperate, and picked a needless quarrel. Thank God, it is I who have the punishment. My dear friend, as I lie here, leaving a world that no man ever loved more, I have come to understand you. For you and your mission have been much in my thoughts. It is strange how good can be done, not at the time when it is intended, but afterward; and you have done this good to me. I say over your words, 'Contentment with Renunciation,' and believe that at this last hour I have gained something like what you would wish me to feel. For I do not think that I desire it otherwise now. My life would never have been of service, I am afraid. You are the last person in this world who has spoken serious words to me, and I want you to know that now at length I value the peace of Santa Ysabel as I could never have done but for seeing your wisdom and goodness. You spoke of a new organ for your church. Take the gold-dust that will reach you with this, and do what you will with it. Let me at least in dying have helped some one. And since there is no aristocracy in souls—you said that to me; do you remember?—perhaps you will say a mass for this departing soul of mine. I only wish, since my body must go under ground in a strange country, that it might have been at Santa Ysabel del Mar, where your feet would often pass."

" 'At Santa Ysabel del Mar, where your feet would often pass.' " The priest repeated this final sentence aloud, without being aware of it.

"Those are the last words he ever spoke," said the stranger, "except bidding me good-bye."

"You know him well, then?"

"No; not until after he was hurt. I'm the man he quarrelled with."

The priest looked at the ship that would sail onward this afternoon.

Then a smile of great beauty passed over his face, and he addressed the stranger. "I thank you. You will never know what you have done for me."

"It is nothing," answered the stranger, awkwardly. "He told me you set great store on a new organ."

Padre Ignacio turned away from the ship and rode back through the gorge. When he had reached the shady place where once he had sat with Gaston Villeré, he dismounted and again sat there, alone by the stream, for many hours. Long rides and outings had been lately so much his custom that no one thought twice of his absence; and when he returned to the mission in the afternoon, the Indian took his mule, and he went to his seat in the garden. But it was with another look that he watched the sea; and presently the sail moved across the blue triangle, and soon it had rounded the headland.

With it departed Temptation forever.

Gaston's first coming was in the Padre's mind; and, as the vespers bell began to ring

in the cloistered silence, a fragment of
Auber's plaintive tune passed like a sigh
across his memory:

For the repose of Gaston's young, world-
loving spirit, they sang all that he had taught
them of Il Trovatore.

After this day, Felipe and all those who
knew and loved the Padre best, saw serenity
had returned to his features; but for some
reason they began to watch those features
with more care.

"Still," they said, "he is not old." And as
the months went by they would repeat: "We
shall have him yet for many years."

Thus the season rolled round, bringing the
time for the expected messages from the
world. Padre Ignacio was wont to sit in his
garden waiting for the ship, as of old.

"As of old," they said, cheerfully, who saw
him. But Renunciation with Contentment
they could not see; it was deep down in his
silent and thankful heart.

One day Felipe went to call him from his
garden seat, wondering why the ringing of

the bell had not brought him to vespers. Breviary in lap, and hands folded upon it, the Padre sat among his flowers, looking at the sea. Out there amid the sapphire-blue, tranquil and white, gleamed the sails of the barkentine. It had brought him a new message, not from this world; and Padre Ignacio was slowly borne in from the garden, while the mission-bell tolled for the passing of a human soul.